Alix Ohlin

Signs and Wonders

Alix Ohlin is the author of *The Missing Person,* a novel,
and *Babylon and Other Stories.* Her work has appeared
in *Best American Short Stories, Best New American
Voices,* and on NPR's "Selected Shorts." Born and
raised in Montreal, she teaches at Lafayette College
and in the Warren Wilson MFA Program for Writers.

www.alixohlin.com

Signs and Wonders

Signs and Wonders

STORIES

Alix Ohlin

Vintage Contemporaries
Vintage Books
A Division of Random House, Inc.
New York

These stories originally appeared in the following publications:
"Signs and Wonders"(as "Stranger Things Have Happened") in
Failbetter; "Forks" (as "Midnight, Tuesday") in *The American Scholar;*
"Robbing the Cradle" in *Washington Square;* "The Stepmother's Story"
in *The Sincerest Form of Flattery: Contemporary Women Writers on
Forerunners in Fiction,* eds. Jacqueline Kolosov and Kirsten Sundberg
Lunstrum (Lewis-Clark Press, 2008); "The Idea Man" in *Southwest
Review;* "Who Do You Love?" in *Five Chapters;* "The Teacher" in
Daedalus; "Vigo Park" in *TriQuarterly;* "The Only Child" in *Ploughshares;*
"You Are What You Like" in *Gulf Coast;* "The Cruise" in *World
Literature Today;* "The Assistants" (as "These Foolish Things
[Remind Me of You]") in *Southwest Review;* and "Fortune-Telling"
(as "Chinese Restaurant") in *Columbia.*

Library of Congress Cataloging-in-Publication Data:

Ohlin, Alix.
Signs and wonders : stories / by Alix Ohlin.
p. cm.
"A Vintage contemporaries original."
ISBN 978-0-307-74379-4
1. Short stories. I. Title.
PS3615.H57S54 2012
813'.6—dc23
2011050885

Book design by Claudia Martinez
Cover design by Abby Weintraub
Front cover photograph © Tony Tilford/Nature Picture Source
Author photograph © Michael Lionstar

www.vintagebooks.com

Printed in the United States of America

10 9 8 7 6 5 4 3 2 1

So there is only one thing for the lover to do. He must house his love within himself as best he can; he must create for himself a whole new inward world—a world intense and strange, complete in himself. Let it be added that this lover about whom we speak need not necessarily be a young man saving for a wedding ring—this lover can be man, woman, child, or indeed any human creature on this earth.

—CARSON McCULLERS,
The Ballad of the Sad Café

Contents

Signs and Wonders

Signs and Wonders

So the important thing to know from the start is that she was miserable. She hadn't always been, of course. She'd gotten married in a flurry of sex and promises, wearing a white dress so hideously confectionary that she felt like a parody of herself, a joke told in crinoline and lace, and even that made her happy, because it was silly and she knew they'd laugh about it later. Which they did. Then they had a baby, who was beautiful and perfect, then later on became less beautiful, less perfect, in fact troubled, for a time Ritalin and methamphetamine addicted, but subsequently, amazingly, pulled himself together and managed, despite the rocky years, to graduate from college and find a decent job at a zoo, tending to the turtles.

Which brings us to the misery, twenty-six years on. On the day she discovered she was miserable, Kathleen was forty-nine years old and a tenured professor of American literature at a college in suburban Philadelphia. Her husband, Terence, was fifty-two, and also tenured, in the same department at the same school. Their son, Steve, had been clean for three years. The mortgage had been paid. Financially, emotionally, and logistically, things were going pretty well. She and Terence were in a meeting, discussing whether or not to allow English majors to graduate without taking a course in Shakespeare. Tempers on this topic ran high, as they almost always did; the professors were a testy bunch, desirous of offense. Terence, the chair, argued this requirement was retrograde, absurd; everyone knew that English majors nowadays went on to marketing or advertising or law school.

"That's true," Kathleen said wearily, feeling obligated to support her husband. At one time, she'd worked hard to stake out her own positions, to be seen as objective and fair. She soon realized, however, that no matter what she said she would always be perceived as taking Terence's side; even when she voted against him, this was interpreted as some kind of obscure but Machiavellian strategy the two of them had cooked up together. So she opted for the path of least resistance, which was to pretend, both at work and at home, that Terence was the most brilliant person she knew.

"Now, I love Shakespeare," he said. Kathleen wondered if this was true. She hadn't seen him read a book, any book, for pleasure, in the last decade. What he truly loved was reality television. He liked to root for the schemers and alliance forgers, praising them for their cunning amorality. *Play the game,* he would urge them out loud in the den, his voice tight with drama.

"I could happily spend the rest of my days," he went on, "reading the plays and sonnets over and over again. But I'm a scholar. And we're not preparing scholars, by and large, after all."

"Surely you don't mean to suggest that only literary scholars need to read Shakespeare?" Fleur Mason said. "Surely *even you,* Terence, aren't *that* hostile to literature?"

Her *even you* hung in the room's ensuing silence. In this group there was no such thing as a passing remark; each one was noted, parsed, enshrined. Fleur Mason looked right at Terence and didn't flush. Young, square-shouldered, and passionate, she wore ruffled skirts and lace blouses and a gold cross on a chain; she seemed like someone who'd spent her childhood alone in a room, writing poems about trees. She didn't belong to today's world but refused, violently, to admit it.

"Surely even you, Fleur, aren't so defensive and small-minded as to think that questioning literature's practices is the same as being hostile to them," Terence said smoothly.

It was almost five, and the others looked indiscreetly at their watches, anticipating blood-sugar crashes, child-care crises, cocktails tragically delayed.

"Maybe this is more than we want to get into right now," Kathleen said diplomatically, for which she received a few grateful glances. But not from Fleur and Terence, both of whom were breathing hard.

Another half an hour passed, with no resolution reached on the Shakespeare requirement. Finally, after some in the room progressed from stuffing papers into their bags to standing up and moving to the door, Terence tabled the issue and adjourned the meeting, promising that next month they would communally endure the punishment of having to discuss it again.

Kathleen went back to her office, hoping to wrap up a few things, but all she could think about was her feverish irritation with Fleur Mason. It was ridiculous for her to be so difficult, so adamant. She obviously had to know that letting Terence have his way was the easiest course of action for everyone. Fleur had, in fact, always driven Kathleen crazy. She was single and thirty-seven and appeared to have no life outside of her job. She had a laugh like a demented clown's; it rose too suddenly and lingered too long. There was also the profound and unforgivable stupidity of her name.

By six thirty everyone else had left, including Terence, who played squash with his friend Dave on Tuesday afternoons. Fleur's office had once been Kathleen's, and she still had the key. She walked down the hall, let herself in, and stood there for a moment, energized with hate. The room smelled like dust and Yankee Candle. There were framed *New Yorker* cartoons with literary jokes on the walls. And there was this: Fleur kept a bird in her office. God only knew why this was allowed but she'd brought in the bird—it was a parakeet—one semester when she was, she said, spending more time here than at home, and didn't want it to be lonely. Now the bird was a permanent fixture, chirping all day long. Fleur put a blanket over the cage before leaving, and the bird went to sleep. Or so she said. When Kathleen lifted up the blanket, it wasn't sleeping, just staring back at her with tiny, waxy, jelly-bean eyes. She opened the office door—there was no one around—and then the cage. She reached in and grabbed the bird in her hand, and in the instant before she threw it out into the hallway, where it confusedly took flight, its yellow wings scraping the walls, she could feel the frenzied, angry beating of its miniature heart against her palm.

She went home and cooked shrimp scampi, which she ate while listening to Terence hold forth on Shakespeare and the irrelevance of canonical literature in today's digital world. When she glanced outside, a cardinal was sitting on the branch of an elm tree, looking back at her. She thought of the parakeet, trapped in the hallway of the Humanities Building or, alternately, flying around the campus, making its yellow way through a world it had never before seen. She felt remorseful, but also still corked with hate. Not a single thing had been exorcised from her soul.

At that moment, she understood—how belatedly!—that she detested not Fleur but herself, her own life, and most particularly her husband and his relentless occupation of that life. And that she'd hated all of this for a very long time.

"Terry," she said.

He cocked his head at her, birdlike, chewing. Sometimes conversation seemed like something he'd read about in a magazine, never experienced firsthand. To him, her preferable role was that of mute audience. Anything she said in response, even her agreement, was liable to piss him off, and he'd storm away from the table, never clearing or washing the dishes, to scour the cable channels.

"Never mind," she said.

For days she kept this knowledge to herself, clutching it to her body like a money belt. *I hate my husband.* She'd been fighting it for so long! Now that she knew, her relief was tempered only by the dread of telling him, then leaving him. She could picture so perfectly the scenario of her escape: she'd buy a little condo and furnish it simply but cozily, in reds and yellows, and she'd have fresh flowers and no stereo system or flat-screen TV, none of the consumer electronics Terry spent his weekends shopping for. But it was hard, if not impossible, to imagine how to get from here to there. His anger was scorching, and his speeches long-winded; she'd have to budget days, more likely weeks, to let him get it all out.

Then, one Sunday afternoon, Steve called to say he'd received a job offer in California—head turtle-keeper at a large municipal zoo—and was moving across the country to take it. Both Kathleen and Terence were happy for him, and not a little surprised that he'd managed to do so well.

"It's weird," Terence said when he got off the phone, his face thoughtful. "It'll just be the two of us now."

"It's been the two of us for a while," Kathleen pointed out.

"I know, but now it seems like he doesn't really need us anymore. He doesn't need"—Terence's gesture encompassed the house, the living room, the framed photographs, all the archival, institutional memory of the family—"any of *this*."

And from the way he said *this*—because, after all, as a professor of literature, she paid attention to the placement and nuance of words—she knew Terence was every bit as miserable as she was. So she spoke, for the first time in years, with genuine affection.

"Honey," she said, "let's get divorced."

They stayed up late making plans, more excited about this stage of their lives than anything since their honeymoon, practically. They couldn't stop expressing surprise and joy at these revelations; the discovery of shared misery was nearly as thrilling as that of mutual love had been. Terence said he wanted to take early retirement and drive a motorcycle to Central America. *What a cliché,* Kathleen thought. Then, realizing his behavior no longer implicated her, that she didn't need to be concerned, she told him it sounded like a great idea.

Because it was still the middle of the semester, because they wanted to sell the house and each buy a new one, because the start of a new life was a luxury that ought to be relished, they decided not to rush it. They spent spring break with their real estate agents, looking at houses in different neighborhoods. They stopped eating dinner together, and sometimes Kathleen just had a bowl of cereal and read a magazine, while Terence went out for a burger with his friend Dave. Dave had never been married, started drinking at noon on Saturdays, had false teeth, and believed himself irresistible to women. What Terence saw in him was a mystery, but she no longer—thank God—felt required to plumb its depths.

The week after spring break, Kathleen was at home grading papers when the phone rang. A man identifying himself as a police officer asked for her by name.

"What's this about?" she said.

"I'm afraid there's been an accident," he said. "Your husband is at the hospital."

"What kind of accident?"

"It's hard to say," he said.

"What do you mean? Is he okay?"

"He's not able to give us a statement at this time. I think you'd better come down right away."

When she got to the hospital, the officer was standing outside the room she'd been told was Terence's, along with a doctor and a rail-thin young man in a dirty hooded sweatshirt whose connection to the situation was unclear. They all started talking at once, and Kathleen stood there unable to understand any of the cacophony—questions, explanations, complications—until finally her teacher instincts kicked in and she said, "Stop. All of you." She pointed at the cop. "You first."

"Your husband appears to have been the victim of a crime," he said. The guy in the hoodie tried to interrupt, but Kathleen shushed him. "From what we understand, he was waiting at the stoplight by the Everton Mall when an individual wearing a ski mask entered the vehicle and asked Mr. Schwartz to exit. Mr. Schwartz appears to have refused. An altercation ensued."

"You're saying Terry was carjacked? At the mall?"

"As you know, there has been an escalation of violent crime in this area," the officer said gravely, "linked to the increased presence of illegal drugs."

The guy in the hoodie could no longer be contained. "I'm coming out of Sears and I see this guy dive into your husband's car. He's yelling '*Pterodactyl! Pterodactyl!*' and grabs your husband and pulls him out and starts beating him and then he leaves him in the middle of the road and screeches off in the car and he actually, uh, runs over your husband when he drives away."

"Pterodactyl?" Kathleen said.

"I think he was hallucinating—you know, tripping?" the man said. "My theory is that in his mind he was being pursued by this, like, animal, and getting away from it was the top priority?"

"Your husband's injuries are quite severe," the doctor added. They were in a rhythm now, this information committee, filling in the picture for her. "He's nonresponsive at this time."

"You're saying he's unconscious?"

"He's in the state you might know as a coma," the doctor said.

"Jesus," Kathleen said. "Can I see him?"

All three men nodded, as if giving her their collective permission.

Inside the dim, white room, Terence lay swaddled in tubes and gauze. Between the bandages, his skin looked bloated, purple, etched with rupture. He was Franken-Terry, a monster version of himself.

"Dear God," she said out loud. The machines beeped. She couldn't bring herself to touch him or even say his name.

The department gathered round. Everyone came to the hospital bearing flowers, cards, audiobooks. Lots of audiobooks. It seemed to have been universally agreed upon that the sounds of literature would bring Terence back to consciousness, a notion that Kathleen found both touching and ridiculous. She herself pictured his brain as rotten and pulpy, fruit that had been dropped on the ground. Playing books on tape seemed hardly adequate. It would be like reciting Beckett to a flesh wound.

But she thanked everyone and accepted the gifts with all the graciousness she could muster. Still, she couldn't help feeling she was just playing a part. She and Terry hadn't told anyone of the impending divorce. For one thing, they'd wanted to wait until the semester was over; for another, knowing that the gossip would rise in the halls to storm force, they each wanted to enjoy the secret knowledge of this surprise for a little while before unleashing it. The desire to spite their colleagues was one goal they still shared.

In a gesture meant to be kind, the department arranged for someone to take over not only Terry's classes but also hers. Kathleen called both real estate agents and told them they had to stop looking at condos. Her world shrank to the house and the hospital room, an orbit of two planets. At the hospital, she played Terry tapes—who knew, they might help—that were mostly, it turned out, of Shakespeare plays. Everyone had taken his profession of love for Shakespeare seriously. So Kathleen lost herself in the reci-

tation of *Romeo and Juliet, Troilus and Cressida,* leaning back in
the room's only chair, her eyes closed. Sometimes she forgot where
she was, but then she would open her eyes and see this broken,
silent mummy entombed by machines. It was impossible to know
how much of him was still there. The doctors said there was some
brain activity but couldn't specify what this actually meant or
how long the coma would last. *It's a waiting game,* they liked to
say, to which Kathleen always responded, "Game?" They'd smile
wryly, then leave the room.

She'd kept the news of the accident from Steve at first, because
she was afraid of what might happen to his recovery if he were
shaken too badly. The twelve steps were his only navigational tool
through the world, and she didn't entirely believe they'd keep him
on course. And indeed, when he came, he was a mess—red eyed,
ashen. He was six foot four and two hundred pounds, her son,
yet still managed to be the most fragile human being Kathleen
had ever known. No wonder he'd been drawn to turtles; he too
should've been born with a shell. Overly sensitive to the world, he
had had to swathe himself with drugs so as not to feel it too much.
Now, sober, he was unsheltered, exposed. One look at his father
and he burst into tears, shuddering against Kathleen, his spine
curling. If he could feasibly have crawled into her lap, she knew
he would've done so. Cradling his huge shoulders in her arms,
Kathleen cried too. His grief was the knife that sliced through her
own numb skin.

"It's going to be okay," she murmured to him, over and over.

"It is?" Steve said wildly. "How? When?"

"We just have to wait," she said. "It's a waiting game."

He wanted to know if he should put off his move to California,
to the better zoo with more kinds of turtles. She forbade it. She

told him Terry would want him to go. Which, if he had any brain activity inside the sleeping carapace of his body, he did.

The car was recovered in a wooded area off the interstate. Its windows had been left open, and the interior was colonized by raccoons—Terry had thought that patronizing McDonald's made him a man of the people—and soaked by rain. As a crime scene, it was less than pristine. Because the pterodactyl-seeing man had been wearing a ski mask; because the sole witness, the guy at the hospital, had been drinking; and because even violent crimes are just passing deeds in a world overflowing with them, the carjacking case did not get solved. At first the police called Kathleen regularly; she went to the station, reports were filed. Gradually she found herself calling them; eventually they stopped returning her calls. At night she sometimes dreamed of the hallucinating carjacker, and he was always riding the pterodactyl, hanging on to its leathery neck, laughing as it flew him up and away.

Steve loaded his possessions into a U-Haul and drove west, calling every day, then every other day, to report on his progress and new life. Her departmental colleagues, initially so solicitous, stopped visiting, and then their calls dropped off too. "End of the semester," they said apologetically. "You know how crazy it gets."

She was left alone with the breathing, silent body of her at-one-time-soon-to-be-ex-husband.

Only one person, of everyone she knew in the world, didn't seem to forget her, and this, horrifyingly, was Fleur Mason. She'd been part of the first departmental visit, and in that flurry of conversation Kathleen had been able to ignore her, though she suspected her of having left behind the white teddy bear holding a mug that read *Get well soon!* But she was unavoidable when she came alone, a week later, with a box of chocolates and basket of specialty teas. She stood next to the bed and said cheerfully, "He doesn't look so bad, does he? I think he looks better than last week."

Kathleen missed her job, her students, her son, and, most of all, the sense of a future without constant irritation opening up before her, a future that—like Tantalus and his grapes—seemed to have been ripped away just as she was about to grab it. But of everything she'd gone through, being alone with Fleur Mason in a hospital seemed the most intolerable. And while she'd realized that her irritation was merely a substitute for other hatreds, that didn't mean she liked the woman any better. She still found her presence, her clothing, her voice, her manner—in short, *her*—as intensely aggravating as before.

So she didn't say much when Fleur showed up, just glared— figuring it was her prerogative to be rude. And she also figured that it was better to discourage Fleur now, based on the same principle she used as a strict, even harsh grader on the first paper of the semester, so the students would know she wasn't a pushover.

If Fleur got the message, she didn't show it. She cocked her head and spoke in a high, chirping voice apparently meant to be sympathetic. "You'll get through this, Kathleen," she said. "I know you will. You're a very strong woman, and you'll prevail."

Kathleen said, "Whatever happened to that bird of yours? Did anybody ever figure out who took it?"

"Um, no," Fleur said, clearly rattled. She looked down at the ground and fiddled with the fringed edges of her beaded, ruffled scarf.

"Maybe no one took it," Kathleen said. "Maybe it just escaped."

Fleur was looking at Terence now, at the cage of his body. If Kathleen wasn't mistaken, there were tears in her eyes. "Stranger things have happened," she said.

Each week, Fleur came back. Sometimes she came to the hospital, during visiting hours, but more often, as time dragged on, she came to the house, dropping in on Kathleen on Thursday afternoons after classes were over. She brought a book, or brownies, or departmental gossip, and also, sadly, she brought the annoying gift of her personality and her chortling, exasperating laugh.

Kathleen made no attempt to be polite; she never offered coffee or tea, or even thanked her for coming by. Fleur took to bringing coffee with her, in a thermos, and separately packed containers of milk and sugar, along with cookies that she arranged on a floral plate. Which she also brought. She was a portable concession, a coffee-shop-mobile.

She rarely asked about Terry, seeming to assume that if there was news on that front, Kathleen would tell her. Rather, she asked about Kathleen's week, what she'd been doing, as if she had a life. And because Kathleen was proud, she found herself anticipating this question throughout the week and then developing a life in order to have an answer. She read books, knitted a scarf, watched a documentary film about turtles so that she could understand her son's job better. These things weren't much, but they were better than nothing, and in Fleur's presence she offered them to herself.

Fleur days, as she thought of them, gave her weeks their only shape. Otherwise she separated the days into mornings, which she spent at home, afternoons, spent with Terry, and evenings, with a bottle of wine. Each day was distinguished from the next only by the shift rotations of the hospital staff, all of whom she came to know by name. She asked after their kids and helped them celebrate their birthdays by eating sheet cake in the lounge.

Alone with Terry every afternoon, she played Shakespeare for him and read. She rarely spoke to him. The doctors had told her that the sound of her voice might help, but reading to him would have felt too much like pretending. She sat with him. She watched as they changed his catheter, his bandages. His skin was healing, and day by day he looked less like bruised fruit and more like supermarket poultry, naked and trussed up.

Inside the hard container of his skull, his brain was also trying to heal, she imagined, pulsing gently as it rifled through useless things—childhood memories, sports scores, Marxist theory—in search of some pure cells that would bring him back to life.

It was entirely possible, the doctors said, that he might never wake up. They spoke in measured tones of percentages and possibilities. She needed, they said, to be prepared for every eventuality. But when she pressed them for details—When do I decide? To do what? And how will I know?—they shook their heads and counseled patience.

To say that what she felt, sitting next to him, was complicated would be more than understatement. She believed, with all her heart, that Terry didn't want her there; that he had long hated her just as she had hated him; that her presence had grown to be a burden, even the sound of her chewing, or the rhythm of her steps, inconsequential things that only married people can hate. It was as a gesture of kindness that she didn't read to him, because surely being in a coma doesn't erase the irritation caused by your wife's voice. With all the troubled intimacy of their twenty-six years together she knew this. And this same knowledge also bound them, making her come back every single day to visit this trussed chicken who had been her lover and her companion and her enemy. Because she was all he had left.

At home that night, a little tipsy, she called Dave. "It's Kathleen," she said.

There was a pause.

"Terry's wife," she said.

"Oh, right," he said. It was ten o'clock, and he also sounded drunk. "Everything okay? I mean, how's Terry?"

"He's the same. Why haven't you been to see him? You're his best friend."

There was another pause. "I am?" he said.

"Jesus," she said. "Listen, I have to ask you something and I need you to be honest. For Terry's sake."

She had a memory of Dave, back when she and Terry still had parties, slipping a bottle of vodka to their son and shrugging afterward, saying that the longer you kept it away, the worse kids wanted it. They found poor Steve at three in the morning, puking in the park, and he swore he'd never again touch alcohol. Which was true, actually, he'd only snorted drugs, so maybe Dave wasn't completely off base.

"Sure, anything," he was saying now.

"Was Terry having an affair?"

"Oh, Kathy," he said. "No."

"I'm not asking for the reason you think I am," she said. "I'm not *mad*. I just thought that if he was, he'd probably want her in the room, do you know what I mean? Instead of me? So I thought it would be nice to invite her or whatever. As a . . ." She stumbled to find the right word, then her mind seized it, brilliantly: "A mitzvah."

Dave, like Terry, was Jewish; Kathleen was Irish Catholic, though the question of religion was one they had always resolutely ignored. But Dave, right now, didn't sound pleased to hear her use the word *mitzvah*. In fact, he sounded sober and annoyed. "There's no girl, Kathy. Get some sleep."

She told him not to call her Kathy, but he'd already hung up.

The notion of an affair preoccupied her for some time. In truth she suspected Fleur—nothing else, she thought, could explain her relentless visitation—yet there wasn't anything in their conversations to support it; Fleur gave no indication of knowing anything more about Terry's life than Kathleen did, and she had little curiosity about him, either. She only wanted to talk about Kathleen, her interests and opinions, her mental and physical health. She kept insisting that Kathleen had a life, against all evidence to the contrary. It was, frankly, more than a little weird.

Summer came, and Fleur left town for two weeks to visit her family in Wisconsin. Kathleen had been looking forward to this Fleur-less time for ages. Finally she would have some peace. She wouldn't watch any DVDs or read the newspaper or knit. She would sit around in her pajamas and be miserable without interruption or witness.

It was an unpleasant surprise, then, to discover that she missed Fleur. She felt like she was going out of her mind, in fact. The days were formless, chaotic. Her visits to Terry seemed hollow because there was no one to report to about them. Her evenings collapsed into drinking and endless crappy television—she was appalled by how much of it Terry used to watch; it was such an obvious cry for help—and she woke up at three a.m. sobbing with loneliness and despair.

Dear God, she thought. *Fleur Mason, whom I hate, is my best friend.*

When Fleur got back to town, she came over the next day. Kathleen had cleaned the house, baked muffins, and brewed coffee. Fleur took it all in stride. She described her vacation, then asked Kathleen about her family.

Instead of answering, Kathleen said, "I have to tell you something."

Fleur set her muffin down. "Shoot," she said.

"I was the one who took your bird out of its cage," Kathleen said. Even as she said it she wasn't sure why she was confessing. To kill the friendship or strengthen it: both urges commingled in her mind, her heart.

"I know," Fleur said.

"You do?"

"You're the only one with a key to the office. Except the custodian, and he loves birds. He keeps pigeons at home, did you know that? I also know you didn't want to hire me in the first place, and then tried to terminate my contract in the second year." This was true, though Kathleen had thought it was a secret. "And I know you told people my teaching was terrible and that you didn't want me to get tenure."

"If you know all that," Kathleen said slowly, "why are you here?"

She steeled herself for what she was about to hear, the words like grit that would rub her skin raw. *Because I get to pity you. And that is my revenge.*

Fleur laughed her too-long laugh. "Just because you don't like me," she said, "doesn't mean I don't get to like you."

"What the hell does that mean?" Kathleen said grumpily.

"You're smart and sensible. I look up to you. I figured whatever issues you had with me, eventually you'd get over them, if I didn't let myself get distracted by the other stuff."

"I don't know what to say," Kathleen said.

"And anyway, the custodian found Harry, so no harm done."

"Harry?"

"My parakeet. He found Harry in the men's room and trapped him for me. As I said, he has pigeons and knows about birds. So he called me and I brought Harry home. He's fine."

"Everybody thought he was gone. They said you were heart-broken."

"It doesn't hurt," Fleur said mildly, "to let people feel sorry for you every once in a while."

The next day, at the hospital, Kathleen didn't play any Shake-speare. She opened the blinds—Terry loved the sun and wanted to retire to Florida and play golf all day, after the motorcycle trip to South America—and sat next to the bed. The view was of the parking lot, where a few spindly trees played host to crows and sparrows, but at least the light was bright. She looked at her hus-band. The bandages had been removed, and his skin was per-versely healthy, even pink. On his hands were scabs, raised like tattoos on his knuckles. His beard had grown but the nurses kept it trimmed, so if anything he looked more professorial than ever. She put a hand on the coarse crinkle of hair on his head.

"Oh, Terry," she found herself saying. She'd known him for so long that this familiarity, however abrasive it had become, was inextricable from love. She felt so badly for him, for everything he'd been through—a Niagara Falls of sorry that crashed through her in a torrent, flooding her voice with tears. "My heart, my love." She touched his cheek, his shoulder, the pale skin beneath his papery gown. "Come back to me, love. Come back, please, please, come back, please, please, please."

She spent the night at the hospital, in the chair by his bed, and when she woke up in the morning, the crows cawing outside, she saw that his eyes were open and he was looking at her expectantly, as if she were the one who had just spent so much time asleep.

It had been three months, but to Terry it was as if no time had passed. He said he felt like he'd woken up from a particularly long nap. Of the accident itself he had no memory whatsoever; the last thing he could remember was buying lunch at McDonald's and eating french fries as he drove home. Within three days of awakening he was released from the hospital, though Kathleen drove him back every day for physical therapy for his atrophied muscles and cognitive therapy for his atrophied mind.

She had no idea whether her voice had finally woken him up, hating to think that if she'd only spoken sooner, instead of delegating all the responsibility to Shakespeare, she might have shortened his ordeal. And she was astonished to think that in spite of the bad years and all of the misery, he still needed to hear her voice. The intensity of the grievous emotion she'd felt that night in the hospital had thinned in the morning, but she couldn't help wondering if all the divorce talk had been a mistake, if maybe, just possibly, they still loved each other after all.

But she didn't talk to him about any of this, just helped him get through the days. She fed him and led him to the bathroom, his shrunken body leaning sharply against hers, more connected than they'd been in years. He slept almost fifteen hours a day, and the house was very quiet. When awake, he said little and asked for nothing. He seemed tranquilized. In the mornings he sat out in the backyard, a blanket covering his knees, and listened to the birds. Kathleen had strung up feeders and houses, something he had always discouraged, claiming the house would be swamped with bird feces and noise, but he wasn't complaining now. He was peaceful in his recovery, though it was unclear if this peace was spiritual, related to his near-death experience, or material, a symptom of brain damage. The waiting game was still going on.

It was a still, humid day in July when she brought him outside and left him to sit there in the sunlight. She was almost back inside when she heard him say something. Turning, she saw the tears streaming down his face. She could remember the exact last time she'd seen him cry, at his mother's funeral, ten years earlier. Now he was crying quietly, letting the tears come, his skinny arms resting by his sides. He was looking up at the sky, where she saw, following his gaze, a red-tailed hawk circling high above them. It soared and swung, strong and heavy winged, eyeing whatever prey it had spotted below.

Through his tears Terry spoke again. "Pterodactyl," he said. "Fucking lunatic."

. . .

Gradually, he recovered his brain, his words, and was able to walk around the house, then around the block. Still, they never talked about what was going to happen between them, if their future was shared or separate. Kathleen wasn't even sure how she felt about it anymore. Their shared project, for now, was his recovery, just as for years their son's well-being had been their shared project, one so hulking and important that it had overshadowed everything else.

As soon as he could, Steve flew home to visit. Next to his father he seemed gigantic and healthy. He was loving California and told them all about the turtle habitat, his apartment close to the beach, what seemed to be a promising relationship with a girl who worked in the reptile house.

Across the table, Terry gave him a benevolent, post-coma smile. "That's wonderful, kid," he said. "Now listen. Your mother and I are getting divorced."

Steve laughed, thinking it was a joke.

Kathleen stared at her husband. This was typical, pre-accident Terry, not to consult or even consider Steve's reaction, or her own.

"Sorry," he said to her. "It just came out."

"What the hell?" Steve said, and turned to Kathleen. "Is this for real? Are you seriously leaving him right after his accident?"

"It's not like that," she said faintly. She felt dizzy, as if she were floating disassociated above the scene.

"Or you?" Steve said to his father. "Is this some midlife crisis thing after the coma? You're going to date twenty-year-olds now, to prove you're alive?"

Terry refused to be rattled. "We planned this long before the accident. It just set us back a little, that's all. We know you want us both to be happy, and we think we'll be happier living separately. It's amicable. We'll both always be here for you. Just in two houses instead of one."

"Two houses. That's all you think it is?" Steve said. The veneer of adulthood chipped off, leaving him an angry teenager, explosive and bereft. His chair scraped as he pushed it away from the table and stormed out of the house. Terry and Kathleen sat looking at each other across the table. She opened her mouth and found she had nothing, not one single thing, to say.

The following morning, Steve sat by himself in the backyard muttering angrily, an old habit Kathleen had hoped he'd outgrown. Terry was in the living room, reading and listening to music. He hadn't turned on the television since he came home from the hospital. It was strange, but no more so than anything else, she supposed.

The doorbell rang, and it was Fleur. Since Terry was released she hadn't visited, and Kathleen was pleased to see her. She actually hugged her, garnering a certain amount of satisfaction from Terry's silent but unmistakable surprise. Fleur waved to him, and if Kathleen still had any lingering doubts about an affair, her casual, uncomplicated friendliness dispelled them.

"Welcome back, miracle man!" Fleur said cheerily. "You are arisen."

"Uh," Terry said.

"I've missed you," Kathleen said to Fleur. "Thanks for coming by."

Fleur smiled, as unruffled by this as she'd been by Kathleen's rudeness in previous months, and allowed herself to be led into the kitchen. Kathleen gestured to where her son sat outside. The windows were open, and they could hear his mutterings.

"God grant me the strength to accept the things I cannot change," he was saying. "But still, I mean, come on, what the hell?"

"Don't you think that's weird?" she said. "He's twenty-five years old."

Fleur shrugged. "Maybe I should go talk to him."

"You? Why?"

"Why not?" Fleur said.

She walked outside without waiting for permission. She was wearing a flowery yellow shirtdress, like a housewife from a previous generation, and her wavy brown hair fluttered in the summer breeze. She sat down next to Steve and put her hand on his shoulder.

"Do you want to pray with me?" Fleur said, as Kathleen watched.

Her son nodded and bowed his head. So far as Kathleen could remember he'd never met Fleur, but he didn't ask who she was or why she was there. The two of them held hands in the brilliant sunshine, bird-lover and turtle-keeper. She heard Fleur say, "Dear God," and the rest of it was lost in the wind.

Dear God, Kathleen thought. *Is this the game we're playing now? The accident, the coma, Fleur's visits, the pterodactyl? Are these signs and wonders? And if so, what do they mean?* She couldn't decipher them; she couldn't read her life that way. Over the months to come, as her misery, so long-nurtured, ebbed; as the divorce was filed; as Steve announced he was marrying the reptile girl in California; as she and Fleur remained best friends; as Terry fell in love with a student and almost lost his job before recovering himself and his sanity; as she started to date her real estate agent, Bob, and eventually invited him to move in with her in the condo he'd helped her buy—she still didn't learn the answers to these questions. But she could feel them all around her, the questions of her life, at times beating like wings, at times soaring cleanly through the air, and she could only wonder how it was that she had never felt them before.

Forks

Alan was lying facedown in Center Square, a squiggle of vomit on the pavement beside him, his one good leg folded sideways. He looked bad and smelled worse, and if he'd been anybody else I would've kept walking. But he was Stephanie's brother, so we both bent down and I shook his shoulder. The classical music the city played to discourage loitering trilled around us, and on the other side of the square two homeless guys smoked their cigarettes and watched.

"Hey, kiddo," Stephanie said, crouching next to him and feeling for his pulse, her curly blond hair spilling over her shoulders. Together, we dragged him to a sitting position, against a stone memorial to the Civil War dead. Alan's head lolled to the side. Having seen the family photos, I knew that at one time he'd been a good-looking teenager, green-eyed, with a dimple in his cheek. It was hard to imagine girls going for him now. During his second tour in Afghanistan, an IED took off his left foot, and since he came back, Stephanie said, he'd been struggling. That looked like an understatement.

We hoisted him up and anchored him on our shoulders. His eyes were closed, but I could feel him trying to steady himself, to help us out. It took fifteen minutes to get him across the street and into the backseat of Stephanie's Civic. She wanted to sit back there with him, so I drove us up the hill to Forks Township. Her condo was in a subdivision that had sprung up too fast, and half the houses were empty. With all those carless driveways and skinny, seedling trees, the neighborhood had a creepy feel. As I drove, I glanced at them in the rearview mirror. Her arm was around him, his head leaning against her neck. His eyelids fluttered. He was smiling.

I met Stephanie my first week at the clinic, which was also my first week in the Lehigh Valley. I was a brand-new doctor, and newly single. Robin, my girlfriend since medical school, had said she'd come with me to Pennsylvania but then, at the last minute, took a job in San Francisco instead. She'd barely even apologized. "San Francisco, Tom," she'd said, spreading her palms, the difference between California and eastern Pennsylvania too manifest to require explanation. So I moved alone. The job was at a large practice with a staff of young doctors, including me, who rotated through before pushing on to bigger hospitals in other cities. I myself didn't plan on being here long. What I hoped was to set up my own practice in a nice suburb of Philly, maybe Cherry Hill, where I'd grown up; this place was just a stopover.

Stephanie was the head nurse on my first shift. Her hair was pulled back in a ponytail that fought to contain it; it frizzed around her forehead, and she kept lifting her hand to smooth it down. She showed me around the place, introduced me to every-one, and from the offhand way she said my name I understood that she had my number and didn't count on my staying long either. She was a good nurse, unflappable and smart. Two weeks after we met, I was walking to my car when I noticed her leaving at the same time.

"Hey," I said.

"Doctor."

"Call me Tom, please."

"Okay, Tom," she said. Her tone was not inviting. She was wearing a lumpy brown cardigan over pink scrubs and Crocs, as unattractive an outfit as I'd ever seen, but somehow I still kept straining at its outlines, wondering just what it disguised.

"Buy you a drink? I don't really know where to go around here, but maybe you can tell me."

She cocked her head to one side, not smiling. I was expecting her to shake her head, but instead she said, "Let's go."

She took me to a sports bar, and over drinks she was quiet. At one point, I caught her looking at her watch. But then she leaned over to me in the booth and suddenly we were making out. She tasted like chicken wings and rum.

She never sought me out at work, and we didn't flirt there, but whenever I'd ask her if she wanted to grab a bite or a drink, she said yes. Stephanie was a local, born and raised in Macungie; her father had worked at Bethlehem Steel until it closed, her mother as a secretary for the school district. They didn't have a lot of money, and she'd put herself through nursing school working as a waitress. As soon as she told me that, I felt like I could picture her no-nonsense way of taking orders, a change belt wrapped around her thin hips.

"I bet you got great tips," I said.

She looked at me, her mouth in a straight line. She had these deadpan expressions that took me a while to figure out, and I liked her for that.

"Enough for school," she said. "And a car. And a couple trips to Mexico."

We'd been dating for around a month when she called and asked me to help her with her brother. She hadn't said much about him, just that he'd been injured while serving and she wasn't sure what he'd do now. He was younger than her by a few years, and I had the feeling she'd always looked out for him. They'd gone to high school with a guy who was now on the police force, and he'd called her when Alan passed out in the square.

On the short drive back to her place, we didn't say much. I could hear her talking to him in the backseat, just simple things. "You don't look good, Alan. We're going to take you home and get you cleaned up. I'll make you some grilled cheese. Or whatever you want." As if she were his mother. Her arm was around his, their blond heads clustered together, and I felt like their chauffeur, some hired hand. When we got there, she guided him into the bathroom. His clothes stank, and his arms and chest were crowded with tattoos and bruises. He looked tough, but he was pliant while we stripped him.

Together we bathed him, as if he were a dirty overgrown child, and he started to come around a little. He didn't seem upset that we were manhandling him. He was very polite. "Thanks," he kept saying, and "I'm sorry." When he was more or less clean, we helped him out of the bathtub and Stephanie asked me to get him some fresh clothes from a dresser in her bedroom. Apparently they were his own clothes, because they fit just fine.

"This is Tom," Stephanie told him, once he was dressed.

"I'm sorry we met like this," Alan said. He held out his hand and we shook. His blond hair was lank, and his green eyes were bloodshot, rimmed with exhaustion. I'd have given him a B12 shot and locked him in rehab for a month, but he wasn't my brother.

"No problem," I said.

She fed him a grilled cheese sandwich, as promised, and put him in her spare room. Then she and I went to bed.

"Are you okay?" I said.

"It's not the first time," she said, shrugging helplessly. "His leg kills him."

"What's he on, medication-wise?"

"He's been on everything. He always says it doesn't help."

She was undressed for bed, and her back was covered in tiny freckles. I set myself to tracing them with my index finger, making constellations out of them, a triangle, a star. I loosed her hair from its ponytail, and it sprang to life, a million curls clouding her shoulders. She lay down and folded herself against me, pulling my arm across her stomach. I wondered if she was crying. But she turned, and kissed me, then moved down my stomach and took me in her mouth, and I closed my eyes, not thinking about anything else at all.

After that night, I was deep into Stephanie's life, and I liked it there. We started spending most weekends together, and I met her parents, who were sweet, tired people, too impressed that I was a doctor for me to be comfortable around them. She showed me around Bethlehem: the shuttered factory they'd turned into a casino, the quaint cobblestoned Main Street, the shambling towpath along the Delaware canal. Sometimes we went hiking in the Poconos, the mountains' dazzling green bisected by the truck-heavy rumble of I-80. The whole place seemed hardscrabble to me, gritty and rural, and as much as I liked Stephanie, I had a hard time imagining staying there for long.

As I got to know her, I realized how closely her life and Alan's were intertwined. She was constantly bailing him out, helping him get job interviews, putting him up for the night when another in his series of housing arrangements—he'd get a new roommate or a new girlfriend, then argue with them and move out—crumbled.

I answered the door one night in December to find him standing on the doorstep, swaying a little. Over one shoulder was a blue backpack he always had with him, and sometimes I wondered if it contained all his worldly possessions.

"Yo," he said. "I don't think we've met."

"We have, actually. More than once."

"It was a joke, Doctor Tom."

"Oh," I said. He was just as deadpan as his sister. "Come on in. Steph's cooking."

When she saw him coming into the kitchen her face lit up, nothing deadpan about that. She was always happy when he came, no matter what condition he was in. For the first few minutes, we were so distracted by the commotion of cooking and getting all the food on the table that we didn't notice how high he was. But then I realized he wasn't eating, just holding up his fork and looking at it, as if inspecting it for cleanliness. He seemed transfixed. After a while the two of us watched in silence.

Finally he noticed, and put it down. "It's beautiful, you know?" he said.

"It's Mom and Dad's old set," Stephanie said. She passed me

some garlic bread, nudging me to hand the basket to Alan. She wanted him to get something into his stomach.

"No, I mean forks in general," Alan said musingly. "There's this perfection to them. You know what word I've always liked? *Tines.* The *tines of a fork.* It sounds so perfect, like little chimes. Like a trinity. Like a trinity of chimes."

"Oh, kiddo," Stephanie said. "What did you take?"

Alan smiled at her. He was the most affable addict I'd ever met. "I feel good," he said. "I got a little help from Ludo."

This was a guy from Allentown who'd served in Alan's unit. They hung around together a lot, though they often fought, Ludo driving off and leaving him stranded at a bar, or a McDonald's at midnight, or a truck stop in Ohio, halfway through some road trip they'd cooked up and then abandoned.

I could see he wasn't going to eat anything, and Stephanie's eagerness for him to be there like a normal person was tearing at my heart. "How about you lie down for a bit?" I said.

He smiled at me, his green eyes warm. "That's not a terrible idea, sir," he said. He settled himself on the couch, and in a couple minutes we could hear him snoring. At first Stephanie just sat there, staring down at her spaghetti, tears glimmering in her eyes. But I reminded her she didn't want to get sick, that she had to keep her strength up, and she nodded and lifted her fork. She was sensible like that.

After dinner, I did the dishes while Stephanie made up the spare room for Alan, then crashed in front of the TV. To my surprise, when I went back there to check on him, he was awake. The bedside lamp was on and he was reading one of her *Cosmo*s.

"Guess what?" he said when he saw me. "The female body has a hundred pleasure receptors."

"Must be nice," I said.

"Seriously," he said. "I know maybe three."

"Yeah." This wasn't a topic I was interested in pursuing. "You need anything?"

"Where's Steph?"

"Sleeping. She's had a long day."

"I hear you," he said. "I hear you." He was sitting propped up against the pillows, his legs straight out in front of him. With his shoes still on you couldn't tell which one was the prosthetic foot. He saw me looking.

"You're a doctor. Tell me why it's the one that's gone that hurts."

"The nerve endings," I said. "They call it ghost pain. The Oxy-Contin should help."

He snorted. "I'm not going to lie to you, OxyContin's like baby aspirin to me at this point."

I didn't know what to say to this. "How's the physical therapy going?"

"How do you think?" He closed his eyes, and a small smile played across his face. "I was in this tank once, me and Ludo," he said. "We were going through this patch of desert when we heard all this artillery, it sounded real heavy. And then it just stopped. Ludo tells me to stick my head out and see what's going on. I say no way, I'm gonna get killed. We argue about it for a while. Finally I say okay and stick my head out the top. I look around and I can't see a damn thing. Not one single person for miles. All I see is this brown desert. After a while, none of it makes sense to me. You know how if you look at a word too long, you can't tell if it's a real word? I couldn't even tell the difference between the sand

and the sky. Finally Ludo pulls me back down. The weird thing is, we never did hear anything about combat engagement that day. Nobody ever said one word about it."

"Was that where you got hurt?" I said.

"No," he said. "That was somewhere else."

He was so quiet after that I figured he'd fallen asleep. I was about to switch off the light when he finally spoke. "You got anything on you, Doctor Tom?"

"Sorry."

"Don't hold out on me," he said. He opened his eyes and there was no affability there, no sweetness at all. "Don't you fucking hold out."

I could see how much he hated me. For being a doctor, for fucking his sister. For having both my feet, for waking each day without pain. "I don't have anything," I said, and left.

Steph kept inviting him over for dinner. I think she hoped that the more time he spent with her, in her calm, organized orbit, the more it would rub off on him. Or maybe she was just hoping to keep him decently fed. When invited, he always showed up, always toting that backpack, mostly sober, sometimes not. Once I woke up at midnight and went to the bathroom only to find him passed out next to the sink. I poured cold water over his head to wake him up. He came around slowly, shaking his head, and grabbed at me. He'd lost weight, and he was scrawny, but his arms were strong and ropy with muscle. I went through his backpack. He had five different medications in there but all the vials were empty. Other than the meds, there was nothing in the backpack except a dog-eared copy of *Sports Illustrated* and wallet with a Costco card in it.

"Please get the fuck off me," he said, pushing me away.

"How much did you take?"

"I couldn't sleep."

"Did you throw up?"

"I don't think so."

"Do it now."

"I'm sleepy now, man."

"Do it now, or I'll have to take you in and pump your stomach."

"Okay," he said, "Okay." He stuck his fingers down his throat until he gagged. He seemed practiced at it. I sat with him for an hour or so, leaning next to him against the wall and making him drink water, until I felt like he was all right.

Midnight, Tuesday. It was February, an icy night with the roads as slick as rinks, when we got the call from St. Luke's. Someone had found Alan behind a bar. It seemed possible he'd been there an entire day and night before he was discovered. The temperature hadn't been above freezing for a week. By the time we got to the hospital, he was awake. The skin on his face was peeling, his lips cracked and bloody.

"Hey, kiddo," Stephanie said. As she leaned over him, covering his hand with hers, he bared his teeth at her like an animal.

"Leave me the fuck alone," he said.

Stephanie had just worked a double shift. Exhausted, she started to cry. "Alan," she said.

I touched her arm. "Why don't you take a minute?"

She hung her head. She didn't want to leave him, but she was about to lose it. She nodded, resigned. "I'm going to call Mom and Dad," she told him. "I'll be right back."

As soon as she was gone his mood seemed to clear, and he grinned at me. The dimple in his cheek was still there when he smiled, incongruous against the chapped skin. I'd never seen him like this, his moods so all over the place.

"I only got frostbite in one foot," he said. "So that's an upside."

"It's good to stay positive," I said.

Just as quickly as it had arrived, his manic mood left and his grin evaporated. His green eyes were steady. "You could really do me a favor, you know," he said. "Man to man." He didn't say anything else. He cocked his head in the direction of his backpack.

I knew he probably had a whole pharmacy in there. He'd been at the VA hospital in Wilkes-Barre, and they were trying out some new meds, seeing if they could control his pain any better. Stephanie had told me she was hopeful it was going to work, but she said this every time, about each new treatment and every fresh promise from Alan. At work, I'd seen her treat patients with cool professionalism, helpful as she could be, distant as she needed to be. With her brother, it was always going to be different.

"Help me out, Doctor Tom," he said.

He had that deadpan expression, but it wasn't disguising some flash of humor. It was just dead. "Please," he said.

I picked up his backpack and placed it on his bed. It was heavy, and I didn't ask what was in it. I brought him some water, then turned off the light and closed the door behind me. The hallway was deserted, and I found Stephanie and took her down to the lobby and made her drink a cup of coffee, keeping her down there as long as I could. The nurses went to check on him, but not in time.

I'd been a doctor for less than a year.

I wouldn't say he looked peaceful. I would say he looked shrunken, and ill-used, and older than his age, which was twenty-six.

I held Stephanie in my arms while she cried. I knew then, feeling her lean into me, feeling my own sadness catch fire from hers, that I loved her, and wanted to marry her, and I stored this feeling away in my heart for a happier day, assuming that we would get to one eventually.

There was a small service, at which Alan and Stephanie's mother cried dryly, hopelessly, and Ludo gave the eulogy. He said Alan had saved his life by walking in front of him one day, that otherwise, he would have been the one who got injured. "It sucks," he said.

After the first week, Stephanie didn't cry all that much. She threw herself into work, double and even triple shifts; she would have worked even more if rules hadn't forbidden it. In the evenings she cooked for me and ate very little herself, and I tried to be there for her, to listen if she wanted to talk, to hold her at night when she turned to me. On weekends we went on walks, and to the movies. Once, we went to Atlantic City and drank too much and gambled and slept together, and when she smiled for what seemed like the first time in months, I began to feel the clouds parting around us.

Then one night I came home at six and Stephanie was lying on the couch sobbing violently, her shoulders shaking with the force of it. I got her a tissue and she blew her nose into it, honkingly.

She sat up, her knees pulled up to her chin like a child. "It just sort of hit me," she said, "that he's never coming back."

There was nothing I could do to comfort her. She wouldn't let me touch her. I wondered if on some level she knew, or suspected, what I'd done. "Leave me alone," she kept saying, and she sounded just like her brother. I left the house, drove around for a while, stopped at a bar. I started thinking about my old life in Philadelphia, the friends I had there, and the women I'd known, and it seemed like I'd been under some kind of spell, living an unreal life. I had these thoughts, but when I got back to the condo, Stephanie had composed herself. She fixed us each a drink.

"I'm sorry," she said. "It's just so hard."

"I know," I said.

I put my arms around her, and we sat together on the couch. She leaned against my shoulder, her hair brushing my chin. I looked out the window at the half-empty subdivision. No lights showed in the houses nearby, and the blackness of the street blended into the inky night. There was no horizon. It reminded me of the story Alan had told me, about not being able to tell the difference between sand and sky. It sounded almost beautiful to me, to be lost for a moment like that, with no one to tell you which way was up.

Robbing the Cradle

They were making a baby. They were going about it in the traditional way. In a ceremonial moment, Lisette put her birth-control pills away in a shoe box that she then buried in the back of the bedroom closet, underneath the silver pumps she wore only to weddings. She had loved Dan for five years, two of them as his wife, and would have said, if asked, that she couldn't possibly love him any more than she already did. But this turned out to be false; what had come before was only a beginning, a small green bud. Now that they were planning a family, a new tenderness grew between them, sweet but not spineless, because it was also taut with possibility. When he held her, when he lingered on top, inside her, his light sweat sticking to her belly, when he came, sex itself seemed entirely different. It was wonderful and terrible and holy, to be in love and to know there will soon be a person in the world embodying that love. Half of each of you, combined.

Fueled by this intense, thrilling notion, they had sex all the time. In the supermarket, they held hands. In the evenings, when Lisette was at work with the youth orchestra, running the teenagers through Tchaikovsky, she ached for her husband, for his hair and smell and skin. Thinking about him, wanting him, she found a sensual component, if not sexual, in the stroke of a bow across a cello's wide flank, a kiss to the lip of a flute. Everything was a body, everything seemed ripe. The kids, who were between fifteen and eighteen, braced, head-geared, rippled with acne and colt-ish energy, used to both annoy and entertain her. They'd gotten along well, joking and teasing and even liking one another. But now she felt maternal. She was nicer, more patient, and physical, too—a little pat on the shoulder or brush of the arm letting them know how special they were. There was nothing inappropriate in it. Her energy was all for Dan, and what brimmed over was just extra caring and love. Sensing this, the kids responded. Instead of complaining about the Tchaikovsky being too hard, or hating the modern pieces (which is what they usually did at the start of the season, so that by the time the Christmas concert came around they'd be sure to score major victories in technique and sophisti-cation), they bent their heads and practiced, practiced, practiced.

When Dan came home from work each afternoon—he taught math at the same high school where she rehearsed—they made love before dinner, in between his day and hers. It was like being newlyweds all over again. Sometimes, Lisette thought back to their wedding day, when she'd felt a squeeze in her chest so strong she'd almost thought it might be a heart attack. She and Dan had exchanged vows in front of all their friends and family, then leaned close and whispered a private vow just to each other, some-thing no one else could hear. These days were like that moment all over again: they moved inside a rosy cloud, a bubble of promise, the family-to-be.

This went on for a year.

Each month she expected to get pregnant, and each month she didn't. She couldn't understand it. She was young, healthy, ready. By the sixth month, she started to think of her period using her grandmother's antiquated term. *The curse.* She paid more and more attention to the slightest shifts in her body's chemistry, its devious ecosystem of hormones and blood, tending to it even as it steadily let her down. She took vitamins, supplements, evening primrose, folic acid. She became an expert in ovulation and cervical mucus. She gauged, with a scientist's exactitude, the swell of her breasts, the frequency of her tears, all the symptoms that presaged another failed attempt. When the curse came, relentlessly punctual every month, she would lock herself in the bathroom and cry.

Those nights, once she returned to the bedroom, Dan would hold her. He never cried. He always had hope. He said, "It hasn't been that long." He said this for six months, seven months, eight.

At the year mark, they made doctors' appointments. Lisette's results were normal. When Dan's came back, he was very pale. He looked as sick as she'd ever seen him; even his bushy brown beard seemed to have wilted like some underwatered plant.

"It's me," he said. "I'm the one letting you down."

The test was conclusive. His sperm—the doctor, with ill-advised jocularity, kept calling them his *guys*—were unlikely to ever produce a child. He didn't have very many, and the ones he did have were not highly motivated. His guys were underachievers. They wouldn't get their lazy asses off the couch. If they were a sports team they'd be in last place, with no possibility of a turnaround, even with the best coaching.

So that was that. No treatment existed. Nothing could be done. They didn't make love for the next two weeks. When Dan came home from work he'd go out for a long run, snaking through the curving streets of their town, and after that he'd make dinner or eat what she'd made and immediately afterward go upstairs to his office, pleading homework to correct, lesson plans to revise. On rehearsal nights, instead of waiting up for her, as he usually did, he'd be in bed by the time she got home, feigning sleep. On the weekends he went for marathon runs, returning soaked with sweat and aggravation, no tension having been released. He'd been a track star in high school, won a scholarship to college, graduated with honors. He offered free math tutoring after school to kids whose families couldn't afford it. He'd never cheated, taken a shortcut, or quit a job because it was too hard. This was the first time he'd failed to meet his own standards.

As for Lisette, there were things she had to jettison. The vision of their children, their genetic cocktail, his brown eyes and her ash-blond hair. Of course she had already named them, kissed them, rocked them to sleep. In her mind—knowing it was dangerous, but unable and unwilling to stop—she'd dressed them up for Halloween, celebrated Christmas with them, watched them graduate from high school, wept as they left for college. She'd had months to embroider their beautiful, complicated lives. But now she had to bury them, erase their memories, throw away the notebook in which she'd kept the list of names: Evan, Veronica, Nicole, Jacob. Good-bye to their futures, good-bye to all of them whose faces she had seen so clearly.

So this is heartbreak, she thought. *Something cracked beyond repair.*

It was sad. She cried in the night, and first thing in the morning, and cried again when she gently laid the notebook in the kitchen trash and ferried the bag out to the curb. But Dan's white, lightly freckled back turned away from her in sleep, the blank fragility of it, was the saddest thing she'd ever seen.

At a certain point, she just couldn't take it anymore. Losing him, his touch, their closeness, was more than she could handle, especially on top of all the other grief. So in the middle of the night she reached over, his body wakelessly responding, and by the time he opened his eyes she was on top of him, moving, kissing his neck. Also crying a little. And it was weird, but he put his hands on her, and it seemed to help.

"I'm ashamed," he said afterward. "I can't believe I can't do this."

"It's going to be okay," she told him, and knew as she spoke the words that it was her job to make them come true.

After that night, they discussed some possibilities. They were chastened, serious, calm, as if they'd aged twenty years between the conversation in which they'd decided to start trying and this one. Lisette, her resolve firm in spite of her heartbreak, told him that she wanted to raise a child with him, to have a family, and there were other ways of doing it. Did he still want a family? He nodded, with the same grim look on his face as when he caught a student cheating: the situation was bad, and there were no excuses, but a good teacher moved past blame to look for root causes and better solutions.

This is when they started talking about other men's sperm. They talked about adoption too, but Lisette couldn't get excited about this option. She wanted to have a baby inside her, to feel the link of flesh and blood, the umbilical cord, the kick of tiny feet. Yet at the fertility specialist's office, she balked. Looking over the sperm donor files, she couldn't imagine this scenario, either. There just wasn't enough information. It was like shopping online for the least returnable of all items. The data given—weight, height, education level—was wholly inadequate. She needed touch and texture, the expression in a man's eye, the specificity of gesture. How he sits in a chair, or holds a glass in his hand.

Though she knew she had to be the strong one, to pull Dan along toward their future, she broke down after the afternoon with the donor files.

"I can't make a baby this way," she said to him, tears streaking hotly down her cheeks. "I couldn't even buy *pants* this way."

If her baby was not to be a stranger, she needed so much more than this.

At work, things shifted once again. Whereas she'd once seen the kids with their instruments as sensual embodiments of a bright future, she now saw each and every one as a reproach, as something she might not be able to have. Everything youthful about them— their braces, their high-pitched giggles, their stupid, stammering in-jokes—made her angry. She'd always hated window-shopping, because there's no point in looking at things you can't buy. She snapped at them, telling them they had no talent.

"You're lazy," she said. "You think you can coast, but you can't. You're going to embarrass me, and yourselves."

They were surprised, but rolled with it. They were used to mer-curial adults. They knew that it wasn't the people around them but the activities in which they were relentlessly enrolled—swim team, orchestra, driver's ed—that gave their lives structure, on which they could rely.

Packing up her bag one day after class she heard two boys talking around the corner in the hallway.

"What was up with Ms. Gilson today? She's so bitchy. I think she hates me."

"I bet she's on the rag. You know how women are."

Lisette stood there, shaking for a moment, then lost it. She dropped her stuff, her legs pulsing with adrenaline, and hurried down the hall after them. When they saw her—it was Tyler, violin, and Mark, French horn—they turned and blushed so hard that in another mood, she would've been compassionate. Instead she grabbed Tyler's forearm and clenched it, hard, feeling the flesh give. If she'd been bigger and stronger, she might have broken it and flung his whole body against the wall.

"You think you know how women are? You think you know?"

"Sorry," he said, his voice cracking.

"Do *not* let me hear you talking like that ever again. Either of you. Do you understand?"

They nodded.

"Get out of my sight."

They weren't going anywhere—why *wouldn't* they go?—because, she realized, her hand was still on Tyler's arm, her nails digging into his skin. She released him, feeling her fingers cramp. "Go," she said.

Once they left the building she stood in the hallway with tears running down her cheeks. Angry at no one more than herself, for losing control, for embarrassing herself, for not having the life she thought she was going to. Then the janitor came, swishing his mop over the tiles, and she wiped her face and went out to the car.

Mark was gone but Tyler was still there, fiddling with his bike at the rack, his violin packed into a wire case mounted on the back. His dad had made the case for him, and when he first started with the orchestra, three years earlier, he'd asked her to come out and see it, assuring her that it secured the violin safely, with no chance of damage. Seeing him there, Lisette felt terrible. Tyler was a gentle, sensitive boy with a dry sense of humor he'd probably inherited, along with his looks, from his father, an engineer. When they first met he'd been stick-thin and given to striped polo shirts, with a strange habit of plucking the front of those shirts nervously, over and over, fraying the fabric just above his right nipple. He'd grown out of this, and filled out in general; he was a young man now, affecting a vaguely punkish look, skinny jeans and Chuck Taylors and a wallet attached by a thick silver chain to his black studded belt. She wanted to tell him that you couldn't be punk and play in a New Jersey youth orchestra. She wanted to tell him that she was sorry.

"Tyler," she said, walking up to him.

"It's okay," he said immediately. He didn't want to have to hear the apology, which would embarrass him all over again; he wanted to go straight past it, back into normalcy.

"I'm having a rough time," she said brusquely. "It's nothing to do with you."

He nodded, looking down at his bike.

"I'll see you, okay?"

He nodded again. As she was walking to her car, he called her name, and she was so rattled that it wasn't until later, pulling into the driveway, that she realized he'd called her not *Ms. Gilson* but *Lisette*. She turned around.

"Whatever's, like, bothering you—you deserve better."

This made her laugh. "How would you know?" she said.

That night she couldn't sleep. Dan snored lightly next to her, a sound as profoundly comforting as any she'd ever known. He was her husband, and almost more than anything else she wanted him to be a father. Her pelvis ached with such emptiness that she couldn't stop palming it, soothing it, trying to ease its pain. She knew it was psychosomatic but it felt absolutely, unequivocally real. As real as hunger, or thirst, or life and death.

She'd made up her mind before she even knew what she was contemplating. It was like falling down a flight of stairs—no gap between the moment your foot slips and when you're lying in a heap on the floor below.

This is what she did: at the next rehearsal, she smiled at Tyler. And he smiled back. Just like that, in the passage of one second, she knew she had him. Before a single word had been spoken, or a single gesture enacted, or a plan even hatched. And it was so easy. It turned out all the banks in the world were giving away free money, and all you had to do was ask.

Her body, now, was a cunning machine. It had its hunger and emptiness; it would be taking matters into its own hands. She let it go about its business, not stopping to ask any questions.

"What's got you so happy?" Dan said to her that night, over dinner.

She looked at him in the candlelight, her sweetness, the love of her life. He was craggy and tired-looking, with bags beneath his eyes. She saw his features overlaid not with the young man she'd first met in college but with the old man he would someday become.

"Nothing," she said. "Just happy to see you."

That night, in bed, she ran her hands through his hair, her fingertips tracing his shoulders and back, and coaxed him into sex. She had to believe that, as close as they were, as much as they meant to each other, some part of him had already entered her, was already inside.

After smiles, a little extra attention. Tyler seemed to be waiting for it, to know and accept what was happening. He stayed after rehearsal, packing up his instrument slowly, dropping his sheet music and studiously, laboriously rearranging the pages. She remembered this kind of unspoken agreement between people conspiring to be alone from the old days, so ancient now, before Dan. It had been ages since she took up a flirtation. But she still knew the deal, remembered how it was done. She, too, was slow, and they walked out together into the fall evening, and she offered him a lift. She realized that he'd purposefully stopped riding his bike to rehearsal just in case this would happen, and she felt a rush of gratitude so warm and intense that it was almost like love. He sat in the passenger seat with his long legs cramped, knees high and awkward, violin case tucked between his feet. Outside his house, he thanked her for the ride. He barely looked at her. And that was all.

But from there they built a routine together. Perfect collaborators, they brought a relationship into existence, and nursed it into the world. Soon he was the one she looked to when explaining a concept, a beat, what she wanted, and he would nod. He was the first violinist, and she had him leading the strings in rehearsal while she worked separately with the woodwinds or percussionists. She relied on him. And he waited for a ride home and during that ride told her about his classes, his plans for college. He was a bright kid and had gotten into Princeton, so excited to be leaving home, and for all that entailed. What the other kids thought, if anything, she had no idea. If asked, she would have said he was a natural leader. She would have told his parents, *He'll go far.*

At the Christmas concert, the orchestra tackled the Tchaikovsky with shrieking abandon and labored gamely through the Hindemith in front of their families, who smiled dazedly until it was over, then started clapping a little too late. Afterward, she stood for a while chatting with Tyler and his parents. The mother was a bottle blonde, short, well preserved. The father, of whom Tyler was the spitting image, still had all his hair, had stayed trim, and seemed, when he laughed, to have good teeth.

In the car driving home, Dan wouldn't look at her. Just before they pulled up to the house he said, "What the hell are you doing?"

She said, "Going home?"

"I mean with that father. Staring at him. Laughing your head off. Flirting."

"I don't know what you're talking about," she said.

He parked. He still wouldn't turn his head. "I've never seen you like that," he said. "You've never acted like that before."

She was defensive, angry, proud—and how perverse was that? Proud of her husband, who knew her well enough to sense, right away, that something was going on, though he couldn't have been expected to figure out how low she'd sunk. "I was just being myself," she said.

.   .   .

There were no rehearsals over the holidays. On January 15, the first evening they came back, she slept with Tyler in the rehearsal room, on a table. There was no first kiss, only her hungry body and his teenage one, his thin biceps working, his angular hip bones cutting into her thighs, his skunky, hormonal smell mixed with the scent of Doritos and hair gel. It was so different from sex with Dan as to constitute a completely new operation, more like coaxing a squirrel out of your garage, everything jumpy, a little feral and uncontrolled. But she was patient and showed him how she wanted it done, same as conducting. The act itself was over very fast, with most of their clothes still on. To tell him not to say anything to anyone would have insulted his intelligence, so she didn't.

Afterward, he kissed her neck, a dry, close-lipped kiss, like a thank-you note.

In total there were three times, all of them in the rehearsal room after everybody else had gone, twice on the table, once in a hellacious, back-aching position involving two folding chairs and a French horn case. He seemed to want to experiment, either already tired of their routine or else wanting to make things more exciting, perhaps degraded, in accordance with whatever fantasy he had about adult sex, and she tried to accommodate him. It was the least she could do.

She hoped three times would be enough. After each one, she took stock of her body, weighed and surveyed it, but she couldn't tell any difference, and was desperately afraid.

Dan came into the bathroom as she weighed herself, squeezing her breasts. In the mirror, their eyes met.

"You're beautiful," he said mechanically. "You aren't fat."

She smiled at him. Fat was what she wanted, but he couldn't know that yet. "Thanks, honey."

The way she said it—her ease and placidity—alerted him. He cocked his head. "What's going on with you, anyway?"

"I don't know what you mean."

"You dress differently. Walk differently. You have this vacant smile all the time."

"I'm still wearing the same clothes."

"You're wearing dresses instead of pants. In *January*. You're putting on makeup every day."

"Maybe it cheers me up."

"For God's sake, Lisette, do you think I don't notice? Are you seeing someone else? Is it that father from the Christmas concert?"

"Oh, honey," she said, and turned to him, away from the mirror.

"Don't touch me right now," he said. "Just don't."

He spent the night in the guest room, the one they'd planned on turning into a nursery. The next evening, when she got home from rehearsal, he'd moved his clothes in there too. And he himself wasn't home: no note, no message saying where he was. At midnight, she heard him come in, run the water in the bathroom, and get into bed.

She thought she'd give him some space. She was far enough gone, at this point, to think that space was what they both needed.

Then, strangely enough, they lived for a time as cordial strangers. They ate meals together and inquired politely about each other's day. The shell of their former life held fast even as its contents were emptied. Dan lost weight, looked exhausted. Once, in the middle of the night, she got up to pee and heard a strange sound from his room, like choking or throwing up. She paused outside the closed door to listen, realizing, gradually, that it was the dry, painful twisting of sobs torn from a man unaccustomed to them. She put her palm on the door, then opened it.

"Go away," he said immediately. "Just go away."

In the morning, they acted as though this hadn't happened.

Three weeks later, she peed on the stick and got a positive result.

"Oh, thank God," she said out loud.

That night, she made steak and mashed potatoes, Dan's favorite meal. When he came home from work and saw it, he took a wary step back. He had the look of a dog that's been beaten and can't help expecting the next blow. And this, she knew, was the next blow. But it was also a gift—eventually, he would recognize it as such himself.

"I'm pregnant," she said. From the other end of the table, she could see herself reflected in his eyes—a torturer, a demon—but she stood with her fingers clenching the back of the dining room chairs they'd bought as newlyweds.

"Whose is it?" he said.

"It's ours," she said.

"Lisette, are you crazy? What have you done?"

"It's a miracle," she said firmly. "It's our family."

He stood there shaking his head. "We're not a family anymore, Lisette," he said.

To Tyler she said: "My husband knows. It's over."

They were in her car, after rehearsal, their breaths visibly streaming toward the dashboard. She crossed her fingers inside the mitten of her left hand. This was the chance she'd taken: that he could let go as easily as he'd latched on. If he fought, if he cried, if he struck out in anger, he could ruin everything. She'd given him that power over her life in exchange for what she needed. It was the biggest risk she had ever taken.

For one quiet, dark moment he looked into her eyes, then turned away. He reached his hand up and absently plucked the front of his winter coat. Seeing this nervous gesture again, she felt a great tenderness she could only describe as maternal, twisted as that was. And Tyler: he'd been fumblingly sweet, he'd stroked her hair, but she knew he wasn't in love with her. She'd given him experience and some passing satisfaction and he already knew how to separate these physical facts from the emotional ones. There was a girl who played the flute, and Lisette had seen how he looked at her, queasy with wanting. The girl didn't reciprocate, though, so Tyler had taken what he could get. The only question now was whether he could leave it behind.

He said, "Okay." He could.

He was seventeen years old, bound for Princeton in the fall. His skin was clearing, his shoulders getting broad. There would be a lot of other women in his life.

In the months to come, she found a doctor, alone, took her prenatal vitamins, alone, bought a crib and baby clothes, alone. Dan wasn't with her for the first ultrasound, didn't hear the baby's heart beat, didn't read *What to Expect When You're Expecting*. On the other hand, he didn't move out, either. So that was something.

.   .   .

At the spring concert, she and Tyler shook hands. She was showing now, wearing sack dresses most of the time, but it didn't seem
to register on him. She led youth orchestra sessions in the summer too, but he was going to hike the Appalachian trail with his
dad. This, then, was good-bye. He said, "I'll miss you."

She smiled. She couldn't wait for him to leave. "Enjoy college,"
she said.

Just then a woman whose son played clarinet came by and put
her arm on Lisette's shoulder. She was warm and friendly, a busy-
body, Dana. She taught biology at the high school and let the girls
leave the room when they claimed to be too freaked out by dis-
sections.

"Oh, Lisette!" she said. "I can tell just by looking. Are you? You
are, aren't you?"

Lisette nodded, blushing despite herself.

"Congratulations! When are you due?"

"September."

"How wonderful. Congratulations again."

Lisette turned back to Tyler, expecting to have to explain—but
he'd already gone off to the refreshments table, where Kim, the
flautist, was eating a brownie.

That night, though, the doorbell rang at eleven. Dan was
upstairs, sequestered in his room. When she opened the door,
Tyler was standing on the porch, his brown eyes anxious. Her heart
pumping, she stepped outside, closing the door quietly behind her.
The last thing she wanted was for Dan to come down now.

"It took me a while to process what that conversation was
about," Tyler said. "Is it what I think?"

"I'm pregnant," she said. "Dan and I are thrilled."

He stepped closer. In the vague glow of the porch light his eyes glinted, the fear in them naked. "It's not—"

"No," she said. "It's not."

He breathed a theatrical sigh of relief, his shoulders rising and falling. For a moment she saw doubt clouding his mind, and then she saw him dismiss it. His eyes cleared and he began to walk away, his palm raised in a gesture of salute, separation, good-bye. He wanted nothing more than to put distance between himself and a pregnant middle-aged woman. He would never ask her another question, she was sure, because he had his whole future in front of him, luxurious, unspoiled; because she'd told him what he wanted to hear; because she was an adult and he was, after all, a child.

The summer passed slowly, the weather sticky and hot. She worked in the garden and took birthing classes. The doctor asked her if she wanted to know the sex of the baby, and she said no, figuring that Dan wouldn't want to know either. Dan spent most of the summer away, first visiting his parents, then on a long fishing trip with his college friends. While he was gone, she moved his things back into the master bedroom, his socks and underwear back into the empty drawers, his shirts back into the empty half of the closet. In the spare bedroom she assembled the crib, the Diaper Genie, a little white bookshelf, a mobile. She had been collecting these things for months. Above the bookshelf she hung a framed copy of their wedding picture, she in her white dress, Dan grinning down at her, on the day they said their vows and bound themselves to each other forever.

When Dan came back, he stood in the hallway outside this room, his hands on his hips. "You are something else," he said, his tone almost admiring.

She stood a few feet away from him, keeping a respectful distance.

"Honey, I love you," she said. "This is going to happen. There *will be* a baby."

"Lisette," he said. "Do you understand how close I am to completely hating you? Does it even matter to you anymore?"

For the first time, a cold shiver swept all over her, cooling her blood, and she felt faint to her fingertips, even her toes. In all this time she'd never thought that she would lose him. So intent, so focused on the goal, she'd set everything else aside. She had the urge to beg him, to cry, to make him pity her, or to yell at him, but none of that would work with Dan; he'd see it as manipulative and hysterical at once. His personality was rigorous and pure; his strictness undercut her own tendencies toward obsession and intensity, kept her moored. No, melodrama would make the situation worse and then she *might* lose him forever. Staying calm was the only way to manage him, hoping that he would come back to her in his own time, willing him to forget the price she'd paid and remember instead what she had purchased with it, that golden, shining good, their future.

So she said nothing, and he left her.

When the school year started, he was living in a shabby efficiency next to the hospital. Dan was seen, of course, as a villain—who leaves his wife while she's pregnant?—and he had to endure this gossiping disapproval on top of everything else. She didn't speak about him to the people they knew, a silence that was interpreted as high-minded. If she had thought too much about any of this, it would have crushed her. Therefore she thought only about the baby. Her body had to be nurtured; there could be no stress, only good food, sleep, rest. It wasn't the life she'd dreamed of, but it was in motion. She'd done her body's bidding and now would do its caretaking, too.

She gave the hospital Dan's cell phone number, in case of emergency, but she didn't call him when the contractions started, or when she took a cab to the hospital. By the time the complications started, the doctors talking about breech birth and emergency Cesarians, she was too out of her mind with pain to call him, so it was the nurse who did, telling him to get there as soon as he could.

Lisette, in a horror of sweat and pain, barely recognized his voice. It was so much worse than she'd ever imagined it could be, the worst thing that had ever happened to her, and she sobbed and screamed. It felt like punishment for all the bad things she'd ever done. She didn't think, *Baby,* or *Help,* or *Be strong,* or *Breathe.* She just thought, *Make it stop.* Eventually, she lost consciousness or was sedated, she didn't know and didn't care; she only wanted to escape the grasping, evil hands of the pain.

When she woke up, she was alone. Her body, which had been her guide for so long, was numb. Outside the closed door she could hear distant hospital sounds, people walking, garbled announcements, phones ringing. The room smelled somehow musty and antiseptic at the same time. It smelled of sickness and solitude, like a place that had never been aired out. She was so weak she couldn't move her hand to press the call button. She wondered if Dan was still around, or if he'd never been there and she'd hallucinated his presence. She knew without a doubt she had failed, that the baby was dead and everything she'd sacrificed had been for nothing. The whole experience had been so terrible, there was no chance that anything as fragile as an infant could possibly have survived it. Maybe she was dead too. Maybe this was hell, specially tailored for her particular desires and sins.

Then the door opened and Dan came in, with the baby wrapped in a little blanket. His eyes were red from crying. He placed the bundle in her arms, and she found the strength to hold it without even thinking or trying.

"Oh, baby," she said, tears running down her face.

"It's a boy," Dan said. He pulled up a chair and sat next to her. He put his hands on the bed next to her, not quite touching her leg. "I didn't know if you had a name picked out."

She shook her head. The baby was teeny, wrinkled, dark haired, red. She kissed his perfect, impossibly small forehead. Her body recognized him, wanted him close. "He's so quiet," she said. "Is he okay?"

"He's fine," Dan said. "He was crying before. The nurse is coming in a couple of minutes with a lactation specialist. They're just giving us a moment together."

"That's nice," she said, still crying, then tore her eyes away from the baby long enough to look at him. "Thank you for being here."

"You're welcome."

They were stiff as strangers.

Reaching over, Dan put his finger inside the blanket and drew out one of the baby's hands. "Look how tiny," he said, his voice catching. "It's amazing."

"It is," she said. "It really is."

The baby opened his mouth and began to wail, and Lisette

tried to open her gown but couldn't quite manage to, with the baby in her arms, so Dan reached over and helped her, both of them unable to stop looking at the boy, whose little mouth was wide open, seeking what he needed.

Dan said softly, "That's it. There you go." And he put his hand on the baby's back, leaning in close to watch.

She knew then that he would come back to her. Because they were a family, and because they had exchanged vows on that wedding day that now seemed so long ago. They hadn't said: *I will ask you for things no person should ask.* Or: *I will hurt you so much it will suck you dry.* What they'd said was: *I will love you forever.* And every word of it was true.

The Stepmother's Story

On the plane, in that dizzy, fitful sleep that feels like slipping underwater, she dreamed that Lucas died. She saw his blue lips, his closed eyes, the damp blond hair plastered to his pale nine-year-old face. He was floating somewhere, and his dark sweatshirt billowed around him like a cloud.

"Luke!" she said out loud, waking herself up.

"He's fine," Jason said immediately, from the window seat. And, as always, he was right: her two stepchildren were just across the aisle, their blond heads islanded in headphones, watching the in-flight movie. Molly was laughing at an animated squirrel falling on the ice as it chased a nut. Lucas was scowling. He considered himself above children's comedy and, as if sensing he was being watched, pulled his hood over his head and slouched down in the seat, his face invisible.

"You okay, Jude?"

"I'm good," she said. She wasn't going to tell him about the dream, because it was morbid and bizarre, and because, now that she was shaking the shreds of it from her mind, she thought she knew where it came from. Two rows behind the children, the seats had been removed and a stretcher bolted down there, a blanket and pillow covering the mattress like an empty hotel bed. When Judith, boarding, stared at the stretcher in surprise, the flight attendant explained quickly that it wasn't being used. A person had been transported from Edinburgh to New York, and now, in the opposite direction, it was being returned. *A person,* she'd said, and Judith wondered at all the specific meanings this vague term was designed to avoid: patient, victim, corpse. Which was exactly the kind of thought that Jason would smile at and tell her to dismiss. He wasn't dismissive of her, but he'd been through an agonizing, bitter divorce and had chosen—this was how he put it, on their first date—to look forward, to believe in life and happiness and the future. Judith was drawn to him just as the sun draws you outdoors on a perfect day you can't bear to waste. Her own divorce had left a permanent smudge on her life, a shadow she couldn't quite shake; even now, in love and remarried, she often felt it lurking inside and had to tamp it down.

Molly laughed, and the sound was like a butterfly, something delicate and uncontainable flapping its wings in the cabin's air.

"Still five hours left," Jason said to her, squeezing her arm. "Try to get some rest."

By the time they landed in Scotland, cleared customs, and found the hotel, the children were exhausted, their eyes circled and hollow. Judith felt a pang of guilt. This trip had been her idea; she'd wanted them to do something different from the Disney World vacations of their past. On this trip, she'd thought, they'd start becoming a family. But maybe it was too much, too far? For the millionth time she wondered if she was making a stepmother's mistake. The room had two double beds and an extra roll-out the hotel had brought up, and the kids collapsed, Lucas in one bed, Molly on the roll-out, without fighting. They fought much less often, in fact, than Judith had expected, and she didn't know if this was because of everything they'd been through or was just the way they were. Molly was like her father, sunny, adaptable, friendly; she liked to sit on the floor while they watched TV and have Judith braid her hair. Lucas was darker. Sullen and withdrawn, he had few friends and spent most of his time at home playing graphic, violent video games. He skirted Judith as if she were a piece of furniture in the center of the room. Whenever she tried to talk to him, he answered in grunts and single syllables until she gave up. Because he was dark, because he was difficult, he was the one whose acceptance she most craved.

At nine o'clock, the kids groggy and pliant, they ventured out for dinner. It was July and still light, a pearly, enduring twilight that made the Gothic architecture and cobbled streets look like the setting of a fairy tale. Judith had been to Edinburgh once before, the summer after graduation when she and a girlfriend had Eurail-Passed through ten countries, but all she remembered was meeting some guys from Portugal at the hostel and staying up drinking with them all night, trying to teach them how to pronounce "Loch Ness Monster" correctly. In the morning they'd gotten back on the train. Now she was pleased to be here, with this new family of hers—an instant, add-water-and-stir family, as her friend Maggie had put it. They chose a homey-looking pub and ordered sandwiches. Outside, tourist couples strolled past the window fronts. She looked at Jason and smiled.

.   .   .

They slept late and missed the complimentary breakfast, which Judith thought was perfectly fine, given what she'd heard about its black pudding and haggis. In a coffee shop around the corner they outlined a sightseeing plan for the day. Molly wanted to know if they could see some sheepdogs; she was the kind of girl who had pictures of kittens and horses in her room. When Judith asked Lucas what he wanted to do, he shrugged.

"There must be something," she said.

He shrugged again. "I don't know anything about Scotland," he said, "so how can I pick?"

Instantly, she felt a tidal wave of unreasonable annoyance wash over her. With his intractability, Lucas drew from her a volatile, explosive emotion such as she'd never experienced with another person. She was trying so hard and he would never even meet her halfway. She wanted to yell at him, *Why won't you cooperate?*, to shake his arm, and he looked at her and could see it in her eyes. His lip curled, taunting her. *I dare you,* his expression said. Between them was the electricity of unspoken anger. Meanwhile, Molly and Jason were buttering their toast.

"I guess if there were Scottish *video games*," she said, "you'd want to play those." And instantly regretted it: she, the adult, was supposed to keep her cool.

But Lucas's lip curled further into a sardonic smile, and his dark blue eyes—they were an otherworldly color, almost purple—twitched and he said, "Scottish video games are probably, like, Grand Theft Bagpipes."

"Or Killer Haggis," she said.

"Black Pudding Attack," he said, and then they were all four laughing, Judith's tension snapped and gone.

Everybody had warned her about the hardships of a blended family, but nobody had mentioned its pleasures: how fun it could be to sit in a coffee shop with your family, all of you jet-lagged and laughing at some dumb joke.

Just as quickly as it had arrived, the moment slipped away as Lucas put his cutlery back on his plate, his breakfast untouched, and stared out the window.

"Okay," Jason said, doing his best to move them all along with his warm, sunny smile. "Let's hit the sights."

And they did: the castle, the Royal Mile, the parliament building. The kids yawned through various tours and were placated with gift-shop trinkets and snacks. Jason bought Judith a cashmere shawl when she wasn't looking, and she scolded him for the expense and then hugged him; though they'd been married a year, she still felt strange kissing him in front of the kids. Sometimes she thought about Maggie's reaction when she told her she was dating a divorced guy and that the kids seemed "great."

"Those poor children," Maggie said, and Judith, who'd only just met them, felt defensive on their behalf.

"They seem to be coping pretty well," she said. "They say kids are resilient."

"Yeah, they do say that," Maggie said. "But is it just because the kids don't, you know, actually explode?"

Judith imagined she meant that kids can't explain themselves, because they often have no words to describe the things that had happened to them. "I don't know the answer to that question," she said. She still didn't, and thought that probably nobody did.

"Hey," Jason said, "come back to us," and she realized that she was still holding the soft, pale blue cashmere to her cheek.

But all in all it was a good day, and they slept well that night and felt better the next morning, when they climbed the 287 steps to the top of the Walter Scott memorial, panted with the accomplishment, heard from a tour guide about his famous *Lady of the Lake,* then looked down at the gardens below. The Edinburgh skyline was shrouded in a gentle haze. And then it was time to climb down. Jason was holding Molly's hand, and they glanced around for Lucas, but couldn't find him.

The panic was not immediate. They just assumed he was exploring somewhere and had forgotten to let them know he was wandering off. They walked around for a few minutes calling his name. Then Judith and Molly stayed put while Jason canvassed a broader area. He was gone for fifteen minutes, then half an hour, then came back and left again for another half an hour. As Judith and Molly sat there, other tourists came and went, taking pictures, chattering, and she was offended by their blithe ignorance. Finally she saw Jason climbing back up the steps, and he was holding out his hands in a hopeless, *empty* gesture. Even though she was too far away to see his eyes, she could feel his heart turning over, and his alarm ignited hers, and her heart was pounding and she allowed herself to actually think the terrible thought that Lucas was missing.

Such a sweetheart was Molly that she stayed silent and polite through the lengthy interview at the police station, downed the muffin and milk a kind secretary brought for her, and didn't cry. Jason, on the other hand, was falling apart. Judith had never seen him like this. She thought he'd permanently exorcised violent and dark emotions from his life but it turned out that they were all simmering underneath. When the police officer said they couldn't do anything right away, his recognizable personality, the self she knew and loved, disappeared, and he became an entirely different person.

"Listen to me, you Scottish motherfucker," he said. "My son's somewhere out there, in a city he doesn't know, in a foreign country, and he's nine years old. You need to find him, do you understand? I'll stand right in front of you and yell my fucking head off hour after hour until you do something about this."

The police officer, a kindly, portly, gray-haired man with a bristly mustache, was unshaken by this outburst. He persisted in a long line of questioning, his Scottish accent underscoring, somehow, the methodical rhythms of his speech: had Lucas ever disappeared before, what kind of a child was he, had he been known to speak to strangers, had they had an argument? Children could be testy and difficult, especially when traveling or particularly tired. As he spoke he held Lucas's passport open to the photograph, his stubby thumb so close to the image that, Judith could tell, it was driving Jason insane. Finally he stood up and snatched the passport out of the officer's hand.

"I'm done answering questions," he said. "Find my son."

What to do in a foreign city where your child could be anywhere? Jason couldn't sit still, and Judith thought she understood. She offered to take Molly back to the hotel while he looked for Lucas. It was early evening now, suppertime.

Jason agreed to this plan with a mechanical nod, then crouched down and gave Molly a hug. "Everything's going to be fine. Okay, honey? I think Lucas probably just took a wrong turn and got disoriented."

Heartbreakingly, the child tried to act like she believed him.

She and Molly took a black cab back to the hotel and ate in the restaurant downstairs, each of them just pushing food around the plate for ten minutes, then went back to the room. Somewhere in the city, she knew, Jason was retracing all their steps from both today and yesterday, scrambling frantically through the quaint cobblestone streets and alleys, the crowded maze of a very old city. All those Scottish words they'd laughed and wondered over: what was a close, exactly? What were mews?

As if echoing her own thoughts Molly suddenly sobbed, down in her little cot. "I wish we'd never come to Scotland. Why did we have to come here?"

"Oh, honey," Judith said, kneeling down and putting her arms around her. Molly's body felt hot beneath her Dora the Explorer nightgown. "Everything's going to be fine." The lack of conviction in her own voice embarrassed her, and she drew the girl closer, pressing her lips to her head. "We'll find him, don't worry."

She was so intent on sounding sure that it took her a moment to register how stiff the girl's posture was; then she felt a strange pressure on her stomach and realized Molly was fighting her, that her tiny hands were pushing her away as she cried hysterically, her pretty face distorted and monstrous. "This is all your fault," she said. "It's all because of you. Get away from me. Get away."

Judith dropped her arms and awkwardly settled Molly back on the cot, where she curled into a sad little crescent, crying even harder when Judith touched her or adjusted the covers around her. Slinking back to her own bed, with no idea what to do, Judith pulled the blanket over herself. Molly's tears subsided and she fell asleep, but Judith stayed awake, watching her, feeling like the worst person ever. It *was* her fault.

For hours she waited in bed as the city outside faded into blackness, wondering where Lucas could be and where Jason was. In a daze, she remembered the dream she'd had on the plane and saw Lucas's pale face. *I'm so sorry,* she told him in her mind. She started crying and was somehow still crying when she woke up, a few hours later, to see Jason asleep in the other bed, above the covers, still wearing all his clothes.

In the early morning light she could tell Jason agreed with Molly that this was her fault, and was amazed at her own foolishness, thinking that his sunniness, his composure, his ability to be optimistic even in terrible situations, were permanent conditions. He could only take so much and now, over the breakfast table, as they tried exhaustedly to make a plan, she saw how much he hated her. He was sitting across from her, with Molly in his lap.

"We should check in with the police first," she said, hoping to sound helpful. Jason nodded dully.

"And then I guess we could make color photocopies of his passport picture and put them up around town with our hotel information. Maybe someone's seen him."

"There are so many flyers up for plays during the festival," Jason said. "People will think it's part of that."

"There must be local TV channels," she went on. "We'll send a picture to them too." She felt she was speaking to him across a vast, oceanic distance. He was silent, his whole face drooping.

Finally he said, "Damn it. I've got to call Paulina. She'll know what to do."

It was the first time he'd ever said anything like that about his first wife, at least in front of Judith, and she felt their future buckle beneath the weight of his words.

The same kindly police officer as before told them there was no news and suggested they go back to the hotel to wait. When Judith raised the question of the local news, he shrugged as if to say they could do whatever they wanted to. So she and Jason called the local news station, spoke to a secretary, and dropped off a photo. Molly was quiet throughout all this, her face drawn and pinched. The streets swarmed with tourists, actors handing out handbills for plays, people dressed in kilts and togas and other costumes, a hive of activity that seemed more sinister with every passing moment. They returned to the Scott monument, and Jason and Molly walked around the crowd holding up pictures of Lucas and asking people if they'd seen him. It had been hours since either of them so much as looked at Judith.

At the top of the monument, looking over the city, Judith thought that it had lost its fairy-tale charm and now was foreboding and sinister. In her mind she again saw Lucas's pale face, the one in her dream, floating in space.

But he's not in space, she thought suddenly. *He's in water.* The water of Leith: the words came to her and she supposed she'd read them in the guidebook, though it wasn't something they'd ever discussed going to. Muscling through the crowd, she tugged on Jason's sleeve and saw, in a heartbreakingly clear second as he was turning around, that he hoped it was Lucas tugging at him, and that when he realized it was her, he felt not just disappointment but hatred, because she'd extended a moment of hope and just as quickly extinguished it.

"I'm going to look for him down by the water," she said.

"What water? Where?"

"The water of Leith walkway."

"Where's that?"

"I don't know. I just have a feeling, Jason. I can meet you back at the hotel."

"A *feeling*?" He tugged on her sleeve in turn but his touch wasn't gentle and surely couldn't be mistaken for a child's. "What do you know? What aren't you telling me?"

"Jason," she sighed. Next to him Molly was shrinking against his leg, as close as another limb. She was fading, this once-bright girl. How much more could she take? "I had a dream on the plane. I didn't tell you about it. I saw Lucas in some water."

"You're telling me *about a dream*?" Jason said, his face twisted, agonized. "Judith, my child's missing and I don't know where he is or how to find him and you're telling me about some dream?"

"I'm trying to help, Jason, I promise."

"I don't see how rambling on about this is helpful at all." Underneath this was everything he didn't say: that she didn't know what she was talking about, she didn't know his children, that she was overstepping herself.

Instinctively she backed away, as though he might strike her, a fear she could tell incensed him even more. "I'll just meet you at the hotel later, okay?" she muttered, and quickly walked off, blinking tears from her eyes.

By asking directions she was able to find her way to the water, a stream that wound, through various neighborhoods, to the harbor town of Leith. A little wooden sign attached to a stick— something she might, in another mood, have found quaint— pointed the direction and gave the distance. Seeing it, her heart sank. There were miles of path to cover.

But what else was there to do but look? She began to walk, peering, with every step, into the water. Each mossy black stone or floating piece of litter drew her careful inspection. The path changed, as she went, from stone to dirt and back again, rising up to cross city streets, then submerging itself again. Tourists and dog-walkers gave her a wary berth, but her attention didn't waver. The long green tendrils of trees were reflected palely in the water. She saw no fish, no life at all.

After around an hour she became distantly aware that a man behind her was observing her every move. Now that she noticed him, she realized he'd been there for quite a while. She wasn't afraid of him, only annoyed to be distracted. Without hesitating, she spun around and said, "What do you want?"

He was in his late twenties and wearing a nondescript outfit: brown corduroys, blue shirt, darker blue windbreaker. His pale face had a ruddy, windswept look, and he only lifted his eyebrows, apparently unruffled.

"Good afternoon, madam," he said. "My name is Lieutenant John McCrary."

"You're a policeman," she said. She was pleased: another pair of eyes to help. "I'm looking for my son. You can help if you want."

McCrary fell in step beside her. After a few quiet minutes he said, "I understand he's in fact your stepson?"

His tone was so soft that she almost missed the accusation in it.

"Yes, that's right," she said. "His parents are divorced. His mother's on her way to Edinburgh, flying in from New York."

"And you've come to look for him here, because . . ."

Judith sighed. They were wasting time. "Because I have a hunch. You've heard of a hunch?" She stopped and spread her palms in appeal. "Anyway, it's just good to do *something*." She could hear herself trying to sound reasonable, convincing, despite the subtle tremor in her voice.

"This hunch you have," McCrary said, still softly, "where did it come from?"

She saw, then, what he meant: that only the guilty have secret knowledge of any crime. Standing before him, with the damp air cooling her cheeks, she felt his indictment join Jason's and Molly's. A mother might have an intuition, but the stepmother could only be the villain. That's how fairy tales go.

"If I could tell you where it came from," she told him, "it wouldn't be a hunch. Anyway, believe whatever you want. Follow me if you have to. I really don't care."

Another hour passed with she and McCrary walking together, a walk that in another context might have been romantic—the low-hanging branches, the glimmer of birdsong, the old buildings hunkering over the water. She experienced these things as quick flashes, whenever she momentarily turned away from the water to rest her eyes. McCrary said nothing, though she felt him watching her, and it angered her that he wasn't paying more attention to the water.

She thought she saw Lucas, but it was a soda can, or a seagull. She thought she saw him, but he wasn't there.

It was three o'clock when they reached the harbor at Leith at the end of the walk. She could go no farther. In front of her was the sea. She hadn't found him; he was out there somewhere all alone, and she had failed. She stood staring at the spot where the gray water met the gray sky. The wind was cold and her tears stung her face and her heart ached for him.

She stood there for so long that McCrary, apparently, lost patience. She sat down on a rock and, glancing up, noticed that he was gone. Though she'd resented his accusing presence, she felt abandoned by his departure. Now she, too, was alone. Somewhere in the city, Jason and Molly were probably still walking the streets, the closes and mews, calling Lucas's name.

Then she saw him.

In the gray water his dark blue sweatshirt looked like a rock or a wave. It was the movement of his hair across his cheeks that caught her eye, an image that recalled, exactly, the dream she'd had on the plane.

He was in the water below a pier, where a kid could easily have fallen off while looking down. Without thinking, she threw herself in and swam out to him. It took her longer than she expected and she was already tired by the time she got close to him. Catching him was yet another difficulty; she was calling his name but couldn't tell if he heard her.

Then she was wrapping him in her arms and heading back to shore. She didn't know if he was conscious, or even alive. His arms and legs were stiff and she could barely make any progress, holding him with one arm and paddling with the other. She swallowed some water and lost a contact lens, the world now a blur of waves. She could no longer see land and seemed to be caught in a current, or was she almost there? She had one hand beneath his sweatshirt and his bare back didn't feel human; cold, inert, it barely felt like anything at all.

She swallowed more water and was choking and couldn't breathe when miraculously, his arms circled around her. He was strong and holding on, and with both hands free she knew they'd make it. She knew, too, that the dream she'd had on the plane had been only part of the premonition, that the stretcher also figured in it: a stretcher that could carry Lucas home again, to health, to safety, to his father and sister and mother.

McCrary, who'd gone off to find a restroom and a sandwich, and who swore to his superiors that he'd been gone for less than fifteen minutes, discovered them on the beach. Lucas was crying and shivering. Judith wasn't breathing. She'd worked one arm inside the sleeve of his sweatshirt, apparently and correctly believing that this would bind them together. Trained in CPR, the policeman did his best, but couldn't revive her; the ambulance came, but not in time.

"I was lost," Lucas said, "and I kept getting more lost no matter what I did."

He'd only walked off for a couple of minutes; he was upset about something, he couldn't even remember what. He was afraid they'd be mad at him for walking away. And he was too afraid to talk to strangers, because he'd always been told not to. Then he was both tired and confused. He'd spent the night huddled in an alley, crouched inside his sweatshirt.

His father asked him question after question: *Where did you go next? Why didn't you ask a policeman?* And he asked one question over and over again: *How did she find you?*

The boy had no answer. Only nine, he didn't have the words to explain any of this mystery, how it had happened or what it meant, what it was like for him to be there in the water, blind and frenzied and drowning, and for the woman to somehow come to him, as if out of nowhere, and carry him ashore.

The Idea Man

Beth met Fowler at a party of sensible adults. She was divorced, her children were in grade school, and she had started to collect antique milk glass. She'd inherited a few pieces from her aunt and was now adding to the collection, rows of pale, frilly jars and gravy boats on her kitchen shelves. Why collect glass? Because it was there. It provided the only available momentum in a life that was losing speed. The party was full of other divorced people, eyeballing what they might be forced to settle for the second time around. When Fowler came in, the energy in the room crackled. He was wearing black jeans, a dirty white button-down shirt, and a sweater vest. His hair was long and tangled. He was very tall and too thin, as if he'd been starved or rack-stretched.

"Sorry I'm late," he said to the room at large. "You're not going to believe what happened to me on the way over here."

It was the best entrance anyone had made all night, and Beth inched toward him. He seemed eager for his audience yet uncomfortable with it, and he kept staring at the floor while telling his story.

"I'm walking down Fifth Street," he said, "and these guys come out of nowhere, these two young kids. They start yelling at me, right? They're calling me a *faggot*. They're telling me to get my *gay ass* out of their neighborhood. They're telling me that *gays deserve to be punished by God*."

"Wow," a woman next to Beth whispered, as if starstruck.

"And the worst thing about it," Fowler went on, "is that my first reaction—as if it mattered—was to tell them I'm *not* gay. Not that they cared. They threw me down on the ground, punched me in the face, took my wallet, and finally they ran away. I lay in a puddle for fifteen minutes before I could get up."

He finished his drink and held it out for replenishment. People crowded around him and patted him on the back, then stood back when he winced. A man with a crew cut said, "Hey, wait a minute." Beth had been talking to this guy earlier. He was a newspaper editor and had an appetite for fact. "How come there's no marks on your face?" he said. "How come you're not even dirty—or wet?"

"I cleaned myself up a bit," Fowler said.

"Did you call the police?"

"No, I just came over here," Fowler said.

"Why didn't you call the police? I mean, that's a pretty serious thing to have happen."

"I didn't want them involved."

There was a pause in which everyone's credulity evaporated. The newspaper guy squinted and said, "Did this even really happen?"

"Of course it *happened*," Fowler said.

"*I* think you're making the whole thing up."

It wasn't that much of a challenge but Fowler shriveled in the face of it. His tall, thin frame curled in on itself, disappearing like paper on fire. "You're right," he said. "I made it all up. I went to a dark place inside myself. I apologize."

Beth looked around the room. No one seemed that surprised.

"Fowler," the newspaper guy muttered, shaking his head.

Beth got Fowler another drink. He took it and looked deeply into her eyes, then seemed to shudder. "What's the matter with you, exactly?" she said.

"It's under investigation," he said, "by a task force of analysts, scientists, the legislature, and my ex-girlfriends. I'll let you know when they release their findings. Excuse me." He walked out of the room. Ten minutes later he came back, wiping his mouth. "When I'm upset I throw up," he said.

Fowler told her he was an ethnomusicologist, studying the performance practices of a tribe in Africa. She pictured drums and tribal costumes. Fowler told her that the tribe's language was remarkably clean of diphthongs. She didn't know how this compared to the Western diphthong situation, and didn't want to ask because she was afraid the explanation might be overlong. Instead she asked him if he wanted another drink.

"More than I can say," Fowler said.

When she returned he was being questioned by a woman in a cashmere poncho. They were discussing Plato's cave. Fowler said, "I used to live in a cave. In South Jersey." Then he winked at Beth.

The woman looked perplexed. "I just thought you might know something," she said, and left.

"I'm the idea man," Fowler explained modestly. "I'm the intellectual go-to guy."

"I think it's your vest," Beth told him.

"What ideas do you want from me?" Fowler asked her.

"Tell me what a diphthong is," she said. "I learned it once but I've forgotten."

"You combine two sounds together to make a new one," he said.

"That's it?"

"In a nutshell," he said. He drained the third drink and looked into her eyes again. He wasn't distracted or looking over her shoulder at the other possibilities, and this she liked.

"Do you want to come over to my house tomorrow night?"

Fowler nodded. He seemed accustomed to sudden invitations.

"All right," Beth said, writing down her address. "Don't get beat up on the way over."

The kids were at their father's and she served beer and Indian food, using several complicated recipes that required the purchase of special spices. Fowler ate little and didn't say much, either. The mood was cordially awkward. Then the kids came home unexpectedly, having forgotten their backpacks and homework, and refused to leave. They were forever leaving their possessions in the wrong place and screwing up the custody schedule. It was their way of participating in the chaos of the divorce, proving that they, too, could cause upheaval. They settled themselves around the table, eating the food Fowler was ignoring. Sometimes she felt this was her finest parental achievement—that her kids weren't picky eaters.

Megan, who was younger, sat next to Fowler and touched his long, wavy hair. Mike, who was older, sat on the other side of the table and talked to him. She'd thought they'd be jealous, resistant, freaked out that a strange man was in the house. Instead they took to Fowler immediately. They seemed to think of him as a stray animal she'd brought home. He talked to them about the music of Africa, which he'd refused, or been too shy, to discuss with her.

"Here's a charming tribal folktale I'll share with you," he told them, and they watched him with their heads balanced on their chins. Why they were sitting at the table instead of watching TV, Beth couldn't figure out. Fowler had that effect on people. They wanted to hear what he had to say.

The story he told was about a snake that ate a goat that ate a lion, or maybe it was a lion that ate the goat—she missed parts of it while clearing and washing the dishes. The children listened seriously. Later, after he'd gone, Megan asked whether Fowler was homesick. Further questioning revealed that she thought he was from Africa.

Maybe she wasn't wrong. Fowler did seem to live in Africa in his mind, which was where most of his living went on. The functions of his body were secondary. On their third date—the children again at their father's, having sworn to take all their possessions with them—Beth led Fowler into her room and to what had once been the marital bed. He allowed her to touch him, passively watching her, his body responding, then crawled on top of her and again looked deeply into her eyes. "You're beautiful," he said. "I'm so into you." Without a doubt he was sincere. Then it was over, and he put his clothes back on and took a book out of his bag.

Her friends thought Fowler was a hobby she'd taken up, like volunteer work or a subscription to the opera—something to broaden her horizons, post-divorce. They didn't disapprove but didn't expect it to last long, either. Nor did her children take him seriously as a father figure. They tugged at his sleeves and sat on his lap and told Beth when he needed more water or wine. Once the two of them were playing in their bedroom and Beth, passing by in the hallway, heard them arguing over some project that kept collapsing and needed to be rebuilt. She peeked in the door: they had their old jars of colored putty out and were trying to sculpt a Play-Doh cave. Fowler had told them it was the most perfect place in the world.

But she thought she might be in love with Fowler. She looked forward to his coming over, and when he was gone she waited for him to come back. Her body fat felt curvaceous; she slept better at night. She told her children jokes she knew they wouldn't understand. She bought a new dress, not minding that Fowler would neither notice nor care. She began clipping articles out of the newspaper for him, stories she thought he might find interesting. A man driving through the city had set his pants on fire while lighting a cigarette in his car; things escalated and somehow the whole car exploded. "We're investigating the pants," a police officer was quoted as saying.

"Maybe he was a liar," Fowler said, as she'd known he would, and she smiled.

"Do you want to move in?" she asked him.

Fowler said, "Oh. *Oh.*"

"It's okay if you don't want to," she said. "It's just that you spend so much time here already."

"Right. True."

"It would save you some back-and-forth," she said. "It's a matter of convenience, really."

Fowler looked deep into her eyes, into her soul, as was his wont. "Well, let's not do it out of *convenience*," he said.

She blushed. "I mean, I like having you here. I'd like to have you here more often." He drew these statements from her, from a well she'd thought had long ago run dry.

"I snore, you know," Fowler said.

"I'm past minding," she said.

She went to his place to help him pack up. She'd only been there once before, after a party where she'd gotten a bit drunk, and her impression had been of a scholarly hobbit-hole, cozy and knowledge filled. In a sober light this turned out to be overly positive. It was a studio apartment with books along one wall, floor to ceiling, and what she'd thought were bookshelves were boards and cement blocks. There was a bed and, in one corner, primitive instruments, gourds and sticks of wood. Fowler went to the closet, got out a suitcase, and packed his clothes. He owned two pairs of jeans, three white shirts, a sweater vest, and a blazer. This was his wardrobe in its entirety. Once he was done he closed the suitcase and looked around.

"I might as well just leave the rest of it," he said. "I'll probably wind up coming back here to work."

Although she considered Fowler a scholar, a person who lived in the mind, Beth didn't exactly think of him as someone who worked. What he did was less like a job and more like an atmosphere he moved in, a thick clear jelly that surrounded him and in which he was suspended, like aspic. Her ex-husband, after hearing about Fowler from the children, had called her up and said, "Just who is this guy? What does he *do*?" Fowler's not a person who *does,* Beth wanted to say. Instead she said, "He thinks." Her ex sighed and asked her to put the children on.

But now she had the same question. "What kind of work, exactly?" she said.

"I'm writing a book," Fowler said, looking at her with the same expression with which he'd told the lie at the party: a little sheepish, his eyebrows and shoulders raised, as if he expected to be found out. But she didn't care if he was lying, or if he wrote a book or not. She opened the door for him, and he picked up the suitcase and led her out.

They developed a routine. During the day Fowler went back to his hovel, and Beth went to work. She was an office manager, and all day long she coordinated appointments and ordered supplies; then, at home, she coordinated her children's appointments and bought groceries. Management was her specialty. When work was over Beth made dinner and Fowler either read or spent time with the children, if they were there. Their favorite story was about a turtle who steals a calabash from the gods that contains all the wisdom in the world. He hangs it around his neck and hurries home. But then he comes to a tree trunk lying across the road, and he can't cross it because the calabash gets in his way. For some reason—stress, excitement, lack of time—he forgets that he can put it on his back, and instead he gets so frustrated that he smashes it. And ever since that day, Fowler told the children, wisdom has been scattered all over the world in tiny pieces. Beth couldn't understand why her children liked this defeatist story, though Fowler did a great imitation of the turtle smashing the calabash into a million pieces. Later she discovered they had no idea what a calabash was. They thought it was a little animal, and the ending a killing scene. They were bloodthirsty in their misunderstanding, but she didn't want to correct them, because they enjoyed it so much.

Fowler said he had to go to a conference and discuss his work with other ethnomusicologists. Beth bought him the ticket and sent him on his way. What she hadn't realized was how much she'd miss him. The children moped too. The days were long, the nights longer. The world felt empty. One afternoon she left the office early and went to Fowler's apartment, her excuse—not that anyone was asking—being that she ought to take in the mail. The room was dusty and the gourds were thick with grime. She thought maybe she could clean them for him, so she took an abandoned T-shirt and began wiping them off. The gourds varied in size and shape, from large and round to long and phallic. Touching these last ones reminded her of Fowler in bed, and she missed him more than ever.

She picked a gourd up and fondled it, and while putting it back she dropped it on the floor. Fortunately it was sturdy and didn't break. But it could have, and she knew she was crazy if she thought Fowler would appreciate any cleaning she did. He didn't care about cleanliness any more than the other mundane details of the world. Quickly, as if he were coming home at any second, she returned everything to its original place and left.

When Fowler came back he knew at once what she'd done. He was sensitive to any change in his environment, any object out of place. He came over to the house late at night and said, "You were in my apartment."

"Yes," she said. "I wanted to do something nice for you."

He didn't believe her. He thought she was there to check up on him, to prove he was not in fact writing his book. Convinced that she didn't trust in him or his work, he ran to the bathroom and threw up. Beth followed and talked to him through the door. She couldn't understand getting so upset over something so minor, but this was Fowler all over, almost too sensitive for the world.

"It was just because I missed you," she said.

"You want me to be something I'm not."

"I want you to be here, with me."

"I'm not conventional, Beth. My work is abstract. I'm not the man in the gray flannel suit."

"But I don't care," Beth said.

"Everybody cares," Fowler said. She could picture him crouched on the tile floor, his long thin limbs curling and twitching like an insect's. "They don't see how much of it is here, inside my head. How much real work is going on. Everybody thinks I'm lying about the book, that just because I occasionally tell *stories* I can't also be *truthful*." When upset he was prone to italics. "But the book is real and truthful. It's the most real and truthful thing about me. Maybe the *only* thing." He was moaning, kind of.

"I was just cleaning," Beth said.

"Everyone wants to see *results*. They want *objects*," Fowler said. "They don't measure the quality of *ideas*."

She saw that she'd hit a nerve and there was no hope of unhitting it. She also saw that explaining she had no investment in the quality of ideas wouldn't help. But she thought that maybe she could distract and soothe him alternately.

"I'm happy you're back," she said, putting her hand on the door, trying to put sex in her voice. But Fowler wouldn't budge.

He stayed in the bathroom until she went to bed, and then he went back to his place.

In one of Fowler's stories—not that they were *his,* but that's how she nonetheless thought of them—a mosquito falls in love with an ear. Why an ear? The story doesn't explain. The mosquito doesn't consider the union's prospects unlikely. It has an idea about the ear and will not be denied the rewards of that idea. It doesn't understand why the ear won't reciprocate its affection and only when repeatedly, permanently rebuffed does it start to bite.

Beth, similarly, began to bite. She called Fowler and begged him to come back, and when that didn't work, she harangued him. She told him the children missed him, involving them in a way she'd sworn she'd never do. She told him he was being irresponsible, distant, uncommitted, sounding like an article in a women's magazine. Fowler would come over for dinner, but didn't spend the night, and then he came over less and less often. He was more comfortable in his hovel, in his Platonic cave.

She blamed him. Of course she did. She told herself and all her friends that he valued ideas more than people, that he'd taken advantage. "I think he's almost *autistic,*" she told them, and her friends nodded sagely.

One day she realized she hadn't heard from or spoken to Fowler in a week, and she knew it was over. She felt exiled from a country she'd once been a citizen of. When her children asked her where he was, she lied. "He had to go back to Africa," she said. "They missed him there."

Reports of Fowler filtered down to her every once in a while. He'd been seen with a divorced real estate broker whose own house had many extra rooms. He'd arrived drunk at a dinner party and announced that he no longer ate meat. Later someone caught him standing over the stove, spooning cassoulet into his mouth.

"Fowler," said the woman who told her this story, shaking her head.

Once Beth saw him on the street, too far away to wave at, his long hair tousled in the wind. He crossed her mind all the time, then only occasionally. But he never disappeared completely. Instead he shrank to a figment of himself, partial and pale, stored on the shelves of her brain. He was a thought that cluttered the night, an idea once held close, now scattered and gone.

Who Do You Love?

Adam Leavitt fell in love with me two weeks before our college graduation, and I never knew what brought it on. One minute we were part of the same group of friends, loosely bound by the parameters of dining hall tables and Saturday night parties, and the next thing I knew he was staring at me with the intensity of a lion stalking its prey. He was a musician, and intensity was his thing. He had curly blond hair that fell in ringlets over his eyes, and he wore the same outfit every day: jeans, motorcycle boots, and the piercing, blue-eyed gaze of a man with heartbreak and death on his mind. He staged solo performances in boiler rooms. He had a tattoo of a Chinese symbol on his arm (this was back before every sorority girl had a dainty one etched on her lower back) and another on his neck, some kind of mythological animal, its claws reaching up toward his ear.

One night I went over to his room to borrow a book and he'd lit at least twenty candles in this tiny room that could barely contain a futon—a fire hazard if I'd ever seen one. He handed me the book, his blue eyes glowing radioactively. I thought, *Why me?* I felt like there might be a hidden camera or somebody behind a curtain waiting for me to fall for this prank.

"Janet," he said intensely. I worried there was going to be a romantic speech. Let me give you some context. This was the early nineties, at Harvard, in a dorm where we all wore black turtlenecks and thought we understood Derrida, or thought that a display of understanding Derrida was important. I had friends who stayed up all night discussing whether all penetration was rape. There was a couple whose abusive S & M relationship was considered by some to be a radical subversion of the heteronormative paradigm. We were serious about these things. There was no place for romantic speeches in our world.

I grabbed the book and said, "Sorry, I have to go."

After we graduated and I moved to New York, he sent me a postcard, a black-and-white photograph of himself, unsmiling, glued to a piece of cardboard. On the back it said, *Thinking of you, wishing you well.* What it meant, I understood, was *I'm over it, good-bye.*

Eventually I left the city, went to graduate school in the Midwest, and then moved back again, this time as an organizational psychologist. While in grad school I'd met and married my husband. All the French theory in my head had evaporated when I graduated from college; I'd come from middle-class suburbia and those were the values I returned to, undergraduate philosophy sliding off me like the extra pounds from dining-hall food and Everclear punch. My husband had attended a state school where they hadn't waded knee-deep in identity politics and irony. He professed his love to me in an e-mail, after a chatty message about some repairs he was having done on his car. He was forthright and direct. *PS,* he wrote, *I love you.*

In person, this became his thing. At the end of a phone call: "Well, I've gotta go," he'd say. "PS, I love you." Sometimes he'd even hang up, then call back to say it.

After the wedding, he joined an Internet startup that was targeted immediately by enthusiastic investors, and all of a sudden we were floating in money. We had salaries and stock options and a brand-new car. My husband began speaking in acronyms. I'd thought *PS* was cute but it turned out to be the tip of the iceberg. He had code for everything. BRB, he'd say when he was going to be right back. IMO, when offering an opinion on current events.

One night, at a dinner party, I heard him say, "LOL!" He wasn't laughing, or even talking about it using real words; he was using the *code* for laughing instead of just chuckling, as if throwing back his head and laughing would be too much trouble, and take too much time. *What would Derrida say about that?* I wondered. It made me hate him—my husband, not Derrida.

You might think it's a small thing, the use of Internet-derived acronyms in ordinary conversation, and of course you'd be right. But it became an emblem of everything about my husband's new and prosperous and grown-up self that I didn't recognize. And it swelled up right in front of me, inflating like a balloon, until it obscured everything that had once drawn us together. My irritation was so gigantic it filled the horizon; it made me miserable every single moment of every single day, and soon enough, so was he. *What kind of love is this,* I thought, *that can be eclipsed not by infidelity or loss but by irritation? What kind of person am I?* We got divorced.

My husband cashed out his stocks before the Internet bubble burst, we sold our car, and he moved to California. I stayed in New York, the city's hard times seeming entwined with my own. After a while people asked me when I was going to start dating again, but truthfully I couldn't get interested. It seemed to me that I wasn't relationship material, that all those dreams I'd had back before getting married—of a house with a yard, a life with children, a couple growing old together—were meant for other people, not for me, in the same way that I just can't wear orange. Sometimes my husband and I talked on the phone, and we were friendly, solicitous, but our failure hung in the air between us, even across thousands of miles. I still thought of him as my husband, not because I still wanted to be married to him but because he was the person I'd chosen to marry, and the subsequent collapse didn't change the facts. Our failure made me more of an adult than getting married had. I was thirty-six but felt middle-aged, as if the best I could hope for was to *maintain*. I spent my disposable income on facials and manicures, grooming my carapace, which was how I thought of my body, something to be buffed and polished but never used, like a car in a showroom, gleaming inside glass walls.

A year passed, and I had a new position as an organizational consultant. I went from company to company with a laptop and a pad of yellow lined paper for taking notes. My job was to improve company performance by assessing its existing climate. I handed out questionnaires and conducted interviews, and in the process, I'd inevitably find out who was competent, overworked, or lazy, resented, or loved. Part efficiency expert, part psychiatrist, I diagnosed the health of these companies, and recommended treatment for their future well-being. Sometimes, people got fired.

I was introduced to the staff of ICS, a corporate marketing firm, by Melissa, a short, skinny woman in her thirties whose long curly hair made her look even smaller. An animal lover, she had her employees bring in pictures of their pets and post them in the lounge; this, she told me, created community. At the weekly staff meeting, she said, "This is Janet. She'll be with us for a month or so, conducting interviews. Janet, you're welcome to put up a picture of your pet in the lounge."

"I don't have any pets," I said.

Everyone in the room shifted uncomfortably in their seats. Afterward, I was shown to my temporary office, and was looking over the departmental flowcharts when a voice said, "Janet."

I looked up. Adam Leavitt was standing in the doorway, his hands in the pockets of his black pants. His hair was shorter, darker, with a few gray strands in it. He was wearing a white button-down shirt, and above the collar I could see the claws of his tattoo.

"You work here?" I said. I was too surprised to sound friendly, though I was happy to see him. "I didn't notice you at the meeting."

"I was in the back." Stepping forward, smiling, he placed his index finger in one of the flowchart boxes on my desk. "It's just a day job," he said. "I still play out at night. You look good."

"Thank you," I said calmly, not without pride, as if he were complimenting my car.

"Let's have lunch."

"I just got here."

"I didn't mean now. I meant at lunchtime."

"Right," I said. On my notepad I wrote down *lunch*. "You can show me where to go."

"I'll give you all the inside dope," he said, and before leaving he shot me a look that reminded me of college—a shade more intense, somehow, than a lunch date ought to provoke.

Three hours later we walked to a deli, bought sandwiches, and ate them sitting across the street in the kind of shoe-boxy Midtown park where corporate workers sit on or next to corporate sculpture. Depressingly, we caught up on fifteen years within ten minutes. Our lives went like this: starter job, disillusionment, graduate school, new job, major relationship, stasis. I asked him about his music, and he shrugged and muttered something about a record deal that fell through. He'd worked at ICS for five years and the line between its being a day job and an actual job had blurred to invisibility. He didn't say he was miserable about it, but I could tell. After we finished eating he gave me a postcard advertising a show by his band, Das Boot, at a bar in Williamsburg on the weekend.

"Das Boot?" I said.

"We pretend to be German," he said. "But we aren't."

"I didn't know you spoke German."

"I don't. Well, sometimes I use German words, and sometimes it's more of a German mood," he said.

"I'm not sure I understand. What kind of words and moods?"

"Angry and guttural. Sad and guttural. Zeitgeist. Weltanschauung. Heineken."

"Isn't Heineken Dutch?"

"Dutch, Deutsch." He shrugged, and I sensed he'd had this conversation before. "Anyway. It's a hybrid Sprockets-revival faux-language poetry kind of a thing."

I couldn't tell if this was serious or not. I smiled noncommittally and said it sounded interesting, and he laughed.

"Well, if it's not, at least the drinks are cheap," he said. "Maybe you don't care about cheap drinks at this point in your life, but will you come anyway?"

"I don't know," I said, catching in his eye a brief flash of disappointment that didn't seem ironic. "I'll try."

I showed up alone. The bar was dirty, small, pulsing with recorded techno, and close to empty. I saw some people I vaguely knew—acquaintances from college, some in designer clothes, others in studied vintage, with uncut hair. I made chitchat, wishing I hadn't come. Then something hit me lightly on the back of my head, and I reached back to brush away what I thought was an insect. I felt it again and looked down at the floor and noticed that I was surrounded by popcorn kernels. Someone was pelting me. I turned around and saw Adam coming at me from across the room. He literally did come right at me, his chin tucked into his neck. You know how cats walk across the room and stuff their faces right into your hand? They do it to mark you, to release some scent that shows you've been claimed. That's what this was like. He took hold of my arm and said, "You came."

"You invited me," I said. He held out the palm of his other hand, with three wizened pieces of popcorn still left in it. I declined them, and he turned his palm over and they fell to the floor. He was wearing one of the strangest outfits I'd ever seen, a striped sailor shirt with buttons on top of the shoulders, like epaulets, and green pants with buttons all down the sides. These didn't look like clothes bought recently, nor did they look used. I spend a fair amount of time in stores but I had no idea where a person could find such clothes. He looked half a caricature, half a heartthrob.

Which is to say that when I looked at him and smiled, my heart buzzed in its cavity like a fly in a jar. Whatever advantage I had on him during the day, as a professional consultant, evaporated.

"I know," he said in my ear, spittle hitting my left lobe and neck. "But I didn't think—well, anyway, it's good to see you."

A woman with long, dyed-black hair came over and told him they were getting started, and Adam made me promise I'd stay until the end.

"Okay," I said.

When Das Boot came on, they were so loud I thought my head would explode. I quickly tore some bar napkins into small pieces and stuffed them in my ears, feeling a million years old. Even through the paper wads I could hear Adam murmur a string of words into the microphone; it sounded like he was whispering the word *polka* over and over again. The woman with the long black hair hugged an accordion wildly. Behind the band, a black-and-white film I didn't recognize was playing.

They played two or three songs—at least I think they did, but it was hard to tell when one stopped and another began. Adam never once cracked a smile, but I was pretty sure the entire thing was a big joke—maybe his response to his lack of success as a musician, or the cause of it. Or both. There were too many layers. I felt confused and out of my depth, a feeling that made me pleasantly nostalgic for college. And when he sang a song about Wiener schnitzel and Werner Herzog, I laughed. The place was small enough that he saw me laughing from the stage, and this made me happy.

Then they were finished and the recorded techno music started up, and he bounded down from the stage and came straight at me again. "What do you think?" he shouted in my ear.

I took out my napkin wads. "I don't know," I said. "Is that what you're going for?"

"Absolutely," he said. He seemed very pleased with my comment and I thought I saw him blush. I was standing close enough that I could make out the age spots and wrinkles on his face, which looked better on him, I knew, than they did on me. "Let me get you a drink," he said.

He was known by the crowd there and people kept coming up and greeting him. I liked seeing him in his element. There were in-jokes I didn't get and names I'd never heard, and I listened to all of it with a dopey smile on my face. After a while I realized that Adam was holding my hand. He'd just put his hand into mine without looking at me or saying anything about it, still smiling and nodding and talking to someone else. Our palms were hot and greasy, kind of gross. My heart buzzed again. I felt like I was fourteen. Is there an exact opposite to growing up? Can a person grow *down*?

An hour later we left the bar together. We started walking purposefully down the street as if we'd agreed on some destination, then stopped at a grim little park—these apparently being our venue of choice—and sat down on a bench.

Adam put his arm around me. "It's strange to see you again," he said, "after you broke my heart."

"What?" I said. "Seriously?"

"Ever since you, I've been wary of women. I let them chase me, and usually I leave them before I get left."

"Wait a minute," I said. "You never even asked me out. It was just some unspoken thing."

"I adored you. I've never felt that way about anyone else, before or since."

It wasn't the kind of thing you hear every day, and I took a moment to drink it in. "I didn't know," I finally said. We were meeting each other's eyes and then glancing away, light bouncing off corners, all goose bumps and indirection.

"Of course you knew. You just acted like you didn't."

I didn't know what to say next. College was all about banter and flirting but now I was used to speaking directly; my husband and I had been to couple's therapy and learned to use *I* statements to express our feelings. I felt like I was attempting some sport I hadn't played since childhood.

We went to his apartment, not far away. He poured me a glass of wine, and as he was handing it to me he kissed me on the lips. "I want to be with you," he said.

I kissed him back, then stopped. I didn't want him to see me naked: I had veins mapping my breasts and clustered like bruises on my thighs. My skin was creped in some places, bumpy in others. I put my hands under his shirt and felt his muscled chest and then, lower down, the sweetly reassuring padding of his paunch.

In his tiny bedroom, no larger than the dorm room of years past, we pressed ourselves close together and wrestled ourselves into submission. Afterward I exhaled deeply, satisfied and relieved that it had gone so well. Then we slept.

I could say that the poor ethics of the situation—I was making recommendations that would affect him and his friends at work—made the relationship exciting. I could say that it was like recovering some part of my lost youth. Or that it was about sex, or abandon, or fun. And all these things could be true yet still not capture the whole truth of its slippery, sexy reality. Adam and I went driving around Brooklyn in his twenty-year-old BMW, smoking cigarettes and listening to eighties music from our teenage years on cassette tapes he'd gotten free off people's stoops. We had dinners out, in small cheap restaurants; I never cooked for him or asked him over to my place. There wasn't much of the domestic between us, nor a sense of the future. With my husband, almost immediately after getting together we'd started playing house, cooking dinner, washing up, and watching movies at home, curled up on the couch. We had a chore wheel on the fridge. Everything was a rehearsal for the real performance of adult life. Adam and I didn't rehearse. We never talked about where things were going or not going. We went out to dinner, the movies, to parties, then talked about the dinners and movies and parties, and after that I slid my fingers through his hair and took him to bed, or was taken.

But it would be wrong to say, because it wasn't grown-up, or an audition for some permanent household situation, that it wasn't also soulful and moving and important. It was. At night I sometimes ran my hands over his tattoos and marveled at his existence. I learned what he liked in bed, and when I did those things he produced this one special sound that gave me a shiver right through my chest. I was pretty close to being in love.

At work, I soon realized that Adam's days were numbered. From all reports, he did little and had no true function, apparently hoping no one would notice. The company was riddled with these redundancies, and the resentment felt by those who had real work to do was enormous. Whenever I asked about this inequality, I got long explanations of how various departments that once were joined had since been separated, or had been separated and now were collapsed; apparently, a guy who'd left the company ten years earlier had orchestrated this particular structure, which still remained but held no actual contents. History dictated the current molds of any company, much as our adult personalities are informed by our childhood. It was my job to retrain this psychology and reform the molds. And no matter what I said about the company climate and its potential for change and growth, that Adam had done so little for so long couldn't possibly look good.

My allegiance was temporarily torn between him and my professional discretion, but Adam won. He never asked me about my job, much less my conclusions, and after that first lunch we rarely spoke at the office. I was busy conducting interviews, and from what I heard he was busy surfing the Internet, making coffee, and using the company's Kinko's account to produce posters and ads for his band.

But at dinner one night, I brought it up. "Have you thought at all about what might happen at the company?" I asked, putting it as vaguely as I could.

"Not really. I'm not all that attached to the job," he said. I knew he was lying. It protected him from having to worry too much about not being more successful; it was at once a cover story, an excuse, a disguise.

At ICS I spent the final week collating my findings, typed up my notes, and put them in a report filled with charts and graphs. I recommended certain dramatic changes, assessing their future efficiencies with a clear eye. I knew they were necessary; whether they would be implemented was another issue, but I was good at my job, a fact that brought me neither great satisfaction nor anxiety. I'd already lined up my next client, a clothing manufacturer in New Jersey, which would require me to commute on a PATH train every weekday for a month.

There was no doubt in my mind that Adam was going to get fired. I told myself this was the best thing that could happen to a thirty-seven-year-old musician: he'd get six months of unemployment benefits and during that time he could devote himself fully to his music, get to where he needed to be, or decide that he'd had enough of the struggle and reconcile himself to a regular job, one he liked enough to work hard at. I told myself I was doing him a favor, but didn't believe it, of course, and didn't expect that he would, either. The night before I was scheduled to hand in my report, I finally had him over to my place for dinner. I put on an apron and cooked, and he sat on my couch and laughed at me, wearing his crazy, clownish musician's clothes, a blue guayabera and purple cargo pants.

"You're like Betty Crocker or something," he said, laughing.

I felt tears welling up. "Adam," I said, "I adore you."

"Baby," he said, drawing me down on the couch.

"I mean it," I said.

"I wanted you my whole life," he said, his hands roving over my back.

There were things I needed to say and hear, and in counseling I'd learned that you shouldn't preempt communication with sex, but at a certain point you have to say, well, fuck that, and this was such a point. With him inside me I felt centered, anchored, pinned. At the height of things I said, "I love you, I love you," and he might have heard me, or he might've been too wrapped up in the sex to be listening.

He didn't spend the night. At the office the next morning, we didn't see each other. I packed up my files and laptop, then gave Melissa my report in her office, which was filled with pictures of cats she'd adopted or foster-cared for. Many of them were injured and ignored the camera, dismayed by the indignities of their head cones, stitches, and casts. She slapped the laminated cover of the report and said she'd have fun reading it over the weekend.

I felt like I had to prepare this compassionate, sentimental woman for the unpleasant realities inside. "There might be some difficult decisions to make."

She cocked her head at me, and I could tell she knew what I was implying, and that I'd offended her. "I'm sure that with your help we'll be able to make some wonderful improvements to our organization," she said smoothly. "Thank you for all your hard work."

From beneath her desk, I heard a sickly meow.

Melissa paled. "Don't tell anyone, okay? We're not supposed to have animals here, but I really couldn't leave Snickers alone."

I stood up. "Feel free to get in touch if you have any questions."

She shook my hand as the cat bellowed again. "Will do," she said.

I'd grown used to spending part of every weekend with Adam, but Friday and Saturday passed and he didn't call. Late that afternoon I tried his cell, but he didn't answer. It seemed unlikely he'd already been told he was getting fired, but sometimes office grapevines work at the speed of light.

By Sunday night I was going out of my mind, unable to sit still, my skin itching. I caught myself thinking crazy things, like: *The only thing that bothers me is that he didn't even say good-bye.* Or: *I just want to kiss him one more time.* My heart was rattling with upset, jumping around as if bent on escape. But there was no escaping this.

On Monday I headed to New Jersey. I greeted the bosses and set up my office and began arranging meetings. This place had no old college acquaintances to add intrigue to the assignment, which was fine by me. The day went by quickly, and so did the week, but the real me was somewhere else.

Apparently, things were over between Adam and me. I'd gotten the message but the crazy part of me, the heart-skipping, cage-rattling part, wanted a final conversation or, at the very least, one last glimpse. And so on Wednesday morning instead of taking the PATH train, I went to Midtown and sat in the park where we'd first had lunch. Looking at the building, I tried to invent an excuse for returning to the office. Maybe I'd left something there, a pen or some important folder. But I'd trained myself in efficiency, and never left anything behind.

At lunchtime, Adam came out of the building with Melissa. They went into the deli, then crossed the street to the park and unwrapped their sandwiches, balancing them awkwardly on their suited laps. They weren't sitting especially close or touching each other or anything, but I could tell, just from seeing them, that they were sleeping together. So I guessed he'd keep his job.

I'm no spy, and I don't do surveillance. "Hey, Melissa," I said, walking up to them.

"Oh, *hi*," she said.

"Adam, could I talk to you for a second?"

"Of course." He stood up and we walked a few feet away, into the shadow cast by some monstrous, ambiguously shaped steel sculpture. We met each other's eyes—we were adults, we could do this—and his were so, so blue.

"I wanted to say I'm sorry."

He looked perplexed. He didn't seem mad, or even uncomfortable. "For what?"

I'd prepared a little speech in my hours of waiting for him to appear. "Although I couldn't have altered the facts of my report, I could have recused myself, or not gone out with you, or given you some advance notice of my findings, and I'm sorry that I didn't do any of those things. It was inappropriate, and I apologize."

He looked down and laughed, and when his blue eyes met mine again, he winked. In all the time we'd spent together, he'd never winked, and the distance it put between us cut me like a cold wind. "Sometimes," he said, "we were *very* inappropriate."

"Well—"

"Listen, I understand you feel bad, and that's sweet, but you don't have to worry." He gestured vaguely behind him. "I'm not getting fired but Melissa's taking the spirit of your suggestions to heart and ICS will be the better for it."

"I never realized that you were so concerned about the company's welfare."

He stepped closer, and his voice softened. "I think you were the one getting concerned. A little too invested. I just figured it was best not to get even more, you know, when it wasn't going to be what you wanted."

Understanding came over me in waves. "This isn't about my saying your job should be eliminated? It's because I said I love you?"

"I told you—when we first saw each other again—that I don't do that anymore. I leave first, always. You can't say I wasn't honest."

"So this was, like, your revenge?"

"No, Jan," he said softly, and I'll swear there was real caring in his voice. "It's just who I am now."

It wasn't something you could argue with, so I nodded and left. I'd like to say I didn't cry on the subway, but I did. And back in my apartment, I curled up under a blanket on my couch. I asked myself what I was thinking, scolded myself for getting involved with him and for acting like a crush-struck teenager, told myself that I'd survived a divorce and surely I'd survive this, commanded myself to grow up, and when I was done saying all this to myself I thought: *Oh, great, another failure.*

The difference between being a teenager and an adult is, I guess, that the next day, I took the PATH train out to New Jersey and got on with it. The days were okay but at night I could feel my heart pacing like a restless and unhappy animal. It was probably the first time I'd felt lonely in years. Usually I was comfortable spending time alone, but I'd made a space for Adam in my life and my body; now that he was gone, I felt hollow.

This is the only teenage thing I did: I went to a bar in Hoboken where Das Boot was playing. This time the place was crowded and a fake French band was playing. Next up was a fake Japanese band. Fake bands were all the rage. I couldn't find any napkins at the bar, and my ears were ringing. I didn't see Adam anywhere, and should have gone home, but instead I stayed and drank Red Stripe with people ten, maybe twenty years younger. At one point, gesturing to the bartender, I knocked over a bottle sitting in front of the girl next to me, who was very pretty and had silver piercings dotted all along her eyebrows. When I apologized, she put her hand on my shoulder and said sweetly, "I think it's great you still get out."

By the time Das Boot came on, the crowd had shifted and was now almost all women. Adam *was* a heartthrob. He came onstage bare chested and his hair was tied up in tiny pigtails all over his head. A kind of collective sigh blew through the audience. A line from an old, nonfake band went through my head: *Baby you're adorable. Handle me with care.*

His smile swept across the room and then he started to sing, or fake-sing, or whatever it was that he did, and all those girls loved it. Loved him. He didn't know I was there. My heart gave a sickly meow, and I went home.

It was past one by the time I got back to my apartment. I felt as alone as I've ever felt in my entire life. I called my husband, just to hear a familiar voice.

"I'm dating someone," he said. "FYI."

"That's great," I told him, sincerely. "I want you to be happy."

"What about you?"

"I was, but it didn't work out."

"I'm sorry."

"It's okay. Or at least it will be."

We talked for a few more minutes, exchanging news, and then we hung up.

What happened afterward? If I were to assess my life like a corporate organization, examining its climate and function, I would summarize my findings as follows. I never saw Adam again. In the days to come, I cried and cried and cried, like the heartsick teenager who still lived inside me. I cried so much that I grew comfortable with it, and with the pain that gave rise to it. I knew that night, without a doubt, that I loved Adam. And I still, in certain moods and lights, loved my husband, a love that was like a ghost of itself. There was no future for either of these loves, but it wasn't the same thing, I thought, as failure. Because of this: I no longer felt like a showroom car, static and shining with lack of use. Because of this: I was a person whose heart could still move.

The Teacher

On Doug and Carol's wedding day, murder was committed in their small town, which they steadfastly refused to take as a bad sign. They were that much in love. They spent their first married night in the Newport hotel wrapped in each other's arms, gazing into each other's eyes, and so on, but after they'd had sex twice there was only so much more gazing that could be done, and Carol turned on CNN while Doug took a shower.

"Oh, my God," he heard her say as he toweled off. She was sitting at the foot of the king-sized bed, the coverlet loosely bunched around her skinny frame, exposing the delicate bumps of her spine. She was transfixed. A young man had killed his wife and child and was now on the run; cameras were holding steady on a blue SUV going down a strangely empty freeway, headed for the coast.

"I don't know why you watch this stuff," Doug said. He sat down beside her and kissed her bare shoulder. She smelled like candy.

"She went to my high school," Carol said, her eyes wide. "Younger though. So young. And the *baby*. Did you know them?"

"I don't think so."

On the screen now was a photograph of the young couple on their own wedding day, red-eyed from camera flash and booze.

Carol was a preschool teacher and spent all day long singing songs about bunnies and cows. Sometimes they bumped into her students in the grocery store, and the kids were so freaked-out to see her outside of school that they ran away. Other times, to be fair, they got excited and seemed like they were going to pee in their pants. In any case, she came home from being with the kids all day, from playing with their brightly colored blocks and vocabulary-building cards, and she liked, by contrast, to watch violent crime dramas or breaking news about murders, kidnappings, disappearances. An expert on bullets and DNA evidence, she supported the death penalty and often, just before falling asleep, would shake her head and say things like, "He should rot in hell for what he's done."

In Jamaica, he'd booked the "Serenity Suite," which didn't have a TV and was more expensive than a standard room. Once the honeymoon began, as he'd hoped, she mellowed. For three days they ate conch fritters and took naps on the beach, their skin burnishing. They held hands as they walked on the sand at sunset and were lulled to sleep by the sound of waves crashing on the beach, a gentle soundtrack piping through the suite's wall-mounted speakers. But Carol hadn't forgotten the story.

"We probably saw them at the mall," she said one day over lunch. "Or at the movie theater. Do you think they got married at the same church?"

All day long she kept this up, and her fascination started to get on Doug's nerves. When she asked if they could find a TV that night, he snapped at her, she pouted, and they ate dinner separately—he on the beach, she in their room—until he came back and they made up and had sex again and gazed into each other's eyes. By the sixth day of conches and tanning, he'd gone over to her side. At a bar they persuaded some people from Chicago to let go of the Cubs game they were watching by buying them drinks. As they sat there, CNN cycled through world disasters and weather forecasts before turning to the case they were waiting for. And in fact, the young woman and her baby were being memorialized in the very church where Doug and Carol's wedding had taken place.

"Oh, my God," she said.

The camera lingered on the familiar steps of St. Anthony's as the mourners emerged sadly, single file, hunched in their black suits and dresses.

"That's where we had our pictures taken," Carol said. "That's where I tripped on my hem and almost fell. That's where the car pulled up."

The young man had been apprehended. His parents gave a press conference in which they expressed their sympathy for the wife's family and, of course, the loss of the baby. It seemed as if they'd already given up on him.

"Let's stop watching this," Doug said, but Carol didn't hear him, and he didn't bother to repeat it, because they were showing the main street of town; they were interviewing the guy who worked at the hardware store, where Doug himself bought nails and plywood, about the murders.

"They were just like any other couple," the hardware guy said. "They had grout issues in their bathroom."

Doug wrapped his arms around Carol and told her that he loved her.

On the plane back to Rhode Island, burnt skin peeling off their noses and backs, they held hands. They landed in a dense, chilly New England downpour. Debbie, Carol's best friend and maid of honor, met them at the airport. Doug could tell just by looking at her that she was dying to share the news about the murders, and she did a poor job of hiding her disappointment when Carol brought it up first. As Debbie drove them home, erratically, in her SUV—she had adult ADD, Carol had always said—they chattered back and forth about it, not discussing the honeymoon at all. Debbie wasn't so much a bad driver as a bad multitasker; she'd light cigarettes or rummage around the front seat for stuff and only look up at the last second, swerving or braking with sudden jerks.

"And my little brother's ex-girlfriend's sister was in the Girl Scouts with her," she said.

"*Really*," Carol said.

"She said she was just the sweetest person. I mean like seriously the sweetest person you ever met in your life."

"Oh, my God," Carol said.

In the backseat, Doug, having had two Jack and Cokes on the plane, dozed as the women's bright, excited voices filled the air. He was glad for the rain; there was such a thing as too much sun. Debbie's voice squeaked higher, and suddenly was joined by an extra squeak and the squeal of tires, and he jolted awake in time to see the road rise up, like a wave, to meet the side windows, and the last thing he heard before impact was Carol's voice screaming his name.

In the hospital he woke up alone, and that was the scariest thing. There was only the sound of machines beeping, not a single voice.

The door to his room was closed. After a while, Debbie came in. She was wearing a hospital gown and had bandages on her face and arms and hands. "Oh, Douggie," she said, as if he were her child, then tried to stroke his arm with one of her bandaged, pawlike hands. She was an animal, and he hated her. He tried to scream, but nothing came out. Then he went under again. This happened over and over, it felt like. A week passed, maybe more; he was never sure. They waited until he was out of the hospital to have the funeral, again at St. Anthony's.

The year that followed held pain like he'd never known existed. He didn't have words to describe it, not to other people, not even inside his own head. It was a lot more like physical pain than he ever would have expected, the ache and stab of it. It was like a broken leg, but no medicine or cast could mend it. Sometimes he drank a lot and that helped, but only barely and for a couple of hours at a time, and he'd wake up in the middle of the night, sobbing.

He had this house full of wedding gifts. Appliances. Wineglasses. Monogrammed napkin holders, with their initials intertwined.

For a year he went to work and came home, went to work and came home. As he began to come out of his haze he understood what a totally crappy job he'd been doing for months and apologized to his boss, Victor.

"It's okay, man," Victor said, wincing, the expression he used to convey understanding. "What you've been through, nobody should have to survive."

"I think I'm doing better," Doug said.

"Hey, man, that's awesome. That is so great," Victor said, wincing harder. "You know what? Let's go out. Let's get some of the guys together and celebrate your return to the world."

It didn't sound bad to Doug. He'd let his friendships slide over the past year, ignoring phone calls from his best man, from couples they'd socialized with, and repeated ones from Debbie. He preferred the company of his TV, watching all the shows Carol liked. After months of investigation, the guy who'd murdered his wife and child was finally on trial. The continuing news story kept him connected to her, to her lust for punishment and retribution. The murderer had cut his hair and lost weight. He looked younger and sickly and therefore more innocent. *Who cares?* he could hear Carol saying, her voice vibrant with anger. *He deserves whatever he gets.*

"What you deserve, buddy," Victor said, as if eavesdropping inside Doug's mind, "is a little bit of distraction. That's what you deserve."

That night, they went out with a couple other guys to a martini bar in a hotel around the corner from the office. He'd never been there before—they used to go a brewpub, since closed—and for this he was glad. They settled into a black leather booth in the corner. A couple of people were drinking alone at the bar. The waitress, a sweet-looking blond woman in her twenties, dropped off the bar menu. There were seventeen kinds of martinis.

In the past year his tolerance for liquor had ballooned, so it took a few rounds for him to feel any effect, and only after the third could he relax and pay attention to the conversation. His workmates were talking about the waitress's ass. It was a nice-looking ass. She caught them looking at it and gave it a wiggle.

There was another woman they were discussing, also pretty, sitting at the bar. She was wearing a pink blouse and matching skirt and had long, dark brown hair. She noticed the waitress giving them a show and rolled her eyes, but nicely, as if she saw the humor of it. Doug's friends noticed him checking her out.

"Go talk to her, man," Victor said. "She's hot."

"Smokin'," said Wayne from Technology Services.

"Who says *smokin'* anymore?" Victor said.

"I'm just saying she's hot."

"Smokin'," Victor said, wincing for real. "Give me a break."

Doug was starting to feel drunk, and grateful for it, nodding vacantly through all of this. He hardly noticed when Victor and Wayne went to the bar to chat up the dark-haired woman, gales of laughter soon pealing from their little group. He ordered another martini from the blond waitress, who brought it and said, "This one is compliments of the girl at the bar."

"Seriously?"

"I think she likes you," the waitress said.

From the bar, Victor gave him a thumbs-up. Doug tried to grin, but it looked more like a grimace, he knew. His smiling muscles were stiff from lack of use. He drank down half the martini and ate his olives, and by the time he finished chewing the guys were trailing back to the table.

"You're never going to believe this, man," Victor said, "but she gave me this for you." He opened his palm and showed Doug a keycard envelope on which the room number was written in blue pen.

"She thinks you're hot," Wayne said.

"Maybe even *smokin'*," Victor said. He elbowed Wayne good-naturedly, and they both laughed.

Doug could feel the vodka now. "That's crazy," he said, not very distinctly, "we haven't exchanged a single word."

"So what?" Victor said. "She likes the look of you."

He drained his martini. When he looked over at the bar again, the woman was gone. Victor and the other guys walked him to the elevator, pressed the button for him, and then left. He could see his face reflected drunkenly in the elevator's mirror. Leering at himself, he couldn't feel the muscles move, like after a shot at the dentist's. The elevator stopped.

He found her room and inserted the key. Nothing happened. He tried again. Was she in there listening to him fumble? Not a very good advertisement for anything that might happen later. On the third try, the light flashed green and he turned the handle and stepped inside.

She was sitting on the bed, wearing a black negligee and watching CNN, a sound so profoundly reassuring to him that his knees felt weak. She was thin and olive skinned, with pointy shoulders. Her clothes were folded on the chair in a neat pink pile. Only when he saw her with her clothes already off did he understand that his friends had paid for her company.

"Hi, Doug," she said, and turned off the TV.

"You can leave it on," he said.

She pressed the remote again and a man said, "Next up, the story of a lost dog traveling hundreds of miles all by itself to find its way home."

He sat down next to her, unsure of what to say or do. He'd never been in this situation before. "I had some trouble getting in."

"Well, you're here now," she said, and patted his hand. "Are you okay?"

"I'm a little dizzy," he admitted.

Patting his hand again, she stood up and fetched him some water from the bathroom, then turned down the volume on the TV.

"Who are you?" he said.

"My name's Violet."

"Where are you from?"

"New Hampshire."

"I don't know why I'm here," he said. He felt close to tears. This wasn't his thing, and it wasn't going to help.

"Your friends thought you needed some company."

"I do need company," he confessed. "I do."

"Okay, then," Violet said.

He put his head in her lap. But she was bony and her negligee was slippery—Carol always wore cotton—and the whole setup wasn't very comfortable, so he lay next to her in bed instead, his heavy head resting on the pillows.

"My wife died," he said. "She was a teacher."

"I wanted to be a teacher," Violet said. They were holding hands. Her hair smelled good, not quite like candy, more like flowers. "I always liked reading."

"You should do it," he said. "You should be a teacher."

"It's kind of late," Violet said.

"It's not even midnight," he said, and passed out to the sound of her laugh.

When he woke up, the room was dark and silent. It reminded him of waking in the hospital, and he was scared and sad, and his head hurt. "Violet?" he said, his voice sounding like a child's.

"I'm here, honey," she said, from the other side of the room. In the darkness, he could make out that she was dressed in her pink outfit again.

"Please don't leave."

"Okay," she said.

In the morning she was still there, and they ordered breakfast from room service. Violet ate a waffle, licking syrup off her fingers. Without her makeup and in a sober light she looked less pretty than she had and even younger, actually, but somehow more tired.

"You had a nightmare," she said. "You were talking but I couldn't understand what you said."

"I dreamed I was back in fifth grade and the other kids tried to kill me," he said, and they both laughed. "Pretty weird, huh."

"Maybe I shouldn't be a teacher, if kids are that violent," she said. "Maybe what I'm doing now is safer." She smiled at him, then bit her lip. "You seem like a nice guy," she said. "I'm sorry about your wife."

"Thank you," he said.

"My real name is Jane."

"My real name's Martin. Martin Douglas Robinson. I thought Martin was a sissy name when I was a kid, so I use my middle name instead."

They shook hands formally, politely. He thought about kissing her, but he wasn't really attracted to her. That part of him was dead or at least dormant; he took care of its occasional needs by himself in the shower, a quick and efficient system that worked fine in his opinion.

"I guess I better go," he said.

She shrugged, sweetly. In that moment he liked her about as well as he could like anyone, and he leaned over and kissed her cheek. She touched his shoulder, a faint, barely-there caress, like the first drop before you're sure it's raining. She put a card into his palm and folded his fingers over it.

"Call me," she said.

At work that day, Victor and Wayne grinned with accomplishment. They kept walking around slapping him on the back and announcing loudly that they knew something other people didn't. Hungover, Doug didn't say much, a silence taken for gentlemanly discretion. A lot of women came around to check on him, stopping by his office with lame excuses about confirming meeting times or having run out of toner and needing to use his printer. Suddenly there was an aura around him; he was back on the market. He wasn't sure how to feel about this, and he left the office early, looking forward to a night at home in front of the TV.

When he pulled up, he saw a girl sitting on his front steps. It was Violet, or rather Jane. This time she was wearing jeans and a pink cardigan sweater and white running shoes. He stood in the driveway for a second, not knowing what to say.

"You're in the phone book," she said, before he could say anything. "I hope you don't mind I just dropped by. Can I come in?"

"What are you doing here?"

"You're in the book," she said again. She was standing up now, with her hands plunged in the pockets of her jeans, and she looked innocent and vulnerable, or like a person who was trying to look innocent and vulnerable. The year he and Carol started going out, he remembered, she'd been obsessed with a hooker who was blackmailing an alderman in Ohio and had amassed thousands of dollars that his wife thought was safely gathering interest in their kid's college fund. "What a scumbag," Carol had said of the alderman. "He should have kept it in his pants."

"I was just on my way out," he told Jane. "Now's not a good time." Quickly he got back in the car, then drove to a theater and saw two movies back-to-back. When he got home again it was midnight and she was gone. She probably had to go to work, in the hotel bar. He breathed out a deep sigh. Inside, he checked his messages.

"This is Jane Eckman calling," her voice said. "That's my name. Jane Audrey Eckman. I really am from New Hampshire. I'm not a creep or a crazy person. I just wanted to call and tell you that. I'm sorry I freaked you out today. I just didn't know if you'd remember my name. I mean, if I called you, I thought you might not know who I was, so I thought I'd just stop by. I thought you seemed like a nice person, and so I thought I would just stop by. I'm in the phone book too if you want to call me back. Or also you have my card. That's all. Okay. Bye."

Alone in his house, he exhaled. He hadn't even realized he'd been holding his breath. In the pocket of his pants, hanging in his closet, he found her card (*Friends for all Occasions,* it said, with a phone number, next to which she'd written, in blue ballpoint and bubbled letters, *Violet/Jane*) and tore it into small pieces, which he then flushed down the toilet.

The next night, she called again. He wasn't picking up the phone, just in case, and she left another message. This time her voice trembled a little.

"Martin, this is Jane," she said. "I know this is making me

sound crazy, but I'm actually not crazy, I swear. I just—Listen. I don't know a lot of people here. And I don't meet a lot of people either, because where would I meet them? And if I did meet them and they asked me what I do, what would I say? So I guess I just thought, I mean, in your case, you already know from the start. I guess I just thought, I'm kind of lonely, and you seem kind of lonely too, so maybe it would be okay. Anyway, I just wanted to explain that. You have my card. That's all. Okay. Bye."

The next day she didn't call. He'd expected her to, but of course he was glad she didn't. He went out for a beer with Victor and Wayne, to a sports bar, not the hotel, and when he got home he was even a little disappointed not to find a message waiting, but not *really* disappointed, just a little let down. She was lonely, that was all, and he was glad she was leaving him alone now. He'd been through enough.

A few days passed. Life went back to its routine, such as it was. He cleaned his office, cleaned his house. No calls.

Then the verdict came down on the murderer of his wife and child. He was guilty. Absent the death penalty in Rhode Island, he'd probably get life in prison. Protesters outside the prison were demanding he should be killed. The parents of the dead woman were interviewed and declined to offer an opinion, saying only that no matter what happened, their daughter and grandson weren't coming back, and given that, there could be no justice. Punishment, but not justice. Doug turned off the TV and sat by himself on the couch, his hands shaking.

.   .   .

A week later, when he pulled up to the house after work, Jane Eckman was waiting on his front steps again. This time the weather
was warm and she was wearing a pink flowered sundress, like a
girl going to church. It looked like an outfit her mother would
have bought her. For the first time he wondered how old she was.
He almost reversed out of the driveway, but didn't. He got out of
the car and faced her.

"Hi, Martin," Jane said, then swallowed visibly. "I'm sorry
about those phone calls."

"It's okay," he said.

"I came here to ask you out," she said.

"What?"

"On a date," she said.

To this he said nothing, and just looked at her.

"People say sometimes men are dense so you have to be clear.
So I'm here, being clear. I like you. You seem like a nice man. You
told me I should go ahead and try to be a teacher. It made me feel
good, do you know what I mean? I meet a lot of men and most
of them don't seem very nice. So I was wondering if you'd like to
have dinner with me tonight?"

"Jane," he said.

"If you say no, I'll leave now and I won't ever bother you again."

"No."

"Okay, then," she said. She pulled a cell phone out of her purse.
"I'll just have to call a cab. It's okay if I wait out here, isn't it? Sorry.
This isn't a very good exit."

In the living room, he watched her stand in the driveway
until the cab took her away. He couldn't see, from where he was,
whether she was crying or not.

. . .

He thought that was the end of it, but she kept calling. She didn't leave messages, though. She'd just call and hang up, every few days. It was ridiculous, like high school or something. After a couple weeks he made up his mind. He went to the bar in the hotel, but she wasn't there. This went on for another few days, her calling and hanging up, his looking for her at the hotel bar at night after work. Finally he saw her, sitting there, nursing a cocktail. He had two thousand dollars in his pocket, in a small manila envelope. It was money he and Carol had saved for a down payment on a new car. Jane smiled when she saw him.

"Buy me a drink?" she said hopefully.

"I can't stay," he said. He looked around the bar, eyeing it as he thought she would, for prospective marks. Was that what she would call them, marks? He didn't know. "I came to bring you something."

Jane smiled again and he saw she was blushing. She thought he'd come around to ask her out. He put the envelope on the bar. "Be a teacher," he said.

Her smile was gone, but the blush was still there. She didn't touch the envelope. She curled both hands around her glass, holding it tightly.

"My wife and I were saving it," he said, "but I don't need it. Take it and go back to New Hampshire. Go back to school and be a teacher. Meet a nice man and have children." His voice was cracking. The bartender was looking at him, but he didn't care. "Start a new life."

Jane pushed the envelope back at him and stood up. "Is that

what you think I want from you? Fuck you." Her voice rose to a shout. "Seriously, Martin. Fuck you." She got up and rushed out, her high heels clicking spastically.

The bartender shrugged. "Women," he said.

Doug picked up the envelope and went home. While he was taking a shower, the phone rang. *Jane,* he thought, *I'll never get away from her.* After he got dressed, he saw there was a message, so he poured himself a drink and steeled himself to listen to it.

But it wasn't Jane. It was Debbie, Carol's best friend, the one who'd been driving on the night of the accident. She'd called him every few months since the crash, but he'd never called her back. It wasn't that he hated her; he just couldn't stand the sound of her voice.

"Douggie," she said, in her high, squeaky voice, and immediately he was back in the hospital, back in the embrace of her awful bandaged paws. "I know we haven't really talked since . . . Well, maybe you don't want to hear from me. But I was watching the news about that guy and how he's going to jail forever now, and I was thinking about you." Her voice trailed off and he guessed she was drinking, or on the verge of crying, or both. "I was . . ." She hung up.

Debbie was divorced and lived by herself, ten minutes away, in a condo development called Lantern Hills. Every time she told people where she lived she'd say, "We do have some lanterns, but the land's actually flat," and laugh. He'd always found her annoying, but now, all of a sudden, he felt like he'd missed her.

He rang the doorbell and she answered the door in jeans and a college T-shirt—no bra it looked like—and bare feet. Her hair was down, uncombed.

"I got your message," he told her.

"Come in," she said.

She brought him a beer and they sat down on the couch. She looked strange holding the bottle, and two of her fingers didn't bend. There were scars on the backs of her hands.

She waved her stiff hands at him, almost apologetically. "They're full of pins," she said.

"That guy," Doug said, "the one who killed his wife and kids. Carol would have said, *Too bad we don't have the death penalty in Rhode Island*."

Debbie nodded. "That's true, that's so exactly what she would have said."

There was a silence.

"I met this girl," Doug told her. "She was a hooker. But she wanted to be a teacher."

"What?"

He told her everything, from start to finish, though he left out the part at the very end where Jane said she didn't want the money. He just talked about giving her the envelope and telling her to start over, and Debbie nodded and listened with her scarred hands awkwardly semifolded in her lap. With the ludicrous, almost lurid story hanging there between them, he felt closer to her than he had to anyone in a very long time. He felt a tenderness gurgle inside him and gasp for air, and as he spoke and gestured he let his hand brush over hers.

Vigo Park

There's a gun at the beginning of this story, placed here so that you know it's going to go off by the end. That's just the way it is; you've been warned. Call it fate, call it destiny, call it the inevitable consequence of certain destructive but all-too-common human behaviors. There's no changing the ending, however dramatic and/or ugly and/or contrived and/or sad it might seem to you. Better accept it now.

The gun (an ancient Walther looted from some German soldier in World War II, not that this ultimately matters) is in the coat pocket of a man on the 24 bus, which is heading to Vigo Park. It's winter, and he's hunched over, with his hands meeting across his lap, like someone protecting himself from the cold. Underneath his coat, though, he has taken off both his gloves and is touching the gun—which his father, a responsible man, kept unloaded and locked in a cabinet in his house until he died—with his bare fingers. The ring on his left hand makes a clinking sound against the barrel, but nobody on the bus hears it. Despite all that's happened he hasn't been able to bring himself to take it off. Whenever he starts to slide the ring off he sees his wife in his mind's eye, crying on their wedding day when she put it on his finger, tears of pure, liquid happiness. To take it off would be to acknowledge all the ways he has hurt her, and that is more than he can stand to do.

A fat man in a sheepskin jacket sits down next to him at this point, and so he stops touching the gun, which has made him feel kind of masturbatory anyway, sliding his hands up and down the length of it beneath his coat. The bus begins the uphill chug toward the park. People get on; others get off. The day is gray. Earlier there was sleet and later there will be snow; but right now the sky holds itself in dark abeyance above the salt-streaked roads and cars of the city. Even the clothing seems to have darkened in the wintry light: brown and black and navy-blue wool coats trudge up and down the streets, relieved only occasionally by a patterned hat or scarf. Why, he wonders, does winter have to take all the color from the world? The bus turns a corner, and through the dirty window he can just make out his destination.

In the park a woman in a red coat sits watching a child play. It's not her child. She has no child. This, to her, is a source of enormous grief. She had a chance, several years ago, but was talked out of keeping it. Sometimes, when she sees a child the age her own would be, she thinks about kidnapping it, or doing other, even crazier things.

"Life is what you make it," her sister often tells her, and this is just one reason among many they seldom speak. Her sister, who is happy, believes this is of her own devising. She doesn't believe in luck. She tells Rebecca to change the things in her life that make her unhappy, and then she'll be happy. "It's like making coffee," she explains. "Is it too strong? Add more water next time. Learn from the mistakes of the past." These words fall on Rebecca like wet snow: white and substantial one moment, dissolved by the next. "I drink tea," she tells her sister, who sighs heavily and informs her that she's missing the point.

This is where things might get a little hard to believe for some people. Basically the situation is that on the other side of the playground is another woman in a red coat. Like Rebecca, she has long blond hair in a ponytail, and like Rebecca, she is alone. In fact, it's the same make and model of coat, bought from the same department store during the same January sale. It was even bought for the same reason, because most winter coats are dark blue or black or brown and both women thought they might cheer themselves up by relieving the gray color scheme of winter with a flash of red. This not-especially-brilliant bit of fashion psychology has infected hundreds, maybe thousands, of women, and the red coats are flying off the racks; it's the one must-have item of the season—you know how women are, they get these ideas into their heads, these cravings that must be satisfied—and Tori has come to regret her purchase, since seeing it on so many other women has made her feel generic in her thoughts and emotions, frankly, the last thing she needs right about now. Looking across the park she thinks, *Oh, great, another one. Why do I even bother?* Which is a question she's asking herself more and more often these days. This other woman seems to be waiting for someone, as she herself is. Automatically she compares the other woman's looks to her own—maybe ten years older, and thinner, too thin, really, a stick—and decides, after some thought, that the coat looks better on her, Tori. Knowing this victory is shallow doesn't mean she isn't still satisfied. Frank always tells her, after sex, that she's beautiful, in a tone of wonderment and joy she has to believe is genuine. In life you have to believe some things are real or you just die. You die, even if you stay alive.

In the playground children are chasing one another, swaddled in snowsuits that make their legs and arms look like sausages. Sometimes she used to daydream about the children she would have with Frank, give them names and choose outfits for them, but these were daydreams, nothing more. Tommy had wanted to have kids immediately, though he never considered the consequences, never thought about supporting them or not being able to stay out drinking until five in the morning whenever he felt like it. On the day they got married, in his parents' backyard, he held the ring so solemnly before slipping it on her finger that she thought—with a sad, small shock of recognition—he looked less like a new husband than a child with a new toy in his hands. He was a child who wanted a child, and she had to be the adult for both of them, always arguing that it was too soon, that they should wait a little longer, that they had plenty of time, and it was too much for her, she was tired all the time, until she met Frank and saw a different vision of what life could be. There was the death of hope and then the beginning of it, and sometimes in her memory she could no longer separate the two.

She says his name out loud, just to say it. "Frank." She misses him.

At the sound of her voice—and she thought she'd said it quietly—the other woman in the red coat turns around. There's a nod, a chagrined, hey-you've-the-same-coat smile. They don't see themselves as doppelgangers or anything like that. They're just two women with the same coat, okay? It happens.

Tori wonders what Tommy is doing right now. It's his second week of four in rehab, a period of maximum potential hostility, the therapist has said. He had vowed to put everything straight, and so had she, after she told him about Frank. It was a contest there for a while, who blamed who more. "That's what marriage is," Tori's mom explained to her, "a blame game. You blame yourself, and then you blame the other person, and then you blame yourself for choosing the other person. That's the cycle." This is why she doesn't usually confide in her mother, because she makes these depressing pronouncements about life that all too often turn out to be true.

A child runs past Rebecca chasing another—it's hard to guess genders with all the coats and hats and scarves—who trips, and the first child falls on top, both of them laughing and then crying. Where are these children's parents? No one runs to pick them up and reassure them and dry their tears. (In fact they are nominally under the charge of a day-care attendant, who is on her cell phone to her boyfriend in the warm confines of the rec center at the other end of the park. Later, weeks from now, she will be fired for having sex with this same boyfriend in the back of the day care while the children are napping, and she will have to move back home with her parents and endure hours and hours of lectures, none of which will influence her behavior in the slightest.) Without parents to help them, the children help themselves. They stare at each other, wide-eyed and crying, for a minute or so, then are distracted by something else going on a few feet away, and just like that, the crisis is over. Once they run away, though, Rebecca sees that one of them has dropped a mitten, striped, blue-red-yellow.

The only other adult in sight is the woman in the matching coat, so Rebecca picks it up and brings it over to her.

"Excuse me," she said, "one of the children lost her mitten."

"Like a kitten," Tori says.

"What?"

"Nothing," Tori tells her, shaking her head. This is her life. Nothing she says sounds as right as it did inside her head.

"Are you, uh, a mother?"

"Oh, no," Tori says. "I'm just sitting here. Come to think of it, I don't know where their mothers are."

Rebecca stands in front of her, holding the mitten by its cuff like it's something dirty. She doesn't know why, but she feels it's important that she not lay claim to it, or try to resolve the problem herself. Okay, she does know why. It's because she thinks the reason she has no kids is that she doesn't deserve them, she'd better stay away from them, because she might do it *wrong*. By some higher and mysterious authority this much has been decreed. When Gabriel told her she shouldn't keep the baby, that they weren't going to be a family (because of his wife, that long-suffering woman), he said, "There will be other chances." She agreed with him and his wisdom. But in the doctor's office, she felt, no, she *knew*, there would be no other chances. She could have gone off and had the baby on her own, right? After all, other women—stronger ones—did. Just not her.

Tori sees that Rebecca is weirdly paralyzed, helpless. The woman is small and pinched looking, tired in that permanent way that afflicts women on the other side of thirty. Tori used to think this was caused by being a parent. Now she thinks it's just life.

She stands up. "I'm sure we can figure out whose mitten it is," she offers. "Let's just look for a kid with frostbite on one hand."

Rebecca smiles at her gratefully. She's younger, this other woman, around her sister's age, and very pretty—short and voluptuous, with olive skin and green eyes, a complexion better suited to the red coat than Rebecca's pale one. She's wearing lipstick and has a come-hither look. Rebecca bets she's popular with men. Some women just have it, *this thing,* a magnetism that doesn't only have to do with beauty or even sex. It's desirability. Women like that never go two years without a date. They never wind up agreeing to have a drink after work with their older, sweet-tempered, sad-eyed boss, even though they're sensible and morally upright and know much better than to get involved with a married man. Women like that never know the pulsing, toothachey loneliness of an ordinary life.

As she's thinking this, Tori shakes her head as if she wants to deny the claim, and Rebecca notices a little wetness around her eyes, like she's been crying. Although it could be the cold. "Are you okay?" she asks suddenly.

Tori blinks, then smiles. "Sure," she says. "Let's find that kid."

Together they walk through the playground like some kind of police duo, fashionable Mounties in their red coats, looking at the kids and trying to figure out, in the blur of skipping and falling down and crying again, which one they're looking for.

"Hey, hey, kids," Tori calls out. "Which of you kittens has lost a mitten?"

The kittens ignore her. "It's like I don't exist," she says to Rebecca. "Kids don't recognize that I'm alive. Good thing I don't have one, I'd never get it to do a thing I say."

"It's probably different once you actually have one," Rebecca says. "A mothering instinct kicks in, and then you're good at scolding and nagging."

"And giving advice and instilling guilt."

"Exactly," Rebecca says. "It all happens automatically. At least I think so, anyway. I wouldn't know for sure."

Tori doesn't answer. The two women stand for a moment encircled by their thoughts, each examining her own future and its branching flowchart of possibilities. Tori thinks about a life with Tommy and/or kids, and how they might be able to make it, to be happy, but then again might not; also about life with Frank, and/or kids, and how this life once seemed not only necessary but inevitable, until it dissolved. And it's so strange that this can happen, and something so counted-on can just wither once exposed to the air; but it never withered for Frank, who insisted on meeting her here today, for one last time. She loves Frank. She misses him constantly. But Tommy—they've been together since they were nineteen and he's going through rehab, changing everything for their life together. "It's not something you walk away from," she told Frank, and she could almost hear him thinking, *Neither am I.*

Rebecca is thinking about how something drained out of her in the doctor's office, some part of herself that believed in change and possibility, in all the and/or flowchart branches of a long and storied life. She thinks about how she hated Gabriel then, and blamed him, and wrote that letter to his long-suffering wife. But the truth was that in spite of it all she did love him; she didn't idealize him or anything, she simply loved him, and that love was pure and true and strong even though its circumstances were sordid and trivial and absurd.

·   ·   ·

The bus stops at the other end of the park. Coming out of the rec center, snapping her gum (which seems to lose its tensile strength in the cold, and she wonders, briefly, why), the day-care attendant notices a man in a gray wool coat get off and start across the park in the direction of her charges. The only reason she notices him is to think that her boyfriend is better-looking and taller and more muscular, and she can't wait until she sees him tonight. She's got a one-track mind, that attendant.

A child runs up to Rebecca and doesn't say anything, just stands in front of her, a strand of blond hair leaking out from underneath a fleece cap. Crouching down, Rebecca can see it's a girl, who removes her hand from the pocket of her snowsuit and shows it to her, shyly, like an injury of which she is ashamed. Their eyes meet.

"It's okay," Rebecca says mechanically, and the child nods. "Come here."

She fits the mitten over her small, white hand and tugs it up over her wrist, the girl so close that Rebecca can smell the sour yet wholesome scent of her skin. The two of them look at each other, the child still holding up her mittened hand as if Rebecca isn't finished yet. What's left to do? A kiss on the forehead, a "You're dismissed"? What's the protocol? Then she realizes she put the mitten on wrong, that the girl's thumb isn't fitting into its slot. So she has to pull the mitten off and start over again, the child staring all the while. Rebecca's starting to wonder if something's wrong with the kid, with the whole lot of them, and that's why they've been abandoned in the park to play by themselves.

Tori, meanwhile, is standing next to her, standing there in her red coat, her long blond hair snaking down her back. From the back, of course, she looks just like Rebecca. Only one thought exists in her mind: *Frank*.

The man coming toward them, the gun warm in his hand, could be Gabriel or Frank or even Tommy, escaped from rehab. But not all of them; only one. As it turns out, it's Gabriel. It's the sad-eyed ones you have to watch out for—another piece of advice that could usefully have been given to Rebecca, but which she would probably have ignored.

You can see where this is going, right? With the red coats and the blond hair? There are no surprises for you here.

From a distance of ten yards Gabriel sees only Tori's back, and he is so blinded by his belief that it's Rebecca—the woman who wrote a letter to his long-suffering wife—that he doesn't notice the other form crouched down next to her. If he did, he might think it is a bundled coat or a child on a sled; his focus is that intense, the world outside it merely peripheral.

The day-care attendant puts away her cell phone, wonders who all these adults are, then sees him pull out a gun and fire. A woman in a red coat falls to the ground, lightly, almost casually, as if in jest.

The attendant starts to run. Children are screaming, some of them running away. Rebecca drops the mitten and stands up and turns around. She thinks of cars: backfires, accidents. She doesn't take a gunshot into account. Then, seeing Gabriel, she thinks he has come for her, to make a life with her, that he has finally left his wife. All this crosses her mind with certainty in the second before she notices the gun. Once she does, she sees the woman on the ground beside her, crouches again, and turns her over, feeling for a pulse. There is none. The woman still looks alive—that is, exactly like she did only moments earlier—but she is dead.

"Oh," Rebecca says. "Oh. Oh." The little girl runs away.

You knew that the gun was going to go off, and that it was going to kill a woman in a red coat. It was only a question of which woman, and when. And of course why. This isn't some kind of mystery. It's not even a story about the murder, really, or police and jail and a trial. It's about the moment after the murder, when Rebecca looks Gabriel in the eye and he looks back. The bitter, burnt smell of gun smoke is in the air between them. Here's the thing: in that instant, Gabriel knows that he's killed the wrong woman, that his Rebecca—the love of his life, notwithstanding the long-suffering wife, whom he couldn't bear to have hurt—is still alive, and he's so grateful and happy that he smiles. And Rebecca, who with one part of her brain knows he must have come to kill her, with another part of it registers this happiness and smiles back, out of instinct, acknowledgment, and love.

And meanwhile Tori is gone and, somewhere in the world, Tommy and Frank do not know it yet.

Soon, of course, there will be police, jail, a trial. There will be repercussions, grief, and pain of enormous proportions, with consequences radiating out from each of the three people in this park, toward friends and families and coworkers and neighbors and childhood acquaintances they haven't spoken to in years but in whose minds they nonetheless appear and flit around, moth-like, unexplained, from time to time.

You think this is a story about coincidence and/or injustice and/or fate, about the extraordinarily wrong actions of ordinary people. But you're wrong. This is about the moment when one of them realizes he has killed the wrong person, and the two of them, these lovers, very nearly run to each other and embrace. They almost kiss over the dead body of the woman who is not her. It's about the moment in which hope leaps in his heart. The moment in which she vows never to let him go again.

The Only Child

It all started when Sophie came home from college, between her sophomore and junior years. She wasn't happy to be back. She'd grown to love Boston, the depressing, blustery winters, the intricate one-ways and roundabouts, and felt she'd outgrown California and its sunny, childlike weather. Worst of all was her mother. Sophie was an only child, and her mother had always clung to her. She tiptoed into her room at night to watch her sleep. As a child Sophie hadn't noticed, but now that she was older she usually wasn't asleep yet when her mother came in, and she'd look up from her book and say, "*What* are you looking at?"

Which only made her mother smile affectionately and back out of the room. By late June Sophie couldn't take it anymore; she went over to her friend Beena's house and they called up Trevor, their high-school drug connection, and got a dime bag and some Ecstasy, and suddenly it was four in the morning and Sophie drove home at breakneck speed only to find her parents still up, waiting.

"You guys," she said, "you're driving me crazy."

Her mother was crying.

"It's not that bad," Sophie said. "I was just out late. At school I do this all the time. I mean, not all the time. But you know what I mean."

"We have to tell you something," her father said. "We should've told you a long time ago." He was a serious man, her father, prone to ominous pronouncements about issues he had no ability to affect. "This real-estate bubble will burst very soon," he'd say while barbecuing chicken. Or: "Gas prices will go up much farther before they ever go down."

So Sophie wasn't that concerned when she sat down to hear what they had to say. She hadn't steeled herself for any news in particular, and this, in addition to the drugs, was probably why, in the future, she could never remember the exact words in which her parents told her that she was not, after all, an only child.

She had an older brother who'd been given up for adoption, and for all these years they'd never known where he was.

"We were very young," her mother said. "We weren't married yet. You didn't know my parents, Sophie, but they were very strict. We had the baby, then gave him up. Eventually we got married and had you, and that was wonderful. But I've thought about him every day since he was born. I was so happy when we got his letter today, saying he wanted to meet us."

At this point she had to stop talking, because she was crying so hard. She could hardly breathe. Sophie crossed the room and sat down next to her mother, who melted against her shoulder. On the opposite side, Sophie's father held her hand.

The brother she'd never known existed, Philip, lived in New York City and was an investment banker. His adoptive parents had given him a good life, with good schools and love. He didn't want anything from her parents, only to meet them. Her mother wrote back that they'd love to see him and told him about Sophie. Two weeks later the phone rang. Philip was going to be in L.A. on business the following week. He wanted to meet, but not at the house. Her mother said they'd all be there.

That morning her mother put on and discarded every item of clothing in her closet. Sophie was wearing a T-shirt and jeans, and it was her father, who ordinarily never noticed her appearance, who asked her to change into something a little nicer. "This occasion," he said, "is something we'll remember forever. Not many days are like that, pumpkin."

So she put on a dress. She still hadn't decided how she felt about anything. She'd never thought about having a brother. She'd always wanted a sister, someone to confide in and whisper with at night after the lights were out. Someone mischievous and fun, down-to-earth, not dreamy like her mother—though now she understood what her mother had been dreaming about.

They waited at a Taco Bell on the freeway, holding medium-sized Cokes. The three of them always ordered mediums, never smalls or larges. They were a family that took the middle road. The door opened and a man in a suit came in and stood there looking around. Her mother gasped. Sophie felt a strong wind shake her arms and spine, a buffeting force. Red hair and green eyes, freckles, a square face and a round nose, a flush on his cheeks and a wrinkle that ran straight across his forehead. All this time there had been someone in the world who looked exactly like her.

Philip came toward them, unsmiling, and sat down. "This is awkward," he said. "Hello."

"I know," her mother said, then bit her lower lip.

Sophie leaned forward. "Would you like something? We have drinks, I could get you something."

He looked at her—she saw it register on his face, how much they looked alike—and smiled stiffly. "Sure," he said. "Root beer, a large? Thanks."

Sophie felt stung. She hated root beer. Of course she understood this didn't mean anything, but she thought it meant everything. The situation made everything symbolic, made everything, even root beer, carry too much weight.

When she got back to the table her parents and Philip were talking about the weather. They didn't seem able to move any deeper into the conversation, to say the things they wanted to say. She sat there feeling annoyed with all of them and the spindly artifice of small talk. She didn't realize that there were some things that couldn't be said, that these were the most important things, and that everyone except her knew it. After she married her first husband, Lars, ten years later, she would tell him constantly, effusively, how much she loved him and how much he meant to her. And Lars would hold her hand and nod, his silences driving her crazy, so crazy after a while that she went off and slept with his best friend and business partner, Joe, who was short and squat and called her "Cookie" in bed, and the act wasn't even finished before she started hating both him and herself. Afterward she came home and found Lars sitting in the living room with a drink. She could either tell him or not tell him. She still loved him. Instead of telling him she stopped taking her birth control pills and got pregnant, and that's how they had Sara. During her pregnancy Lars broke off his partnership with Joe even though it left them at a terrible financial disadvantage, and Sophie was so angry at this—about to have a child, they needed to be stable, plus there were house and car payments to think about—and hormonal that she cried and raged and threatened to leave him. And Lars said quietly, "But I have to. Don't you see?"

She understood then he'd known about her and Joe all along, that he was trying for a fresh start. And she was grateful, and wanted it to work so badly; but it didn't.

This was later. At the time, at Taco Bell, she had no idea how small talk was protecting them from the scabrous weight of the past. All she knew was that her mother asked Philip for the story of his life, and he told it, and then her parents talked about their business, Sophie's college in Boston, their house, even the perennials they were trying to grow in the garden. It was a conversation people might have on an airplane.

As they were leaving, Philip turned to her. "You and I live so close to each other," he said. "You should come visit me in the fall, when you go back to school."

"I don't know," Sophie said. Her mother, who hadn't wanted her to live in a coed dorm, who worried when she took a cab from school to the airport, was nodding vehemently.

"You can stay with me and my girlfriend. I'll tease you and pull your hair, or whatever a big brother's supposed to do. We'll figure it out. You'll like Fiona, she's nice. All this was actually her idea, me getting in touch with you guys."

"Oh," Sophie's mother said softly, as if punched.

"Not that I hadn't thought about it myself," he added.

. . .

Sophie went back to school and in October, on Columbus Day weekend, she took the train to New York. She'd been there once before, with her roommate, who was from Long Island. They stayed in the suburbs and, during their one day in Manhattan, went to FAO Schwarz. This time she took a taxi from Penn Station to the Upper West Side, where her brother—saying it, inside her mind, still gave her an intense but not entirely unpleasant shiver—lived.

They'd arranged this on the phone. "I'll still be at work when you get here," Philip had told her. "But Fiona will let you in and entertain you until dinner."

"Okay," Sophie said.

"We'll show you a good time, don't worry," he said. "And we can call your mom on the phone while you're here, so she knows you're all right."

Sophie wondered why he said *your* mom. But of course he had his own mom, who lived in Philadelphia and was also a banker. His father was an orthodontist.

The building's doorman asked Sophie's name, made a call, then carried her backpack to the elevator and pressed the button, as if the task would be too much for her. Upstairs, Fiona was waiting with the door open, smiling. She looked like a movie star, with straight, glossy brown hair and manicured fingernails. Grabbing the backpack, she threw her arm around Sophie's shoulder and gently pushed her into the apartment, all the while offering drinks, food, a shower.

"We'll make up the couch for you later," she said. "I'm sorry there isn't a spare room, but this is New York. We all live like sardines. We're going to move soon, I swear, but looking for a place is such a nightmare. Have a seat. It's so great to meet you. God, you look just like him, don't you? Didn't that freak you out?"

It was the first time anyone had mentioned the weirdness of the situation to her. Everybody else, her parents, her new brother, seemed intent on making it seem ordinary, which it manifestly wasn't. At this onslaught of honesty Sophie felt grateful, even close to tears.

"It's incredibly strange," she said.

"Must be," Fiona said. "But also good, right? I mean, here you have somebody else who's part of your family. Somebody else to care for you."

Sophie hadn't considered it that way at all. "I guess I'm still getting used to it," she said.

At eight, she and Fiona went out to a French restaurant. Her brother arrived twenty minutes late, trailing a briefcase and apologies, then insisted on ordering for her.

"Have you had oysters?" he asked. "What about snails? Have you had steak tartare, ever, in your life? I bet you didn't have snails growing up in California."

She hadn't, and didn't want them now, but felt it would be rude to refuse. She thought he was testing her. She didn't realize that he felt he had something to prove, that his entire life—what he'd been given, what he'd become—was under scrutiny. Fiona sat back and didn't talk much, just smiled at both of them. Philip ordered the snails and a bottle of Bordeaux and Fiona pushed her glass over to Sophie, letting her drink most of it. Philip kept asking her questions. What was their house like, what kind of after-school activities did she do, what did she think of her high school, what did she get on her SATs? It felt like a job interview.

"You must be smart, you got into a good college," he said. "What are you going to do after you graduate? If you moved to New York, I could help you. I have some connections. The world's about connections, you know. That's something I didn't realize in college, but it's totally true."

"I was thinking maybe grad school?" Sophie said. She didn't want to let go of the life she'd only just discovered. It was the first time she'd ever felt like an adult, and she couldn't imagine that there would be other places she might feel that way, other ways she could grow up.

Philip laughed. "Everybody here's either dropping out of grad school or just about to go back. You'll fit in perfectly."

He ordered dessert for the table but didn't have any himself. Sophie and Fiona shared it, their spoons digging into the meringue. Close enough to smell Fiona's perfume, she noticed the diamond engagement ring on her left hand.

The next day, Fiona offered her a menu of activities: the Guggenheim, MoMA, the Met. "We don't have to do anything big and touristy," Sophie said. "Just walking around is good."

Philip nodded, and Fiona smiled. "That's such a smart thing to say. It's so true that you see more of a city that way." Sophie felt that she'd done well. "Let's go to Chinatown and then we can have some pasta in Little Italy, maybe walk around SoHo. How does that sound?"

"Perfect," Sophie said.

They took a cab downtown. The streets in Chinatown were mobbed. While holding hands with Philip, Fiona pointed things out to Sophie: Chanel knockoff purses, an art-supply store, the ducks hanging in shop windows. Next they moved over to Little Italy, where they had lunch. All the talk was about what it was like to live in New York, the various difficulties and advantages, the rents, the stresses. It was an urban version of her parents' friends sitting around talking about their houses and yards. Having this revelation made Sophie feel wise. She thought that this was maturity, the ability to see through people. Only later did she find out that anyone could see through people, and the hard thing was not to try.

After lunch Fiona said she was tired, so they went back to the apartment. Before taking a nap, she suggested that Sophie and Philip call California.

It was one in the afternoon there, and Sophie's mother was outside gardening. "Are you having a good time?" she asked, sounding a little breathless.

"Of course," Sophie said, knowing that this was what she wanted to hear, yet unable to bring herself to rave or brim over with stories.

"Put him on?" her mother said.

Sophie handed the phone to her brother, who stood with the receiver pressed to his ear, smiling politely. Was he good-looking? Sophie couldn't say. His face was long, like hers; his nose had a bump in it. If without knowing anything she'd passed him on the street, would she have noticed him, or somehow felt a connection?

"Soph," he said, still smiling, but now holding out the phone.

When she put it to her ear she could hear her mother crying. "Are you okay?"

"I'm great," her mother said, the worst liar ever. "I'm just so happy."

In the background she could hear her father's voice but not

the specific words. Whatever they were, she knew he was trying to comfort her. In the future, after he retired, this tendency would grow even stronger. He'd start cooking for her, three meals a day, even after she got sick, and he'd shadow her from room to room, just as Sophie's mother had once done to her. Her mother, irritable from pain, would complain about this to Sophie while he was in the kitchen straining broth into homemade soup. Once she died, of liver cancer, Sophie expected him to fade into the shadows himself, to lose his purpose, or to move into her own home. By then she was living with her second husband, sharing custody of Sara with Lars and of Mark's son, Henry, with his ex-wife, a rotating parade of children and schedules that had to be carefully regulated and updated on wall calendars lest total chaos ensue. But her father seemed happy in his own routine, walking two miles every day and scrupulously following the news. Not until then did she realize he was the most self-sufficient person she'd ever known, and that her mother, the doter, the worrier, the maker of phone calls, had been the most in need of care.

"It's okay, Mom," Sophie said now. "We're having a nice time."

"Please remember everything," her mother said, "and be sure to tell me later."

"I'll try," Sophie said. She hung up and looked for Philip—wanting to commiserate, for a glance to pass between them—but he was in the kitchen already, talking to Fiona and pouring himself a glass of wine.

They were supposed to go out to dinner again, but after two glasses of wine Philip said he was tired, wanted to order in Chinese and stay home. This sounded fine to Sophie, but Fiona didn't like the idea.

"Sophie's only in town for the weekend," she said. "We should be taking her to the Russian Tea Room or something."

"The Tea Room's closed, babe," he said, with a touch of irritation.

"I said *or something*."

"Anyway, she's cool with it. Right?"

Sophie nodded slightly, afraid of overcommitting to his side of the disagreement. When her parents fought, they did so in their bedroom, at night, keeping their voices down and the door closed. She was thirteen before she figured out that they ever argued about anything, although this, she now knew, was the least of their secrets.

"Of course she's *cool with it*," Fiona said. She was standing with her arms folded in front of her, and Sophie couldn't be sure but it seemed like tears were glimmering in her eyes. "She doesn't know what the other options are. That's why *we* should come up with something. You always want to do the *least difficult* thing."

"And that's wrong?" Philip said. Then he poured himself another glass of wine, clearly an act of defiance. There was a kind of electrical current in the room, like just before a thunderstorm.

Fiona started to cry.

Sophie wanted to disappear, but the only other room was their bedroom, and she couldn't very well go in there. "We can do whatever," she said. "I'm easy."

Fiona looked at her and tried to smile. "You're such a sweetheart," she said, then added bitterly, "It's hard to believe you're related."

"Hey," Philip said.

Sophie tried again. "Maybe we could have dinner here, and then you and I could do something," she told Fiona. "A movie or something. There must be tons of stuff I couldn't see anywhere else."

"This isn't about you and me spending time together," Fiona snapped.

Sophie stepped back. And then again, to sit down.

"You get these ideas, and you can't handle any deviation," Philip said. "Everything has to go according to your plan."

"There's nothing wrong with having a plan," Fiona said. "If you don't have a plan, you don't get anywhere."

"Maybe I like where I am."

"I have to push you to do everything. If it weren't for me, you'd never do anything. You'd just live here alone for the rest of your life. That's what you want, isn't?"

"It's looking pretty good right about now," Philip said.

Fiona went into the bedroom, leaving Sophie and her brother alone.

Philip ordered Chinese without asking her what she wanted, and the two of them watched basketball. He switched to beer and gave her one, which she drank quickly. The second she pulled out of the fridge herself. An hour later Fiona came out of the bedroom carrying her jacket and walked straight out the door without saying anything.

"Are you going after her?" Sophie said.

Her brother shrugged. "She can take care of herself."

Sophie thought of her parents worrying every time she left the house, how her mother sometimes called her first thing in the morning at school, as if she might not have survived the night, and about how they both cried when they left her in Boston at the beginning of college, Sophie herself dry-eyed and itching to be alone. Now she too walked out of the apartment.

"Hey," Philip said, but that was the extent of his interference. After riding the elevator down, Sophie stood in the street wondering where Fiona had gone. Though it was late there were still tons of people out walking around, there were cabs and cars. A person could go anywhere and do anything. It was cold. Nobody looked at her; nobody asked what she was doing. Helpless, wordless, she went back inside. By the time she fell asleep on the couch, Fiona still hadn't come home.

Her train wasn't until noon, and Sophie woke up worrying about how to get through the last few hours of the visit. But Fiona and Philip were in the kitchen making French toast. Sitting up, she saw that he had his arms around her waist, and Fiona was laughing, a low, sweet murmur. Then they started kissing. If Sophie's parents had never fought in front of her, they'd never kissed in front of her either, a discretion she approved of completely. As she watched, Fiona moved one of Philip's hands so his palm lay flat on her stomach, and she rubbed it against herself, as if she were a magic lantern.

She faked sleep until Fiona shook her shoulder gently. Together they stripped the couch, folding the blanket as Sophie been taught to in Girl Scouts, Fiona holding one end and Sophie walking the other up to her and pressing it to her chest.

Fiona's eyes were sparkling. "Thanks for coming to look for me last night," she said.

"Oh, it was nothing."

"It's not nothing. He learned something from you. He doesn't understand things sometimes, because of how he grew up. He thinks everybody gets to choose who they love."

Sophie didn't know what this meant, but nodded as if she did. Then Philip served the French toast. He was in a great mood and kept telling Sophie that she had to come back, that the couch would be reserved for her.

"Consider it your pied-à-terre," he told her.

She didn't know what this meant, either, but could tell he was proud of the phrase. Over the three days they'd spent together she'd at least learned this much about him.

They ate breakfast while reading the newspaper. After a while Sophie took a shower and packed her bag. She was already thinking about school, the party she'd missed by being here, what she'd say to her mother when she called that night.

"Hey," Philip said, "what are you doing for Thanksgiving? You could spent it here with us."

"I'm supposed to go home," Sophie said. She bit her lip, hesitating, then took a chance. "Why don't you guys come out there? Mom and Dad would love it."

"We'll see," Fiona said. She was standing next to Philip, moving her left hand with its bright engagement ring up and down his arm. "I'm not sure I'll feel up to traveling. As you can tell, I'm already pretty hormonal."

Sophie looked at her brother.

"Fiona's pregnant," he said.

"Oh, wow," Sophie said, as Fiona stared at her with an expectant smile. "Congratulations," she remembered to say.

"Thank you! We're thrilled," Fiona said, and her stroking picked up its pace. She was beaming. This was her show; the whole weekend, Sophie thought, had been her show. Even the letter. She thought of how her mother had sounded on the day the letter came, when she said, "I always thought of him, wondering where he was, every minute of every day." Unspoken was the idea that, somewhere off in the world, he had been thinking of her too.

"I should go," Sophie said.

They offered to take her to the station, but Sophie refused. She wanted to be alone, to plan her phone call that evening. *It was as if we'd known each other all our lives.* It was her turn now to leave out everything that couldn't be said. The last thing her brother offered, as she left, was "Keep in touch," as if they were high school friends whom college choices might force apart. Fiona jumped in: they had friends in Boston, so they'd come visit and take Sophie and her roommate out to dinner. Sophie believed her. She would drag Philip to Boston and probably, eventually, to California, taking him everywhere there was family, people to whom he was connected.

Indeed, this is what happened. The child was born and named Andrew, and he looked like Sophie and Philip: the same red hair, the same boxy face. When Fiona brought him to California, she presented him like a trophy to Sophie's mother, who exclaimed happily over him, and said all the right things, and it wasn't until after the visitors left that she locked herself in the bedroom and cried over everything she had lost: a whole child's future, a whole child's past.

On a drunken Thanksgiving years later, Fiona would confess to Sophie that she wanted to have other children after Andrew, but that Philip was against it; too much money and time would be required. "He doesn't understand about family," she said, this initial grain of suspicion having hardened to a sturdy pearl. Sophie, with four glasses of wine in her and struggling through divorce, could only nod exhaustedly, too drunk to remember Fiona as a young woman aglow with her child and her confidence and her love. Whether she remembered it or not, though, this was the end of her own childhood: the day she left Fiona and her brother in New York, Fiona waving good-bye with one hand and holding on to Philip with the other, as if without this tether he might float away into some other orbit. This escape Fiona would not allow. Instead she held his arm and smiled at Sophie, her eyes sparkling fervently, amply sparkling, as if she felt so full of love that she could afford to give some away.

Three Little Maids

George picked her up wearing a suit and tie.

"It's like a date," she said.

"Except it's not," he answered, without a smile. That he could never keep from the obvious retort was Reason #463 they were divorced. Nonetheless, he looked good. Since the angioplasty he'd cut out meat and fried food, and his skin had shrunk to a handsome tautness around his cheekbones, like a man stranded on a desert island. She herself had taken up spinning and had lost at least four pounds in the past month, not that George would ever notice or comment (Reason #464). In the car he put on some screeching jazz music, the kind he knew she hated, and Ruth sighed pointedly and looked out the window as they drove into the city: this was a war of gestures both habitual and genuinely annoying. After the divorce they'd each moved into separate town houses in the West Island suburb they'd lived in for years. Superficially this was for the kids, so they could still come home to more or less the same place; secretly, she thought, it was for themselves, so as not to have to find new friends, grocery stores, dentists. Not that the kids seemed grateful anyway. Matthew lived in Calgary with his two children and hardly ever came home, pleading the expense; Jennie lived in Montreal West and visited constantly, complaining to each of them about the wrongs visited upon her in childhood. She had an encyclopedic memory of her own problems. In reparation she extorted from them both money and support for every new undertaking. Thus far, in her thirty-five years, she'd been a photojournalist, yoga instructor, ceramicist, and canine masseuse, each aspiration more unlikely than its predecessor.

Tonight it was light opera. She'd joined a local company and was appearing in their performance of *The Mikado,* as one of the three little maids from school. When she told her father about the casting, he'd said, "Aren't you a little old for that part?" and she hung up on him. Then she immediately called to bemoan his insensitivity to Ruth, who agreed, though she had thought the same thing. You just couldn't say things like that to Jennie. People who never had children thought that parents were responsible for their kids' personalities. But Jennie had been exactly the same since the day she was born: she had to be pulled from the womb with forceps, hysterical with protest, and her mood hadn't shifted since. Whereas Matthew, who shared her genes and upbringing, was so remote and placid, so totally imperturbable, that Ruth at times wondered if he was paying attention to anything at all.

George and Ruth had to attend all of Jennie's events, or there'd be hell to pay in the form of recriminating phone calls and gifted self-help books about truly loving families. When George first remarried, his second wife, Marlena, used to come as well, but she and Jennie didn't get along and she soon begged off. Ruth envied her. Now it was just the two of them, and after a while they'd started carpooling, because why not? They'd been divorced for fifteen years; they still hated each other, but at this point they were resigned to it.

When they arrived—the auditorium was in a high school, and she had a sudden flashback to seeing the kids, as teenagers, in *The Pajama Game* and *Guys and Dolls*—Jennie was standing in the freezing-cold parking lot, smoking a cigarette and watching for them anxiously. She was wearing her stage makeup, white powder and thick eyeliner meant to make her look Japanese. A black wig was perched on her dirty blond hair like an ugly hat. Her arms were crossed and her shoulders slouched inside an enormous blue parka, beneath which peeked a red kimono. When she saw them she looked at once vexed, relieved, and somehow starved. Had she honestly doubted they were coming? Where had she gotten this eternal hunger for their attention? It was a hole they could never fill, year after year though they tried.

"I thought you might not make it," Jennie said.

"*I* thought you didn't smoke anymore," George said severely.

"I don't, really. This is just nerves."

"You look great, honey," Ruth said. "Can't wait to see you up there."

Jennie grimaced. "Well, it might suck, to be honest with you," she said. She always had enough distance from her various endeavors to know they weren't worthy of her time—just not enough to avoid getting involved in the first place. She took a final drag, dropped the cigarette, and poked a sandaled foot from beneath her kimono to crush it out.

"Break a leg, kiddo," George said.

"I probably will, in this getup," she said, then gave a little wave and tottered back into the building, taking tiny steps across the snow-covered ground.

Inside, people were filing slowly down the aisles, and Ruth wondered if any of them were here for the joy of Gilbert and Sullivan as opposed to supporting their children or spouses or cousins. It was hard to tell from their expressions whether or not they actually expected to be entertained. She and George took seats toward the back. A small orchestra was warming up by the stage, the instruments rising in a jumble of trills and squawks. In the row in front of them a young child sat weeping silently, holding a melted chocolate bar, the chocolate smeared all over his face. His mother took a Kleenex from her bag and wiped his face roughly, without asking why he was crying.

As she looked at the program, George grimaced and started rubbing his arm.

"What's wrong?"

"Racquetball injury," he said. "I'm still playing with Kenny twice a week."

Ruth sighed and returned to the program, realizing she should've known better than to ask. He'd probably only rubbed his arm so he could then brag about racquetball, as if she cared. He'd always been proudest of things she considered trivial (Reason #465). Someone flicked the lights off, then on again, twice. A baby squealed, a resigned hush fell over the audience, and music began to play. Nanki-Poo was looking for Yum-Yum, his true love, but Yum-Yum was already taken, engaged to Ko-Ko. The situation looked bad for Nanki-Poo. The company was having some trouble hitting the high notes, the man playing Pish-Tush had a stutter that repeatedly made him lag behind the music, and the conductor sweated heavily as he fought to bring the musicians and singers into line. The actors' makeup shone under the bright lights. Her memory stretched farther back to when her children were little, dressed up for Christmas pageants and spring festivals, their cherubic cuteness making every missed line and off-key note all the more endearing.

"This is the worst thing I've ever seen," she muttered. George shushed her, but also nodded.

Jennie and another woman joined Yum-Yum onstage and began to sing. Glancing down at her program in the dark, Ruth tried to remember whether Jennie was Pitti-Sing or Peep-Bo.

"Three little maids who all unwary come from a ladies' seminary!" they sang, each a quarter-tone off from the others. They were filled to the brim with girlish glee, they informed the audience, fake smiles splitting their faces. Not a one was under thirty, Ruth thought, and they all looked burdened with concentration, arching their necks as they strained for the high notes. Jennie gestured wildly with her hands and sang louder, though no better, than the other two. Finally the song ended, and her parents, loudly, clapped.

At intermission they split up to visit the restrooms, and by the time she came out George had returned to his seat. She would've liked to people-watch in the lobby, maybe buy a cookie from the bake-sale table, but didn't want to stand there alone, so she went back in. The unhappy child in front of them had disappeared, though another baby farther down was crying full throttle. When she pushed past George, he ignored her. The lights were blinking on and off again.

"What do you think?" she said.

He didn't answer, which was typical. When Jennie was a teenager—fighting with them constantly over curfews, boyfriends, grades—George tried for the first few minutes to reason with her as if she were one of his colleagues and they were negotiating labor costs or shipping charges; but then he'd check out of the conversation and sit stonily at the dinner table, his hand curled around his water glass. Ruth was the one who'd kept soldiering on, while he sat waiting mutely for the war to be over. She'd fight with Jennie and then, once they were in bed, harangue George for not helping. "I can't do this all by myself," she'd say.

"But you *are*," he'd say in return.

And years later, when he was moving out, she asked what, precisely, he thought he'd find elsewhere that was better.

"Peace and quiet," he told her.

So now she gave him his peace and quiet. She didn't care anymore. She arranged her purse on the seat next to her and watched the curtain rise on act 2, which provided a wealth of further complications: deaths and marriages, both real and fake; old people pitted against young; and the Mikado himself, whatever he was. All this was conveyed through trills and patter and high-pitched chortling. During one song she glanced sideways at George, and the look of pain on his face mirrored exactly how she felt inside. She almost laughed, knowing at least they agreed on one basic fact: this show was terrible.

But then, while the Mikado was presiding over some major disagreement, George turned to her in the dark and whispered, "I have to go to the hospital."

"What?"

"I think I'm having a heart attack."

"For God's sake, why didn't you say something earlier?" She bolted out of her seat and people all around them turned their heads to watch. George stood up shakily and she offered him her hand, but he ignored her and limped, as if cramping, up the aisle. The expression she'd thought was a frown had deepened into actual pain. She followed him uselessly out of the building.

Once they were in the parking lot, she said, "Give me the keys."

"I can drive."

"Over my dead body," she said, and he closed his eyes and handed them over.

In his unfamiliar Subaru she spent a moment adjusting the mirrors and seats before shifting into gear; it had been a while since she'd driven a standard, and the car stalled when she pressed on the gas.

"God, Ruth," he said.

"Don't talk," she said sharply, and turned the key again. She switched on the heat as he lay back in his seat and closed his eyes. His taut skin now looked haggard and deathly. "Hold on," she said.

Under the streetlights, the avenues glowed palely with salt. They'd come to the city together in the late sixties as graduate students, she in history and George in engineering. After Kingston, Montreal had seemed exotic and glamorous, and the times were glamorous too, everything in tumult, the world remaking itself. She'd thought that their lives here would lift them into some entirely different sphere. Now she knew that not even Montreal could have that effect. They'd moved to the suburbs and started a family and then dissolved it, as they probably would've done in Kingston or Halifax or anywhere else.

In the passenger seat George moaned slightly, involuntarily.

At the hospital she filled out the paperwork while he was rolled into an observation room. Then she went to a pay phone and called Marlena, explaining as briefly as possible what had happened and where they were. Finally she called Jennie's cell phone and left a message. She decided to wait to call Matthew until she knew how serious it was. After all this had been accomplished there was nothing left for her to do, so she sat in the waiting room, reading a knitting magazine she'd found in a stack on a table. She'd always meant to take up knitting. Now would have been a good time for it.

A green-robed doctor walked in and spoke her name, her married name, in accented English. "I am Dr. Vasanji," he said. "Your husband will be having emergency bypass surgery. We won't know anything for the next few hours."

He nodded and left even before she could think of what she was supposed to ask.

Twenty minutes later, Marlena came rushing down the hallway, her eyes wide with anxiety and her scarf trailing behind her. Marlena was what Ruth called an artsy-fartsy. She wore jewel colors and long skirts and dyed her hair dark red. "Where is he?" she demanded.

Ruth stood up. "In surgery," she said, and then explained everything. But Marlena kept asking questions she couldn't answer— What room was he in? How long would the surgery take, exactly? How bad had the pain been?—and Ruth brusquely told her to speak to a nurse, which she finally did, engaging one in a conversation Ruth couldn't hear.

When she came back, her face was pale beneath her red hair. "They won't tell me anything, either," she said, sitting down next to Ruth. She took off her coat and ran her hands through her hair, then she looked at her. "Thank you for calling me," she said stiffly. "It's late, and they won't tell us anything for a long time. You can go home."

Ruth closed her eyes for a second, not wanting to leave. George was in surgery, and she needed to know what was happening. She could feel the other woman staring at her, willing her to clear out of the waiting room. *Too bad,* she thought. "I called Jennie," she said.

"Oh, dear," Marlena said.

Ruth knew that Marlena would not want to be alone with Jennie. "I left her a message, and I'm sure she'll be right over, after her performance."

"Oh, God, *The Mikado,*" Marlena said. "I bet that's what did him in." Her lip curled in a smile, and she looked at Ruth, as if expecting her to go along.

Ruth looked at her coldly. "It was really very good," she said.

Marlena nodded, her expression knowing and ironic. "I'm sure it was."

They sat together watching the news, and the nurses chattered and ran around. Marlena asked them more questions, her voice louder and more confident now, carrying back to where Ruth sat. Her French was far better than Ruth's would ever be—she'd grown up in Montreal—and she wrangled with the staff fearlessly, pressing them with yet another question every time they shook their heads and tried to walk away. As Anglophones, George and Ruth had always found it somewhat difficult to deal with hospitals, government officials, even store clerks; no matter how many years they lived here, they'd never lost their self-consciousness. Not Marlena, though. At times Ruth wondered if this was what George liked about her, that she was *at home* in Montreal in a way he'd never been.

"What did they say?" she asked when Marlena finally came back.

Marlena shrugged. "No news," she said, although she'd talked with one nurse for at least five minutes. Ruth shifted in her seat, annoyed. Just then Jennie came walking down the hallway, still in her stage makeup, though it was smeared and thin and patches of her skin showed beneath the white.

"What's going on?" she said, and burst into tears. She sat down next to her mother, who held her in her arms as she cried a couple of dry sobs, her blond head shaking.

"It's going to be fine, honey," Ruth said. "We just have to wait, that's all. He'll be okay." Marlena was looking at her with an expression of doubt, clearly displeased by these reassurances. Marlena had raised her own children with rational argument, talking to each as one adult to another; she never offered bribes or made false promises or exaggerated claims. (Ruth had heard about all of this from Jennie.) One worked for Stats Canada, another was an elementary-school principal, and the third was in jail for mail fraud. Ruth pitied them, these adults who'd never had a mother tell them everything was going to be okay, who'd never had the comfort of lies.

Jennie nestled her head onto her mother's shoulder and sighed. "I thought he didn't look good earlier," she said. "He was rubbing his arm when he was talking to me before the show."

"Really?" Ruth said.

"He was."

"He said it was a racquetball injury," Ruth said.

Marlena sighed. "He hasn't played racquetball in months," she said.

Ruth didn't know if she was pleased or displeased that George would still bother to lie to her. The most explicit expressions of his love had always been the least palatable: getting jealous of another man at a party, or complaining that she never dressed up for him anymore. But the fact that he'd lied about his fitness—what could this mean, to either of them, after four decades? She turned it over in her mind for a few minutes, then gave up. She'd known the marriage was truly over when she stopped trying to figure things out; this was Reason #466 why they'd gotten divorced. Although if she weren't still trying, then why was she still counting the reasons?

A doctor came over, not Vasanji but an impossibly young man with wide-set, gentle brown eyes that made her think of a deer. Holding a clipboard, he pulled up a chair opposite the three of them. "I am Dr. Thanh," he said. "I need to ask which if you is the next of kin," he said.

Ruth was relieved to hear English. At least it wouldn't be a French conversation she'd have trouble following.

Marlena held out her hand to him, like a queen, Ruth thought. Her mannerisms were absurd. "I'm his wife," she said.

"There are forms here," he said. "Unfortunately, we must fill them out." His eyes refused to look down at his clipboard, as if the facts there were too impolite to acknowledge. "Regarding your husband's future. In case"—he paused delicately—"the operation is not a success."

"Oh," Jennie said softly.

"I'll take them," Marlena said, and again extended her hand with that ridiculous regal air. The doctor gave her the clipboard and murmured something about returning it to the nurses' station when she was done. Marlena walked across the room and sat down in a chair next to a table.

"Wait a minute," Jennie said loudly. Other people who were waiting looked up and stared at her bizarre appearance. "What are you doing?"

"Filling out the forms, dear," Marlena said sweetly. "It's nothing you need to worry about."

"Maybe I *want* to worry about it," Jennie said. "What is it about? You can't just go off and decide everything yourself, without us. You can't keep us out of this. You can't."

Her voice broadcast unadulterated anger, and Ruth was surprised at the surge of satisfaction she felt at hearing that permanent, unbreakable *us*. For a moment she saw how it must have been for Marlena for all these years, knowing her every action would be scrutinized, that she would forever find herself on the other side of *us*.

"Jennie," she said.

Her daughter ignored her, and Marlena didn't even look up from the clipboard. Pen in hand, she filled out the form. Jennie began to moan, rocking back and forth.

Ruth put her arm around her. "He won't die," she said quietly. "Nothing bad is going to happen. Don't worry."

Jennie wasn't crying but she was shaking, and she held her mother's hand and pressed her body against hers, side to side. She was warm and smelled of sweat and hairspray. As Ruth told her, over and over, that there was nothing to worry about, that this surgery was done all the time, that her father would be okay, she listened and nodded to each statement as if thinking it over very carefully. "Yes," she said quietly to every sentence. Finally she stood up. "I'm going to take off my makeup," she said. "I look stupid."

"That sounds like a good idea," Marlena said from the other side of the room. She meant to be encouraging but it sounded sarcastic, and Jennie's eyes rolled in annoyance as she left. Ruth saw that Marlena, having put down the pen, looked exhausted, with blue veins showing beneath her rouge.

"He's seemed so run-down lately," Marlena said. "I should've noticed."

"George is a grown man. He should know enough to go to the doctor if he isn't feeling well."

"He can't take care of himself," Marlena said. "He needs me."

Ruth didn't answer this, and they were silent until Jennie rejoined them, freshly scrubbed, white residue at her hairline. Her daughter's face was lined and weary and worried; for all her bluster, she was quiet now. Marlena was quiet too. The three of them waited together while George lay somewhere in the building having his chest opened up. The truth, Ruth thought, was that she hardly knew what George needed, except for competent doctors and good luck. But each of them needed him: to push against, to argue with, to care for. Years and years could pass and this fact would never change. They were together in this, three little maids who waited for the man to pull through.

You Are What You Like

It was typical Dilrod to come to town at a bad time. He'd shown up at Jill and Stefan's when they'd just moved in together, right after his first divorce, in need of comfort and a drinking buddy, which for him were the same thing; then he'd visited on the heels of their honeymoon to announce his second engagement, in need of celebration and a drinking buddy, which were also the same thing. Now he was divorced again and seeing somebody new, coincidentally in town on business, and Stefan invited him over, even though the baby was only six months old and half-crazy with colic and neither of them had had a solid night's sleep since she'd been born, or, in Jill's case, a couple of months before that.

Dilrod was Stefan's oldest friend. Since high school their values, places of work, tastes in women, music, movies, and books—Dilrod didn't read, actually—had diverged dramatically, but they'd known each other so long that time itself provided a string of connection. By keeping in touch they were staying loyal not so much to each other as to their own young, reckless pasts, which they somehow hoped—though, Jill thought, they'd never admit this—to meet again.

She ordered Thai for dinner, which seemed like the easiest thing. She hadn't cooked a real meal since Phoebe came. Sometimes Stefan did, or her mother visited for a weekend and built up a battery of stews and lasagnas she left behind in the freezer in individual Tupperware containers, solid Midwestern comfort food that Jill had hated as a teenager but now made her weepy with gratitude.

"This is great," Stefan said, coming into the kitchen. It was only the dinner table set with real plates and place mats and utensils but it seemed, after the chaos of recent months, an unaccountably luxurious, grown-up affair. She'd even put candles out, though Phoebe'd started crying so half the holders were empty. Even so, they smiled at each other. "I'm so excited about this," he went on. "A real meal, it feels like ages."

"I just hope it doesn't mess her up, like that spicy broccoli I had that time," Jill said. "Or those cheeses."

"Yeah," he said absently, turning away, then went off for more candles. Jill sighed. Stefan was amazing with the baby; he coddled her, changed her diapers, rocked her to sleep, did half of everything except the breast-feeding. He was all she could have wanted in a father. But in the past few months—after he went back to work—he'd started making these ironic, self-parodying jokes about having an "old lady" and calling the baby a "rug rat" and being an old-fashioned dad who didn't change diapers. Everybody was supposed to play along with this, because to imagine that's how he *truly* thought or felt would be ridiculous, but of course by dint of making the jokes he was also raising an issue, a thin whine of complaint and protest.

Also, this: he didn't look at her the same way. He didn't look at her much at all.

Maybe this was temporary. It was a time of adjustment, necessarily difficult. They were bound to lose themselves a little. Maybe they'd have a good night, with a friend, and be grown-ups together—though of all people, she thought, it was a shame they had to be grown-ups with Dilrod.

He showed up at eight, an hour late, smelling of vodka and cigarettes, hugging them both a little too hard. His name wasn't actually Dilrod, it was Alan Dilworth; but in high school Dilrod sounded funnier. While she reheated the pad thai in the microwave Stefan made drinks, asking all about the new woman, where they'd met, who she was.

"She's awesome," Dilrod said. "She drove me to the airport so that I wouldn't have to pay for long-term parking. Finally I've met somebody who anticipates my needs instead of putting herself first."

Jill held back a snort. To say this was the source of Dilrod's relationship problems was so off-base as to belong in a different country from the base, a different solar system. What killed her about Dilrod's women was that they were invariably intelligent, attractive, and reasonably successful; they were independent filmmakers, schoolteachers, dental hygienists. She always thought they could do better than Dilrod, but apparently they couldn't.

Though he wasn't, she had to admit, bad-looking. His vibe was teenage prepster gone to seed: chest muscled but stomach slightly paunched, his wispy blond hair like dandelion weed around his head, his eyes a little bloodshot but still a piercing blue. He wore striped collared shirts and frayed khakis. He was in sales for some computer company and had managed to hold on to his position despite the tumult of the past ten years, so he must have been good at it, or at least had a knack for survival. He stood in the kitchen with a drink in his hand, gesturing, his mouth open, so obviously happy to see Stefan that you had to like him for it. He'd added two days on to his business trip just to see them.

"So, dude," he was saying, "you've got to come out and meet her. Come next month, for my birthday. Take some time off work."

"Things are crazy right now."

"You always say that, dude."

"It's always true."

Stefan was happy too, laughing and shaking his head at everything Dilrod was saying. They would never hug each other, these two, nor write or call during the intervals when they were apart; but stick them in a room together and they almost swooned with affection.

She put the food out, and they ate. Phoebe'd been so fussy that Jill had curtailed her diet drastically, restricting all but the blandest foods, and now the shrimp exploded on her tongue. Would all experiences be as dramatic as this when she experienced them again, this time as a mother—spicy food, alcohol, sex? She was still waiting for that last one, waiting for both of them to feel something other than exhausted. Dilrod was telling a long story about his ex-wife and her frightening Croatian mother. Stefan was laughing, harder than seemed warranted. Jill sat back and let her attention wander. Being a mother was all about attention, every moment on a hair trigger, alert for the baby's cry. But right now Phoebe was asleep, thank God, and she'd let herself drink half a glass of wine and her mind go pleasantly blank. She felt her muscles, her body, the container of her physical self, as if for the first time in years.

"Sweetest," Stefan said, smiling, "I think you're falling asleep."

For an hour or so she nodded off with the baby, and when she came back they were arguing. From the other room it had sounded serious, but it turned out to be about movies. In particular, a director whose films Stefan loved and Dilrod thought was ridiculous.

"Any time there's a mansion in a movie," Dilrod was saying, "and in that mansion there's a tent, and inside that tent there's a person listening to Nick Drake—I hate that person and I hate that movie."

"I love Nick Drake," Stefan said, slurring a little. During the time she'd been gone, they'd finished off the vodka.

"You know who I'm into lately?" Dilrod said, shifting in his seat. "Billy Joel. Valerie and I saw him in concert last summer and I have to say he totally rocked."

"You can't sit there telling me that you hate Nick Drake and Billy Joel totally rocked. This is an impossible statement."

"'This is an impossible statement,'" Dilrod mimicked, in a high, girlish voice.

Stefan's red face deepened to beet. Jill stared at Dilrod. She'd forgotten what a dick he was. She could see what he obviously couldn't—how his scorn still lashed at Stefan. When the two of them were together, Stefan returned to his former self, the awkward son of German immigrants who was desperate to fit in. She'd been to Stefan's hometown in Illinois, where he'd slammed beer from funnels and joked with football players and talked about girls in God only knew what way. All those guys were sales executives and lawyers now; Stefan was the outlier. He was a social worker married to a freelance book designer, and his parents smiled stiffly while others in the neighborhood bragged about how well their kids were doing.

College had set him free. That was where he learned—just as she had, around the time they met in a philosophy class—that there were legions of them, the misfit kids from all over the country, the readers, the too-smart and the uncool, the secret music fetishists and film trivia mavens, and that they could get together and form their own army, their own band. Weirdness was their passport to citizenship in this new country, and taste was the stamp on it. Liking Nick Drake—well, that was practically a law.

Nowadays they'd grown so used to living in this country that they forgot, a lot of the time, that not everybody did. They did see, of course, everything that lay outside it; they read the newspaper; their alienation took fervent, political form. But it was also rigid, calcified, taken for granted.

Which is to say that they no longer knew people who thought differently from themselves.

Except Dilrod, who was now ranting, spittle at the edges of his mouth. "And there's some fucking guy in Japan who's in love with a girl and all they do is sing karaoke? I don't buy one word of that. I believe in Superman. I believe in Batman."

"Those movies are so generic," Stefan protested. "Empty formulas."

"Yeah, but they're *good* formulas. Formulas of intense, exciting shit. Formulas that say I don't have to watch some depressed chick sit around a hotel room all day long in her panties. No offense, Jill."

He expected her to say, "None taken," or to get mad. Not wanting to give him the satisfaction, she shrugged. Stefan burst out laughing. This was how he handled it, the gap between himself and where he came from: by treating it as a joke. And maybe it was. He was always delighted when Dilrod showed up. Back in tenth grade, it was Dilrod who'd befriended him, taught him what to wear and what to say to girls. No matter that in college he'd changed his clothes, his politics, his entire direction in life; some part of him would always be grateful. When she went to bed, they were still arguing, and she fell asleep long before Dilrod took a cab back to the hotel.

The next day, Stefan told her that he and Dilrod were going out that night. Well, he asked her, but so politely and submissively that only a shrewish wife could say no. She wouldn't have done that anyway, and resented the expectation that she might.

"You don't have to ask my permission," she said. "It's fine."

"My girls will be okay?"

His saying *my girls* had always annoyed her—like they were his backup singers, or secretaries—but she let it pass. "We'll be great," she said. "So what'll you guys do—go see Billy Joel?"

Instead of laughing, Stefan frowned, defensive. "Don't be a snob," he said.

"Oh, come on. How is that snobby?"

"It sounds classist."

"Don't be ridiculous," she said. "Dilrod has more money than either of us. His dad went to Yale. It's not about class."

She didn't know how to put it, exactly. *It makes him a stranger to us,* she wanted to say. *You are what you like, and he doesn't get what we like.* But she sensed that no matter how she phrased it, she'd still look bad.

"What's it about, then?" he asked, pressing her.

"I don't know," she said. "Something else."

She was nursing the baby when Stefan left, without saying where they were going. Phoebe wasn't fussing and it was, in fact, nice, sometimes, to have her to herself. To be quiet in a pink room with the baby at her chest. To sing a lullaby. It was like a dream of what she thought parenthood could be. Weirdly enough this fantasy only seemed true when the two of them were alone. When Stefan was around she was always worried, wondering if they were happy, if he was happy, if the baby was happy. When it was just her and Phoebe she experienced an animal certainty about life: it was her job to feed this little body, to soothe and shepherd and put her to sleep. It was the biggest responsibility she had ever had; it was enormous, towering; it wiped her out. But it was not, somehow, all that complicated.

It was past three when Stefan came home. She'd just fed Phoebe and was still awake, if a little dazed, when he crawled in beside her. He smelled like alcohol and smoke, and her stomach turned over. She'd gotten ultrasensitive to smells while she was pregnant, and it hadn't gone away.

"Have fun?" she said.

He propped himself up on one elbow and didn't answer, so she turned to him, opening her eyes in the dark. Before her vision could adjust he kissed her. She was shocked by the heat of his mouth, the lust in it. She kissed him back, her tongue on his, and the feeling was like coming home to a place she'd abandoned and missed terribly, though she had forgotten it.

Then, as if satisfied, he leaned his head back against the pillow and fell asleep, snoring.

In the morning, Stefan's hangover looked to be killing him. She could only laugh, but it annoyed her when he just sat there when Phoebe's diaper needed changing. Then again, she reminded herself, there were plenty of times when she was sick, or tired, and he did help. She brought him some ginger ale and Advil and patted him on the shoulder. As the day wore on, he didn't seem to feel any better. He didn't eat anything and sat in front of the television, groaning every once in a while.

"Dilrod really did a number on you, didn't he? What did you guys get up to, anyway?"

"I'm nauseous with remorse," Stefan said.

"Was it rum?" she said. Ever since college rum had made him sick. She'd seen him throw up after a single daiquiri. But he was drawn, sometimes, to the challenge of it.

"I have to tell you something," he said, his tone shifting. She stood in front of him, bouncing up and down with her knees bent. It looked idiotic but kept Phoebe calm.

"We went to a strip club," Stefan said.

"You're kidding. Really? Why?" It didn't occur to her to get mad—it just seemed inexplicable. Men of their acquaintance, hers and Stefan's, didn't do that kind of thing. It was an activity to roll your eyes at.

"It was Dil's idea. You know, to celebrate getting married again. He's not having a real bachelor party this time."

"I didn't realize they were getting married."

"He proposed to her yesterday. On the phone."

Jill laughed, but her husband's expression cut it short. "How do you not think that's funny?"

"So we went to this club," he went on, as if he hadn't heard her or didn't care what she said. "We drank a lot. And we got, uh, lap dances."

She looked at him. In the "uh," that ungainly hesitation, were layers of omission and ghosts of scenes she didn't want to envision, her husband watching, aroused . . . In her surprise she stopped bouncing, and Phoebe fussed so she had to start again. Her knees hurt. What she thought about wasn't some woman contorting herself over her husband, though that was gross enough; what she thought about was their kiss in the night, the heat of his tongue, all that intensity she'd thought was returning for her, to her. She was suddenly so tired that tears rolled fatly down her cheeks before she even knew she was upset.

"Please," Stefan begged her. "It was nothing. I missed you both so much, my girls, I'm sorry."

He pulled her down on the couch and held both of them, and his voice sounded panicked, ashamed, like any old husband who knew he'd done wrong.

When Dilrod came over to say good-bye, he could tell something was up. Jill's eyes were red, and Stefan was visibly stricken by rum and shame. Jill left the room, but could still hear them.

"Oh, tell me you didn't, you pussy."

"I had to tell her," Stefan said feebly. "She's my wife. I couldn't live with it."

"Live with what, you asshole?"

"It was bad enough to have done it. I couldn't keep it secret. I felt disgusted."

"You *should* be disgusted," Dilrod told him. "You're such a fucking fake. Acting so fucking sanctimonious. So *progressive*. You were loving it last night. You were eating that shit up. Now you have to pretend like you're ashamed. You're not. You just want your wife to believe you are."

She couldn't hear Stefan's response, though from his murmured tone she knew he was denying it. But here was the thing: she thought Dilrod was right. In Stefan's jokes about rug rats and the old lady, there was a grain of truth. And in the disdain he claimed to feel for the strip club, there was a grain of longing. Of desire.

"A fucking fake," Dilrod said again, loudly, and the door slammed shut.

Stefan came stomping upstairs, angry. He stopped at the door of the nursery, where she sat in the glider with Phoebe. He looked defenseless, miserable. She wanted to comfort him, but what could she say? He was a fake and she knew it; to deny it was ridiculous; his fakeness was part of him, as much as his dark brown hair and the odd bump on his shoulder he'd had since he was twenty-five. He'd been a football jock, a college philosopher, briefly an aspiring writer, now a professional and a parent. Each of these versions of himself was fragile, dented with the effort required to build it.

"I love you," she said, and he smiled.

But this was not enough, and they both knew it. So she put Phoebe down, turned on the baby monitor, and said she was going out for milk. They didn't need milk, but he wouldn't check. He would grab, eagerly, at the chance to be alone with Phoebe for a little while, to prove himself a doting father.

She headed to Dilrod's hotel, a corporate Sheraton fifteen minutes away. He should've been upstairs packing but was in the bar, just as she'd suspected. Dilrod's drinking would only get worse, she knew, and the marriages, one after another, would fray just like his clothes, then fall apart. Either that or he'd find a woman who liked drinking with him, and then they would fray from the inside. This was his future.

"Hey," she said, sitting down next to him.

"Look who it is," said Dilrod. His tone snaked with menace. She hadn't realized, until this moment, that he probably hated her; that he probably thought she was responsible for making Stefan different, less fun, more into weird movies and guilted-out about strip clubs. The idea hardly surprised her; she'd just never bothered to consider things from his point of view before.

She caught the bartender's eye and ordered a vodka tonic.

Dilrod said, "Mama's stepping out."

"Everybody needs a break once in a while," she said with careful neutrality.

Dilrod smiled mirthlessly. "I'm sure Phoebe will understand."

"There's frozen breast milk as a backup at home," she said, and immediately knew she'd said the wrong thing; upright and defensive was the wrong tone. Then she added, "So how was it?"

"How was what?"

"Last night. With the girls."

"Oh, my God. I'm going to need another drink. Did you come here to attack me too? Pussy-whipping your husband isn't enough?"

She thought of Stefan at home, bent over the baby in his lap. He liked to sing her the ABC song. He read her *Goodnight Moon* every single evening. "That's not it," she said steadily. "I'm just . . . curious." And into the pause left after this remark she said, "Don't tell Stefan." She was a fake too, but Dilrod didn't know it.

He lifted an eyebrow and turned toward her on his stool. "I don't believe you," he said, though she knew he wanted to. It was more interesting, more fun, to be drunk with his old friend's wife in the bar of the Sheraton, and she'd come out after him because he represented something different and more exciting than what she had at home. This, she thought, was a story he'd live off for years.

"Fine," she said, carefully matching her tone to his. "Don't believe me."

They finished their drinks and ordered seconds, or whatever number Dilrod was on. She felt wasted, and her cheeks were flaming; this was more alcohol than she'd had in ages. Dilrod was telling her about one of the girls from last night, her huge ass and her nipple rings—trying to shock her, as if she'd never heard of nipple rings before.

"I just wanted to grab her ass, you know?" Dilrod was saying. "It's like a primal thing that comes over a man. You see it, you want to touch it, and then you gotta pay for it. People who run those places are fucking geniuses. And the women—don't ever let anybody tell you otherwise, they're *in charge*. The men are like little children, begging and pleading. The women have *everything*."

He went on like this, but she stopped listening. She was just staring at him and wondering how much longer she could stay. She loved Stefan, and Stefan—for whatever reason, it didn't matter—loved Dilrod. Useless to explain these choices, their dark and permanent importance, the way they could rule you forever. *You are what you like,* she thought, and put her hand on his knee.

Dilrod's response was both sloppy and mechanical. He leaned over and kissed her, wetly, his lips grabbing at hers like some separate animal. She held the kiss long enough to confirm its reality. As they sat there, mouths attached, her breasts began to leak. At home, she knew, her baby was crying.

She persuaded him to come back with her to make up with Stefan. It wasn't hard. He was glad to have kissed her, but also guilty about it—the guilt inextricable from the gladness. He would never tell Stefan; not telling was his thing.

She held his hand as she drew him through the doorway. Stefan stood up to greet them, and she saw him take it all in, everything she presented to him, as if on a tray: her smeared lipstick, her blouse stained with milk, Dilrod drunk and sloppy, with a secret smile.

"Look who I found," she said, her voice a little breathless.

From the other room Phoebe, perhaps hearing her, let loose a demon wail. As she went to tend to the baby she could feel her husband's eyes on her, following her every move.

A Month of Sundays

There were three of them in the car that night: Lauren, Samantha, and that boy he'd never liked, the one he'd pegged as a bad influence. The first time the kid showed up at the house, his eyes were bloodshot, his hair wet; clearly he was fresh from the shower, deodorant and shaving cream wafting off of him, and this made Mike wonder what smells he'd had to wash away. He was good-looking enough, square-jawed and blond, and Lauren sprinted out to him like a stone from a slingshot. Mike sauntered over, leaning heavily over the driver-side window, partly to get a look at him and partly to remind him that the pretty girl in his car had a father— not just any father, but a former college football player, a man who could cast a shadow, someone who'd come looking if anything went wrong.

"I'll have her home by eleven, sir," the kid said, so polite that Mike wanted to reach in and shake him. *Do you think I'm an idiot? That I was never seventeen?* But Lauren had her seat belt on, her green eyes glowing with please-don't-embarrass-me fury. So he patted the roof of the car and let them go. And he did have her back by eleven, Lauren smiling at him where he was watching TV, yawning as she headed safely up to bed.

These were the scenes he replayed in his mind at night. The dentist had given him a mouth guard because he was grinding his teeth. He lay on his back with a mouth full of plastic, sweating into the sheets. The dentist said it would help with his headaches, and he supposed it did. But it also made a clacking noise that Diana couldn't stand. She was sleeping in the spare room now.

Sunday morning he woke and showered, the house quiet, Diana at church. He'd never gone with her except at Christmas, and once Lauren turned thirteen they didn't make her go, either. Heading to the hospital he stopped, as had become his habit these past months, at Samantha's house. She and Lauren had been friends since the second grade. They'd played on the same soccer team, slept at each other's houses, spent hours on the phone talking through teenage melodramas. He'd taught them both in his middle-school science class, relieved they were good students. Eighteen, and starting at Drexel in the fall, Sam was a stocky blond girl with bright blue eyes obscured by too-long bangs. She slid in beside him, wearing a tank top and jean shorts, and buckled her seat belt without saying anything. Her nose and shoulders were sunburned. As usual, they didn't talk.

Lauren's room was down a dim hallway that smelled musty no matter what the weather was like. The nurses nodded at them. Lauren's skin was pale, her dark hair in a ponytail, her green eyes cloudy. Taking a seat, he read her a chapter of Harry Potter as Sam sat outside. After a while she came in, and he went to the cafeteria for a cup of coffee. When he came back, he saw that she'd fitted her iPod headphones over Lauren's ears and was staring at her intently.

Lauren had always liked music. Her favorite song was "Here Comes the Sun," and every time he heard it his eyes filled with tears.

If she liked what Sam played for her, she didn't show it. The nurses nodded at them when they left.

On the drive home, they chatted a little. Curiously, when he parked in front of Sam's house, they sometimes talked for five minutes or more, the girl suddenly bubbly, as if the fact that she'd soon be getting out of the car, or that their errand was over, relaxed her.

"So a couple summers ago Mr. Harad was giving out free passes to soccer teams?" she said today. "Like for ice cream cones or whatever? And these kids just started bringing in these old passes, saying they'd forgotten about them. So we had to give them all this free ice cream, tons and tons of it. But then he figured out the passes were fake."

"He must've been mad," Mike said.

"Steam was *literally* coming out of his ears," Sam said. "He was screaming at these ten-year-olds, 'You use computers to cheat! Computers are to learn!'"

"I wish," Mike said drily.

"No kidding," Sam said, then opened the door, got out, and waved at him exuberantly, even though they were only a few feet apart.

At home Diana was making Sunday brunch, which they ate while reading separate sections of the newspaper. She used to tell him about the day's sermon, until she realized he wasn't listening. He couldn't help it; he just tuned out. She'd grown up in the Moravian church, whereas his childhood Sundays in Ohio were devoted to football games on TV. By now they had a truce on the subject. When he was finished clearing the plates and loading the dishwasher, he found Diana on the couch in the living room, not doing anything, just sitting. She was thin and dark haired, as was Lauren. She sewed quilts and gardened and coached Lauren's old softball team—all that on top of working twenty hours a week in the school-board office.

She glanced up and saw him in the doorway. "Come here," she said.

They sat together on the couch, Diana's legs flung over his, her head against his shoulder. After a while he turned on the TV and they watched the end of a John Wayne movie. Diana fell asleep holding his hand.

Summers he generally spent fixing up the house, lucky to have learned these skills from his dad, a contractor. This year he was redoing the bathroom on the first floor. One day he and Diana were at Home Depot picking out fixtures when suddenly she grabbed him and pulled him into the next aisle, flattening him against a rack of lamps, pressing against him.

He could smell her shampoo and feel her hummingbird heart-beat against his chest. A chandelier dug into his back. "What are you doing?" he said, laughing.

She shushed him, lowering her face, and he put his arms around her, wondering if she was upset about the bathroom. But they'd planned the renovation even when they thought Lauren would soon be off to college; they needed it for when family came to visit. When Diana finally released him, her eyes were dry, her cheeks flushed. "Sorry," she said, "it's the Kents."

Gazing over her shoulder, he saw Sam's parents browsing through the lawn mowers. They were kind, smart people, both doctors. After the accident they'd come by regularly, bringing food and flowers, eyes soft with pity, but Diana had stopped returning their calls. "It just makes me feel worse," she'd said. This was why he didn't tell her that he took their daughter with him to the hospital every Sunday. It was the only secret he kept from her.

They hid in the lighting aisle until the Kents were gone.

The following Sunday, he picked Sam up again, read to Lauren, and drove Sam home. In front of her house, she said, "Can I ask you something?"

"Sure."

"When I go away to college . . ." Her voice drifted off.

She had a scab on her right knee, like a younger child, and she'd been picking at it; it looked angry and infected, blood oozing out. If she were Lauren, he'd be on her case about it. He waited for her to go on.

She looked vacantly out the window and said, "Should I, like, write to Lauren?"

Gripping the steering wheel, he turned away. They'd never once talked about the accident or how they felt about it. It was what had made their Sundays so comfortable. When he spoke, he was surprised by how unsteady his voice was. "It's up to you," he said. Carefully, then, he brought his voice under control, adopting his teacher's tone. "If it would make you feel good, then I don't see why not. I could read the letters to her."

She blew out a puff of air, spraying her bangs out to the side. "It's just weird, like we said we'd keep in touch, so I feel like I should, but I don't really think she can hear me. And even if she could, wouldn't she be pissed? That I'm going to college and she's not?"

"I don't think she would," Mike said. The truth was in the car between them: that Lauren didn't have the faculty for anger, that college meant nothing to her now. The thought sank him. It was like going down in an elevator into a dark, cool basement so deep beneath the earth that you might forget you could ever come back up. Forget that you'd ever seen the sun. When he was in that place, Diana said he was unreachable. Lost. So far away, in fact, that he didn't notice at first that Samantha was crying, sniffling bubbles of snot that she wiped away with the back of her hand. He wished Diana were here; she'd have handed her a tissue and given her a hug. He patted the girl's shoulder awkwardly. "It's okay," he said.

"I feel like it's all my fault," the girl said.

"It's not," he said, then paused. "Right?"

The events leading up to the accident had always been mysterious. Sam, who'd been sitting in the back, was the only one who'd come out of it intact. The boy died at the scene. At first, the doctors said that Lauren would be all right, that they could relieve the pressure on her brain. Later, they'd changed their minds.

And now Samantha was next to him, her eyes wild and red, her chin trembling spastically. After the accident, she'd been so upset that no one had been able to get anything out of her. Later, she said she didn't remember any of it. Sometimes Mike had wanted to shake the memory out of her. But he'd tried to let it go; knowing what had happened wouldn't undo it.

"Hey," he said. "It's all right."

She took a deep breath, then hiccuped. Not knowing what else to do, he took a card from his wallet—it was from a plumber they'd used last year—and wrote his cell phone number on the back. "You can call me anytime," he said.

She took it gratefully, seeming relieved to have something to hold, and put it in her pocket, smiling at him through her sloppy bangs. "Thanks," she said.

That week he worked on the bathroom, stripping out the tile and removing the old toilet and sink, and ferrying it all to the landfill. The summer was densely humid, and his sweaty clothes stuck to him. At night, his muscles ached. He was deep asleep on the following Friday when his phone rang. It took him a while to understand what was happening, and then to remove the mouth guard so he could speak. When he finally flipped the phone open, he heard only music, some pulsing dance beat.

"Who is this?" There was a scuffling sound, followed by jagged breathing. "Samantha?" he said. "Is that you?"

"Can you come get me, please?" she said.

He looked at the clock; it was past two. "Tell me where you are."

She gave him an address in South Bethlehem, not far from Lehigh. Maybe she was at some party with college kids. He got his keys, then paused by Diana's closed door, wondering if he should tell her; but she wasn't sleeping well lately, and he didn't want to ruin her whole night.

Though she'd called from what sounded like a party, the ramshackle duplex he pulled up in front of was quiet. He'd thought she'd be outside waiting for him, but she wasn't. He sighed. Lauren had never done anything like this. Grudgingly he climbed the splintered wooden stairs and peered in the window. A couple of guys were lying on couches, watching TV, no one else in sight.

He knocked, and when he got no reaction, he assumed they were stoned or something worse. Now worried, he opened the door and went in.

"Don't you knock?" one of them said. The other stayed riveted to the TV. They looked to be in their twenties, one white, one Hispanic, both skinny, slouched on their threadbare couches, their jeans riding down to expose their underwear, their arms sleeved in tattoos.

"I did," said Mike. "I'm looking for Samantha."

The guy who'd spoken shrugged, and the other still hadn't moved.

Giving up, Mike headed to the empty kitchen, then moved upstairs. If the first floor was unadorned, the second was battered, littered with beer cans overflowing with cigarette butts. In one room there was only a bare mattress on the floor. His pulse quick and angry, he opened the next door and saw a fat man in a white tank top ministering to a sick person in a bed. Then his eyes readjusted, and he understood the man was pulling up Sam's dress. Her eyes were closed, her arms flopped out to the side. A strand of her long blond hair was caught in her mouth, foam flecked on her chin.

"Get off," Mike said. "Now."

The man ignored him, his face flushed as he pulled down her underwear.

Mike stepped forward and pushed him off, and he landed hard on the floor, his jeans unbuckled, sprawled there waving his arms and legs languidly, like a turtle on his back.

Turning back to Samantha, Mike pulled her dress down—it barely reached her thighs—and picked her up, draping her arm across his shoulder. "Can you walk?" he said. She didn't answer. She smelled of puke and beer.

Downstairs, in the living room, there was now only one guy left, the one who'd spoken earlier. He was crouched over a bong, filling his lungs. When he saw them, he let out a stream of smoke and smiled. "Girl had a little too much fun, huh?"

At the sound of his voice, Sam came around, gurgling a little. "Thank you for the party," she said weakly.

"You're so welcome," the guy said. "Dude, need help getting her to the car?"

"Shut the fuck up," Mike said, propping Samantha against his leg as he opened the screen door.

The guy smiled again. "Whatever," he said.

After Mike got her buckled up, he started the car. The fat man came running out of the house, shaking his fist. When Mike reached over the girl to lock the door, Sam woke up and smiled vaguely. "Bye," she said.

Pulling into the Kents' house, he saw the driveway was empty. Sam was awake, staring listlessly at the window.

"Where are your parents?"

"They took my brother to visit colleges."

He turned off the ignition and rolled down the windows, a breeze carrying the smell of skunk into the car. Sam sat with her seat belt on, dazed or sick or simply pliant. He knew he should scold her, express concern, or both. Be parental. But it was three in the morning and he was wiped out. A headache pressed its angry iron grip upon him. Leaning back in the driver's seat, he said the first thing that came to his mind. "Did Lauren know those guys?"

She nodded. "Sure," she said. "We partied with them sometimes."

His skin prickled with revulsion. "The night of the accident, were you partying with them?"

She squinted at him. "We never got there," she said simply.

Nights when Lauren was out, he and Diana told themselves not to wait up, that they knew her friends and where she was. Every time they called her cell she'd answer promptly. She was allergic to hazelnuts and they'd trained her to ask about the food in every restaurant or home, even if it was something that didn't seem like it would have nuts in it. Once when she was eleven she ate some chocolate cake at a party and went into anaphylactic shock, her throat swelling, and he'd plunged the EpiPen into her skinny thigh as she stared mutely at him, terrified . . . These memories skittered like marbles across the flat planes of his brain.

"Thanks for picking me up," her friend said.

The fake politeness of teenagers drove him crazy. He looked at her, not knowing if she remembered what had just happened to her, or if he should remind her. "Are you okay?"

"Absolutely," she said, then got out and walked slowly, carefully, up to the door. Only when she got to the front door, framed beneath the yellow porch light, did he notice she wasn't wearing any shoes.

Back home he slid into bed next to Diana, needing her body beside him. He put his palm on her hip, and she nestled back against him. Lying still, he tried to time his breathing with hers. When they were first married, her hair was long, well below her shoulders, and it would get into his eyes and mouth while they were wrapped together in bed. And when she was pregnant, it grew thick and silky, with a heft and shine they both loved; he used to run his hands through it, feeling it slip around his fingers like ribbon. After Lauren was born, she cut it short, because the baby kept pulling on it, and she'd kept it like that. Now the black was spiked with gray. He reached his arm over her stomach and in her sleep she took his hand and put it between her legs, warming it there.

He thought back to when her hair was long. He was twenty-five, waiting for friends in a bar after work, when he noticed this pretty girl sitting alone in a corner. Her friend had flaked out on her; he never met his. They'd been dating three weeks when she invited him over to her parents' house for Sunday supper. She went to church with her parents every week, and they spent the rest of the day together. At the time he thought she went along just because she was a good daughter, not realizing how tenaciously she believed. It had taken him a while to come to grips with that, but he had. On that first night, he was greeted by her father, a portly, jowly man with skin so saggy it was as if gravity were tugging it downward.

He looked at Mike and said, "You must be the young man I've heard so much about."

"I hope so," Mike said, and held out his hand, but the other man didn't take it, just stood there staring at him, his eyes half-hidden by his fleshy lids. Mike heard Diana and her mother talking, and the mysterious clatter of kitchen work. Almost reluctantly, her father gestured for Mike to come into the living room. It was clearly a place they spent little time in, with an uncomfortable-looking, straight-backed couch and side tables riotous with doilies and knickknacks.

"What is it you do for a living?"

"I'm in sales," Mike said. He had a job at a medical supply company, and hated it, how he had to inflict himself on people, the associations with illness and death.

Diana's father grunted, his expression impossible to interpret. "You like it?"

"Not very much."

He lit a cigarette. He didn't offer one to Mike, who didn't smoke and maintained his college habit of running ten miles a week but nonetheless thought it rude.

"Diana says you're from Ohio."

"Columbus. Sir."

"What church does your family go to?"

Mike took a breath. His hands were sweating. The two women were chatting away in the kitchen, their voices too low for him to make out what they were saying. Whatever they were cooking smelled good—pot roast, maybe—but why was Diana leaving him stranded out here?

"We don't go to church," he said. "My parents were raised Lutheran, but they didn't much care for it."

"Ha!" Diana's father barked. "Didn't care for it!" Mirthlessly he shook his belly, exhaling smoke at the same time.

At this, Diana finally came out of the kitchen, her eyes dancing as she took in Mike's discomfort. "Are you tormenting him, Daddy?" she said.

"Not too much," he told her. "I got to make sure he's all right for you, sugar."

"He's just fine," Diana said, and Mike flushed as if she'd said much more.

After Diana's mother brought out plate after plate of food, her father said grace. They all held hands. As they unclasped, her father turned to her and said, "Mike says he's thinking of being a teacher."

Diana and Mike exchanged puzzled glances; her father went on imperturbably. "Knowledge is the thing. It will last a lifetime. Better than material goods." He was a deacon at the church and his voice rolled from him in waves, inexorable as his thick sagging flesh, a deep, rich river of words. "To mold young minds," he said to Mike, "is to better the world. It is itself a kind of religion."

That evening, he and Diana slept together for the first time back at his little apartment, and afterward he said, "What do you think your dad meant about me being a teacher? I didn't say anything like that."

She shrugged. "I don't know. He gets ideas like that sometimes. He calls them inspirations."

Mike ran a strand of her hair through his fingers. "I think I might give it a try," he said.

Seeming unsurprised, she smiled at him. As they held hands, he saw the path his life was going to take: he knew he would marry this girl, that they'd live close to her parents, that he was going to be a teacher. There was a certainty to it all that he would have said, if he were a religious man, felt like a state of grace.

The following weekend he went to see Lauren alone, then came back and changed into his work clothes. He was hanging sheetrock when the doorbell rang. Sam was standing on the front porch wearing shorts and a T-shirt and flip-flops. "Hey, come in," he said, stepping back. The girl stood in front of the couch uncertainly until he said, "Sit down. Do you want some lemonade or something?"

"Um, okay."

He brought her a glass and she sipped it tentatively before putting it on a coaster. He sat down next to her on the couch. She was slouching, her head nodding as if in agreement to something he'd said.

"So anyway," she said, and laughed awkwardly. Her hair hung loose around her shoulders. She was sweating a little. "I came to, you know . . . about the other night."

"Listen, I'm glad you called," Mike said. "I'm glad we got you out of there."

She glanced up. "No, I—" She reached out her hand, as if to touch him, then stopped.

Mike was confused. Why was she here? For a recounting of that horrible night? She shook her head and didn't speak. He waited her out but nothing came.

Finally, she said, "So what are you up to today?"

He gestured at his sweaty clothes, the plaster dust coating his shorts. "I'm redoing the bathroom."

Her eyes lit up. "Can I see?"

It wasn't what he was expecting, but he nodded and led her back there. He showed her where he was installing the new toilet and sink, the tiles and paint colors they'd selected. Nothing a teenage girl should be remotely interested in, but she was acting like it was the most exciting thing she'd ever seen in her life.

"Can I help you?" she said.

"Oh come on," he said. "You must have better things to do with your time."

"I don't." Through her bangs, tears were visible in her eyes. She blinked and sniffled. Without thinking he took her in his arms, and they hugged. She came just up to his shoulders, and she nestled her head almost into his armpit, like some animal burrowing there. She put her arms around him. He could feel the heat coming off her body, and her breasts squishing against him. He didn't move. She reached up and palmed his neck, then leaned her head back and stared at him intently. He felt logy, sedated, as if viewing all this from a great distance. Then she stepped up on her toes and kissed him, slipping her tongue inside his mouth. She was none too adept, but his body responded and he let his hands drop down to the small of her back.

She broke the kiss and took a step backward, smiling at him triumphantly. "I always wanted to do that," she said.

"Sam."

"Look, don't worry about it, okay? I just always wanted to."

Always? He almost said it out loud. How long can *always* be to an eighteen-year-old? Since you were fourteen, sixteen? Since last week?

"I'm going to go," she said. "Thanks for getting me. I owe you."

"No you don't," he said.

She let herself out. After she'd gone, he sat on the box of tiles, wondering if he ought to feel guilty. Was he as bad as that fat man in South Bethlehem, preying on his daughter's friend? She'd seemed so happy, as if she'd proved something to herself, passed a test that only she knew the contents of. That she was grown-up, he guessed. That she was allowed to make mistakes.

On the next Sunday he didn't pick her up. Instead he offered to go to church with Diana, who was taken aback. "How come?"

"I want to be with you," he said, which was the truth. They attended the service together, and then went to see Lauren. They fed her some soup and washed her hair, Mike supporting her neck while Diana shampooed and rinsed it. When clean, it gleamed darkly with health. Lauren seemed to enjoy it, making soft, snuffling noises that sounded contented. He noticed that someone had taken out her earrings, and wondered who'd done it, and when. They'd argued for months about her getting her ears pierced, Lauren wanting to at eleven, he and Diana insisting she wait until thirteen—an arbitrary number in all honesty—before finally giving in. Diana drove Lauren and Sam to the mall, and the girls returned full of pride, constantly fingering their ears . . .

The night of the accident it was the Kents who called them, the police for some reason having dialed the wrong number, and they all met at the hospital, including the parents of the dead boy, whose name, he now remembered, was Evan. The Kents rushed in to see Sam, who was crying in a room down the hall. He and Diana were taken in to see Lauren, who was lying in bed with her eyes closed, breathing quietly. There were lacerations on her face and arms but otherwise she looked fine. Diana touched her forehead gently, speaking softly all the while, letting her know they were there, that everything would be okay.

Now she folded Lauren's hands in her lap, squeezed them, kissed her forehead. She was worn and tired but her strength was remarkable; it nourished him, kept him from falling into the darkness.

Mike stood up and kissed his daughter's cheek. She made a small bleating sound; the doctors had cautioned them not to read too much into the noises she made, but it was hard not to think that she was saying something, that she knew they were there. She was still so pretty. He thought of her on the night of the accident, running out to the car. Sam in the back, her oldest friend. The good-looking boy in the driver's seat, gazing at her with hunger in his eyes. It was a crisp fall evening in the November of their senior year, a clear night with millions of stars speckling the sky. He hoped his daughter had seen that. He prayed she'd felt, getting into the car, a happiness too pure and rare to dwell on, a fleeting but immeasurable sense of the rightness of the world.

The Cruise

Because her aunt was both wealthy and caring, because people seemed to believe that divorce required a period of mourning accompanied and defined by homemade ritual, because Laureen (the aunt) was also kind of bossy and wouldn't take no for an answer, because she (Reena) had been named for Laureen and they were therefore considered by the family and, eventually, themselves to be specially affiliated, because the same people who spoke of post-divorce rituals also said that travel broadened the mind, because the world's wild creatures were disappearing and it was imperative to see them before it was too late, two women went on a cruise to the Galápagos.

"This is going to cheer you up," Laureen said as they boarded the flight to Quito. She had for decades been a highly paid executive secretary who wore black cashmere turtlenecks and tasteful gold jewelry. Now, in retirement, she'd ditched all sobriety, in clothes and otherwise. She was wearing fuchsia pants and a pink striped blouse and had already downed two alcoholic smoothies at the airport bar. She squeezed Reena's hand, and her breath smelled of rum and chips.

Reena's eyes watered, not from the squeeze or the breath. How long had it been since anyone held her hand? She was touched by it. She was touched by everything these days, not hardened by the divorce so much as scraped raw. This year's holiday cards, even the generic ones from the bank and the dentist, had brought tears to her eyes. *It's so nice people care,* she'd tell herself as she put the cards on the otherwise bare mantel in her new apartment. The cruise hadn't been her idea, but she was grateful for it. It was two weeks of something to do every day and night, the hours portioned into particulars. Two weeks in which she wouldn't have to be alone for more than a few minutes, or contend with those terrible, scurrying creatures, her thoughts.

As they settled into first class, Laureen ordered more drinks. She had been widowed young and raised her son, Jasper, by herself. She was briskly competent, always cheerful and independent and brave and Reena didn't want to be like her, she didn't ever want to have Laureen's life. But for now they were cruising, and she was grateful. When the plane lifted off, she felt better already.

The first part of the trip was a blur: two days in Quito of heat, dehydration, bland hotel food, and a dizzying trip up to the Virgen del Panecillo. Sometime after thirty she'd gone from mediocre traveler to complete wimp. Laureen kept after her, cheerleading her through the days. It was infantilizing and Reena liked it. She would have liked to be tucked into bed and read a story at night. She wouldn't have minded a kiss on the forehead. Her mother would never do such a thing, would never have taken her on a trip to get her mind off her troubles, in fact had told her that the divorce was her fault (a belief Reena shared). Laureen's curt dismissal of this opinion—saying of her sister, in front of Reena, "she's very narrow-minded"—typified her general auntly excellence. And now Laureen seemed most intent on getting Reena drunk, which was largely why the first two days passed in such a blur. A brief flirtation with stomach flu or food poisoning, on the day they boarded the cruise ship, came as a relief, giving her some respite from rum.

When she emerged on the second morning of the cruise, the social dynamics of the ship had already been established. And she had been abandoned: Laureen had a boyfriend. His name was Benjamin Moore, like the paint. A sixty-year-old civil engineer from Toronto, he was sensibly dressed in pressed Dockers and a light blue shirt and the equatorial sun had already played havoc with his ruddy face. He and Laureen had had dinner together the first night on board and watched the stars, and were now, her aunt said, "thick as thieves."

"I know all about you," Benjamin Moore said when introduced.

Reena's nervous laugh came out as a squawk. "I'll have to catch up."

"You don't have to do anything at all," he said kindly, by which Reena understood that he did know everything about her frailty and unfortunate life circumstances, and again her eyes watered, which she knew was pathetic and tried to hide by putting her sunglasses on, muttering something about the light.

Besides Benjamin Moore, her aunt had befriended a Japanese couple who spoke excellent, if slow-paced, English and knew everything there was to know about the wildlife photography opportunities to come. And also a German man, taking the cruise by himself and slightly younger than Reena. "He's really into movies," her aunt said. "His name is Hans."

"Yo, what's up?" he said, shaking Reena's hand and smiling broadly. He looked like a younger, pastier, doughier version of Benjamin Moore. She understood that Laureen intended for him to be Reena's cruise-boyfriend, a distraction to enjoy and practice on for her eventual return to the world, a boyfriend from camp whom you missed terribly the first day back home and then forgot about, remembering only the thrill of kisses in the woods.

"Hi," she said. "I'm Reena."

"Reena," said Hans. "We're going bird-watching today!" He seemed very pleased about it, and punched his fist in the air. "It's going to be motherfucking awesome, I think."

Reena looked at Laureen.

"Movies," her aunt mouthed.

Reena could only imagine that Hans had no idea how little the word *motherfucker* was generally used by middle-aged people on package vacations.

They were in open water and the sun was brutal. Reena looked around, suddenly disoriented. It was so hot and she was so far from home.

"Well," Laureen said brightly, "let's go!"

A young white-clad officer named Stavros led them, obedient as schoolchildren, onto one of the islands, where they would begin their wildlife tour. The Galápagos were bare and brilliant. Back in the distance their ship waited, hulking and white and patient. Reena looked at it longingly. Although seeing the wildlife was the whole point of the trip, she found the ship's rituals comforting, the constant availability of food, the orchestrated social events, even their tiny cabin. Everything outside was too big, too bright. *We're at the end of the world*, she thought, and understood why people used to think the earth was flat. Glancing fearfully at the horizon, she felt as if they might sail right over the edge. She started to cry again and hated herself for it. When would this stop? It wasn't even localized pain anymore. Her tear ducts were just in the habit. She set off after the tour guide, hot tears coursing freely down her cheeks. Hans sprang to her side, loping energetically, like a dog. Behind her, Laureen's happy laugh harmonized with Benjamin Moore's lower, rhythmic music.

"This is the frigate bird," the guide said. She was a young, pretty biologist with her hair in a long blond braid, her sturdy legs in cargo shorts planted firmly on the ground. "They're named after a warship and they steal catches from other birds. During mating season, the male's red air sac inflates like a bullfrog's neck."

"What is this air sac?" Hans asked Reena.

She tried to answer him by gesturing, but he still looked confused.

After the frigate bird they spent a long time looking at iguanas, everyone silent as their cameras whirred and clicked. It was as if they were a group of robots, these mechanical sounds their only language. Iguanas, Reena learned, are quite hypoallergenic and would make good pets, if only they were not endangered. Hypothetically good pets. Hans was taken by one that looked like a dinosaur, its neck ringed by sharply pointed, prehistoric skin.

"Motherfucker," he marveled sweetly, almost under his breath.

She wanted to ask him why he was here, if he was pursuing a lifelong dream or escaping some disappointment. But this question—*why are you here?*—was too loaded. After all, she wouldn't want to have to answer it herself.

Laureen and Benjamin were standing next to them, and she

hadn't even noticed. Reena smiled at her and said she was having a good time.

"You don't have to be so polite," Laureen said. "You don't even have to have a good time. Just *be*, okay?"

At this, without warning or choice, Reena burst into a full-grown sob attack.

Alarmed, the tour guide came over and put her hand on Reena's shoulder, her blond braid gently brushing her arm. "Is everything all right?"

Suddenly the world was in motion. Everyone was looking at Reena, muttering and whispering. The endangered species scrambled to take flight. Medical emergency personnel were summoned. Before she knew it, Reena was sitting in the incomplete shade of some equatorial tree, drinking water, taking aspirin, and applying sunblock while anxious crew members loitered nearby, scribbling notes on clipboards, conferring about dehydration and liability. How had she become such a spectacle? She knew what her ex-husband would say, if he were here, if they were still speaking. *You go to one of nature's most spectacular places, and you make it all about you.* He would say that, and he'd be right.

After insisting she was fine at least a dozen times, Reena was allowed to stand up. Laureen took her arm, as if trying to support an invalid. Smelling powerfully of some floral perfume, she was wearing a black-and-white striped blouse, gauzy and slightly revealing of her bra, and red Capri pants, and gold hoop earrings. She looked fantastic. Reena leaned against her as birds disappeared over the horizon. And then they were gone.

.   .   .

Back on the ship, they dressed for dinner. At Laureen's command, Reena had brought two new outfits, clothing with no past associations. She put on a blue dress, hoping to feel pretty. Her skin felt pleasantly scorched and dry.

In the dining room she and Laureen were seated at separate tables, a procedure designed to encourage further mixing among the guests. Hans, sitting on her right, kept smiling and offering her more wine. He asked what she thought about Martin Scorsese.

"Is he the one who did *The Godfather*?" she asked. "Most movies are so violent. I don't go very much."

Judging from his expression, this was the wrong answer.

After dinner, the bar stayed open and people milled around, loose and friendly. Reena stepped outside to get some air. She'd spilled some of her dinner on her new dress; it was just that kind of day. A hand touched her arm, and she turned around with a prepared, chipper smile—expecting Laureen—but it was Benjamin Moore.

"Your aunt's organizing a card game," he said.

"I'm not big on cards," Reena said.

"Neither am I. I thought I'd come out and join you. Is that all right?"

"Of course," Reena said, though it was more confusing than all right.

He inquired in a gentlemanly way about her health, and together they stood looking at the black water and the indecipherable landscape. Darwin, birds, the understanding of our humble origins that science gave us: that was what you were supposed to see. All Reena saw in the dark was water and rocks.

"I have a son who's twenty-five," Benjamin said musingly, not looking at her. "He's gay and he thinks I don't know it, but I do. It upsets me more than I'd like it to. He's an actor on a soap opera. It's on every day at one in the afternoon. He plays what you might call a rake. I have a TV in my office, and every day I sit there eating my lunch and watching my gay son seduce women wearing too much makeup."

Reena had no idea what to say. Maybe this was part of the cruise-ship experience, along with the dinners and the wildlife tours: you went on board and told strangers the story of your life.

"Sometimes they look like their entire faces are coated in Vaseline," Benjamin went on. "Why do they do that? Sometimes I think that if I had to look at those women all day and kiss them and such, maybe I'd be gay too."

"I'm not sure why you're telling me this, Benjamin," Reena told him.

"You can call me Ben," he said affably.

The ensuing silence didn't appear to make him uncomfortable. It lasted so long that Reena felt compelled to speak.

She took a breath, then said, "I got divorced because I cheated on my husband. Electronically cheated. I started e-mailing my high school boyfriend and we fell in love all over again, and my husband found out, and my high school boyfriend wasn't interested in leaving his wife, but my husband left me, and I don't blame him."

What her mother had said: *Reena, you've never known how to take care of things. You were always breaking your toys and messing up your clothes. This is the same, only bigger.*

What Laureen had said: *Well, honey, everything happens for a reason.*

What Reena had said: *I'm an idiot and a fool.*

"This Internet," Ben said, "it's changing our lives."

Reena's laugh sounded like a bark. "Yeah, it's definitely the Internet's fault."

"That's not what I said," he said.

She looked at him. There was no absolution in his voice but no blame, either. She couldn't figure out what he was doing there with her while her charming, vibrant aunt was off playing cards.

"Everything changes and nothing stays the same," he said after a while. They stood looking into the darkness as if there were something to see.

By the time Laureen came out to say good night, Reena was by herself; Ben had gone back to his cabin. "You doing okay, kiddo?"

"Better, thanks."

"I think Hans has a crush on you."

"Laureen, how old are you?"

"A girl's never too old for a crush," she said. This was the kind of statement that made Reena dread the idea of imitating her aunt's life. Shouldn't a woman at some point stop being a girl? Shouldn't there be an end to crushes? It was too terrible to contemplate, all that starting and blushing, over and over again.

"What about Ben, is he your cruise-boyfriend?" she said, trying to shift the focus from herself.

"Maybe," Laureen said coyly. "He's awfully cute. But there are a lot of fish in the sea. Or, as we learned in our nature talk, there are many fewer fish than there used to be. But still fish exist and we can fish them."

"Are you drunk, Aunty Laureen?"

"You bet, honey pie," her aunt said, and kissed her cheek.

.   .   .

Reena woke early, Laureen snoring woozily in the other bed. It wasn't even five yet. She rose as quietly as she could and went out on deck. The sun was pearly, kind. When she was married, this was the only time of day she'd had completely to herself. Then she'd contaminated that lovely solitude with time spent on the computer and desperate, yearning e-mails she now cringed to think of. The man she'd grown so close to, whose words she'd read so feverishly, she could hardly remember. What she missed was the need of him, how it prickled her skin, how she jonesed and ached, her blood in a kind of fury. She'd ruined her solitude with wanting, and then she was alone in a different way.

This morning she was not alone, as it turned out. Ben was there too. She smiled when she saw him, unexpectedly pleased. He looked as if he had been up for hours, and without speaking he offered her a cup of coffee from the leather-encased thermos by his side. She nodded and sipped. In front of them were islands, behind them were islands. Ancient, inhospitable places. It should have soothed her, seeing them, should have reinforced her small-ness in the world. If it didn't, then it was not the islands' fault.

Though the day began on a magical note, later it began to unravel. First there were complications with the scheduled activities and logistical delays that went unexplained, and the crew members smiled tight-lipped as they attempted to behave as if nothing was wrong. Then came rain in great torrents, trapping them on the ship and moving them beyond the awkward pleasantries of early acquaintance into the annoyances of familiarity. You could notice the strain in people's voices, hear previously affectionate couples now snapping and bickering. Everybody agreed that lunch was substandard.

In the afternoon the weather cleared and moods lifted. Scuba diving had for some reason fallen through, and the replacement activity was to visit a beach where sea lions lay napping. Though people complained about the insufficiency of this program—"It's not like we can look at animals *all day*," Reena heard one woman tell Stavros angrily—they all filed onto the beach, because what else could they do?

Laureen was wearing a white swimsuit bedecked with gold jewelry and a red sarong and she looked like some aging goddess, sensual and distended. In her striped blue T-shirt Reena felt sexless and uptight. They embarked in their small clique—Hans, Ben, and Reiko and Tomo, the Japanese couple. Hans was acting peculiar. Deeply flushed, he kept slapping his hand against the side of his leg; as he was wearing long swim trunks, the nylon made a swishing sound each time. Everyone kept looking at him, but he was too agitated or preoccupied to notice.

Laureen nudged Reena. "I think he's jealous of you and Ben," she said happily.

"What do you mean?" Reena said, startled.

"I heard about you two up drinking coffee with the birds. Oh, don't worry about me. I've got lots of opportunities. You play the field, honey. I deed him over to you."

"You *deed* him?" Reena said. Tears clustered once again in her eyes, though this time they were tears of anger, or maybe anguish, she wasn't sure; certainly it felt adolescent and hormonal. "Laureen, could you just stop, please, acting like this is high school? I know you mean well but I don't need to go back to high school."

Laureen put her hands on her hips. "It wouldn't kill you," she said, "to have a little fun. You act like having fun would actually hurt, like you're allergic to it or something. Men like women who like fun. I'm sure Jason and Bobby would have liked a little fun, too."

It was the first time on the trip that either of them had spoken those names. Reena felt sick. She'd never get away from it, how much everything was her own fault.

"Oh, honey," Laureen said. "Forget I said that."

Reena shook her head. She felt as if her arms, her neck, her ears were on fire. If she could have, she would've jumped into the water and swum to the ship, gotten into bed and pulled the covers over her head.

"Hey," Laureen said. "The sea lions."

They lay in a line on the beach, flopped down like cushions, vulnerable and dopey, like overweight puppies. They were almost preposterously cute. Reena immediately wanted to touch them, even knowing that she couldn't, that they weren't pets, wouldn't even be good hypothetical pets. But how could anyone resist them? The fight she and Laureen were having disintegrated, shelved until there was less-pressing cuteness in front of them. Ben took Hans by the arm and walked him down the beach, pointing out some feature of the landscape, a soothing, fatherly gesture. The Japanese couple crouched and bent calisthenically, their telephoto lenses zooming.

Laureen and Reena stood quietly, not too close and not too far, listening to the occasional thwapping of the sea lions' glistening tails. Two raised their heads, but overall they didn't seem disturbed. Maybe they were used to tourists. Or maybe this invasion was so far down their list of sea lion priorities—fish, swim, bask on the beach—that they had no concept of it.

The biologist guide had joined them, and was talking about threats to the sea lions, from skin infections due to polluted waters to plastics that could strangle or choke. She talked about how their mothers nursed younger and older pups at the same time; if the younger one was too much weaker than its sibling, then it would die. She droned on relentlessly, reciting these terrible things so matter-of-factly, without emphasis. Without tears.

Reena's heart squeezed. She reached out and took her aunt's hand in hers.

"Look," she kept saying, even though she knew Laureen already saw. "Just look."

The Assistants

"If I died, would you come to my funeral?"

"Why would you ask me that? We barely know each other."

"That's why I wondered," Martin said. We were drinking Red Stripes, just the two of us, in a dive bar on the Lower East Side. "Would you come? Would you be that person who everybody at the service was wondering about? You know, whispering in the pews, 'Who is she?'"

"Nobody would say that."

"But really—would you come?"

"Would it be in New York?"

"Probably not."

"I doubt it, then," I said. "I doubt I could get off work."

"They wouldn't give you time off for a funeral?"

I drank my beer. "I just started," I said. "I'm just an assistant."

Back then, we were all assistants. We worked at magazines, galleries, or nonprofits. We lived with roommates in tiny apartments in questionable neighborhoods. My bedroom was just big enough for a twin mattress. My friend Sarah shared a room with a guy who was a bartender in Chelsea; she slept there at night, and he slept there during the day. Martin lived by himself, which sounded luxurious until we went over there one night and discovered his studio was a converted supply closet; he washed his dishes in a deep sink spattered with stains. Millie also lived by herself, we assumed under similar conditions, until we went over one night and found she had a corner one-bedroom in the West Village with Pottery Barn furniture and jute rugs. It was a surprise to us, learning that Millie was rich, and it upset me in particular; I was shocked anyone under thirty could live like that, which will tell you something about how young I was at the time. It would have splintered our group, except that things were coming apart already.

Sarah and I worked together, at a literary magazine whose downtown office was a dusty shambles of manuscripts and review copies and file cabinets stuffed with carbon copies of letters, author contracts, galleys, and production details. At first Sarah was my only friend in the city, and she'd gotten me the job. I knew her from high school; she'd gone to college with the bartender roommate, who knew Millie from his hometown in Connecticut, which he'd always presented as hardscrabble and blue-collar but which description, after seeing Millie's apartment, we began to doubt. The five of us invited one another to whatever work-related parties we knew about, improvising dinners out of the cheese cubes and cheap wine; we bartered the tickets and CDs and passes and book galleys that were the currency of assistants, and cadged free drinks at the bar in Chelsea if it was a busy night and the manager wasn't around. Six months after I moved to New York, straight out of school, we'd become a running pack. We hung out on the weekends and called one another nearly every day. When my mother, back home in Toronto, worried I might be lonely, I laughed and said, "I have three roommates, I'm never alone," but the running pack was a secret I clutched close to myself, better than money.

How Martin got involved is something I can't remember. He was tall and gangly and perpetually stooped over as he listened to what other people had to say. He came from the South, with a lilting, musical twang, and was an assistant at a foundation that dispensed grants to artists; this suited him perfectly, because he himself seemed both courtly and impoverished. He wore chinos and bucks and looked less preppy than messy; his clothes didn't fit well, his hair too long and his skin pocked with acne damage. He sweated even when it wasn't hot. I remember one night, Sarah and Martin had planned to see a movie, but she went on a date instead. So Martin picked me up at work and we headed to the theater. After a block or two he abruptly said, "Excuse me," then ducked into a bodega and emerged carrying two tallboys in a paper bag, one of which he was already drinking. "I can't sit in the dark without drinking a bit," he said. He sounded both apologetic and matter-of-fact. He finished the first beer before we got to the corner and the second as we reached the theater. As the movie started, he pulled out a silver flask and sipped.

I liked the flask. I was charmed by this kind of apparatus, the accessory of a more glamorous time.

Afterward, we went to a bar on Ludlow, and that's when he asked me the question about his funeral. I asked if he thought about dying a lot, and he shook his head. He had other fears, he said. Darkness. Confined spaces. Wide-open spaces. Elevators. Escalators. Chewed pens.

"Pens?" I said.

"Those tips," he said, and shuddered. "Bite marks in plastic. People hand you one and expect you to pick it up? With I don't know what germs?" He shook his head again. "That's just crazy."

I looked at him. "It must be hard for you to get around."

He studied me back, his head cocked to one side. His eyes were blue, watery, and kind. I felt the full force of his attention, which was not sexual but not asexual either; it felt complete somehow, as if he were taking in every aspect of me.

"Not you, though," he said, with that soft Southern lilt. "I bet you can go anywhere and do anything. You're made of stronger material."

"I don't feel particularly strong," I said.

"Do you feel particularly weak?"

"I guess not."

"That's what I mean," he said. "You're the most normal person I know."

I did not take this as a compliment.

But he smiled when he saw my frown, and his hair fell over his eyes. "Don't worry about it," he said gently. "I'm sure it'll come in handy eventually."

Wherever he came from, Martin started hanging out with us, and pretty soon it was clear he was there for Millie. When she was in the room he still paid attention to you, but you could tell it was an effort. I couldn't blame him, really; Millie was the kind of person I'd come to New York to be around. Short, with dark spiky hair, she was good at poker and occasionally smoked cigars. Her skin glowed even at three in the morning after a night of drinking. She was an assistant at a gallery on Fifty-seventh Street. If, on a

Saturday afternoon, we dipped into a gallery, Millie would take two seconds before pronouncing the work "shit" or "genius"— there was no in-between, in her opinion—while I tried to figure out why she'd landed to one side of the pendulum rather than the other. I myself had no idea, but I liked the confidence of these declarations.

I think Martin liked it too. She had no fear; he was afraid of everything, including rejection, so he watched her from a distance as she felt him watching, and they were locked together in this as if by contract. She must have enjoyed knowing he was always there, a gentleman beanpole on the sidelines, following her every move with those watery blue eyes. There isn't a woman on this earth who doesn't want to be adored.

At work, Sarah and I were also adored, albeit in a different way. Our boss, Eric, was an elderly bohemian who wore pilled woolen cardigans and too-short pants, and spent afternoons in his office reading manuscripts while twirling his beard between his thumb and index finger, making a little curl that stood out from his chin. By five o'clock his beard would be a tufted mess of curls, all fluffed out like the feathers of some preening bird. Because of this, Sarah and I called him the titmouse.

"Titmouse on the move," one of us would mutter to the other as he came toward our desks, and we'd straighten up to look like we were actually working. There wasn't really any need to talk in code—there was no one else around, and Eric's hearing wasn't great—but this was the sort of thing we found hilarious at the time. *Taking flight* meant he was leaving the office on some errands. *Worms:* he was going for lunch. *Flapping wings:* he was in the photocopier room, looking perplexedly at the machine. Eric seemed to think it was demeaning for him to ask a woman to help with basic office tasks, even though this was our job, a scruple we didn't hesitate to exploit. We let him suffer for as long as we could stand over some paper jam or mailing snafu before we'd come to his aid. The photocopier, the fax machine, the FedEx label—these were newfangled technologies so complicated that in the face of them Eric simply threw up his hands. He'd grown up in a New York where any business deal was done via handshake at a cocktail party below Fourteenth Street. Sarah and I loved him. When the titmouse came back with worms, we'd drop by his office on some pretense and while he was eating we'd get him to tell us stories about parties at George Plimpton's apartment, Mary McCarthy throwing a drink in somebody's face, arguments that spilled out into the streets at two a.m. Eventually it would be midafternoon and he'd glance at the pile of manuscripts at his desk and sigh. "Well, my lovelies, this magazine isn't going to publish itself."

How exactly the magazine did manage to publish itself was a mystery. My job, nominally, was as assistant to the head of sales, Judith, who worked out of her home and besieged me with harried, confusing phone calls. I'd only met her once. She must have been good at her job, though, because she was always finding some fancy restaurant or upscale furniture store to place an ad with us. My main task was to coordinate her expense reports. I used to show Sarah the tallies for lunch or drinks. "Can you believe this?" I'd say. She spent more on cocktails than I made in a month.

Sarah just shrugged. She was Eric's assistant. In high school she'd been an indifferent student, and I didn't even remember her reading many books, but in New York she'd discovered a seriousness of purpose. Her job was to screen the flood of incoming manuscripts. Every time the mail was delivered, it included dozens of slush submissions in manila envelopes, and Sarah visibly shuddered. Her bag was always crammed with paper, her eyes red and shadowed, and she said she dreamed about all the poems and stories and essays floating around in the world waiting to be read. Because I didn't have enough to do, I'd sometimes offer to help her out, but she'd shake her head. Being burdened made her feel important.

In the evenings, we'd meet up with Martin and Millie and some other combination of people—some friend from out of town, or a girlfriend or boyfriend of the moment—and head to Veselka for dinner, or to Brownies to hear some music, or, in the long, humid summer, to the park or somebody's roof. I remember one night in July at the apartment of somebody none of us knew very well. We'd invited ourselves over because he'd mentioned central air-conditioning. It was actually his uncle and aunt's place; they were gone for the summer on some lavish vacation, and he was apartment sitting for them in between semesters of graduate school at NYU. Skinny and bearded, he stank of smoke and talked about Harold Bloom in scathing, urgent terms, and we were willing to put up with all of this in exchange for an evening in that cold, expensive apartment. He served us chilled white wine in fancy glasses, and we took off our shoes and ran our toes over the luxurious carpets as if they were a sandy beach. At least most of us did. Millie just sat on the couch, with her legs tucked daintily beneath her.

The grad student, whose name is lost to me, was also supposed to be taking care of the two elderly cats, sickly and long-haired, who trailed around the couch sneezing. He had to feed them special medicine twice a day, inside of hollowed-out liver treats. Despite all this special care they looked mangy, like they lived in some alley and foraged in trash cans for food.

"Those are the saddest cats I've ever seen," I said.

"They live better than you do, I bet," the guy said.

I flushed, not sure if he was insulting me or commenting on his aunt and uncle. "They do have air-conditioning," I said.

Martin got down on the floor and reached out to pet them, making clicking noises with his tongue. With his long legs and other arm folded up, he looked like a cricket. The cats ignored him.

"Here, kitties," he said, fixated on them, his pale face sheened with sweat. Millie was sitting behind him, and she put her feet down on the floor as she leaned over to sip from her glass of wine. This put the smooth, glowing skin of her calves right next to his face, and I saw how it pained him to be so close. Millie didn't notice. She was arguing with the grad student about Barbara Kruger's art, which she thought was profound and he said was overrated. It was the kind of argument I'd come to New York to witness, perhaps even participate in, but I was distracted by the little drama on the floor and the contrast between Martin's pale, pockmarked chin and Millie's lovely legs.

"Martin," I said softly. "Martin." I shook my head at him, and he stared back blankly.

"Cats usually like me," he said.

We were all drunk. It was so cold in the apartment I wished I'd brought a sweater, which seemed ridiculous given that the night before I'd emptied a tray of ice cubes into my pillowcase before finally falling asleep.

"You're so pretty," the grad student said to Sarah, who was lounging on the couch with a cat wedged between her ankles. "What are you into?"

"Leftist bohemians with wealthy relatives," Millie answered for her, and laughed. Sarah didn't say anything. "Guys with intellectual rather than physical brawn."

"You're a bitch," he said.

"It's not true," I said.

"Of *course* it's not true," Millie said. "It's never true."

"Anyway, you're the one with *wealthy relatives*," the guy said, pronouncing it like a swear, and I realized they had some kind of history, that maybe Millie was into him, or had been, and that's why she was so mad.

Martin looked up as their voices got louder and said, "Hey, now. Come on." Because he was drunk, his Southern accent was stronger than usual. "Everybody calm down."

"Shut up, Martin," Millie said casually. She was still looking at the grad student, her eyes practically shooting out sparks.

Martin's whole face buttoned, closed itself like an envelope. His blue eyes went vacant. Then he did an odd thing. He put one hand on the floor, as if to brace himself in order to stand up, then curled the palm of his other hand around Millie's ankle, grasping it as tightly as a bar in the subway. She looked down at him, surprised, but he was focused on his own operation and didn't say anything. Drawing his face close to her knee, he stuck out his tongue and licked it—more than once, quite thoroughly, as if he were cleaning it. As if he were a cat.

I remember Millie staring at me, eyes wide and frozen, wondering what she was supposed to do.

I remember our host laughing, a shrill squeal like a girl's.

Then Martin said, "Gotta go." He unfurled his tall frame, bowed slightly to everyone, and left the apartment.

"What the hell was that?" Sarah said.

At first it seemed like just another night when something weird happened, like the time when Sarah and I left the office at dusk and a guy in a gorilla suit came up and gave me a hug, or the day in Tompkins Square Park when we met some backpackers from Denmark who'd run out of money, and we bought them lunch and they thanked us by performing Scandinavian folk songs until other people in the park told them to go away.

The next day, Sunday, Sarah and I had a picnic in the park, if you can call two bagels and the *New York Times* a picnic, then on Monday we went back to work, and it was probably Thursday or Friday before we realized that nobody had heard from Martin.

"I should call him," I said to Sarah in the office, my hand hovering over the phone. She shrugged. I left him a message, but he didn't call back. I guessed he was embarrassed, and lying low for a while.

Millie told us that she thought the whole thing was funny. "I was talking," she said, "and I felt something wet, and I thought it was some wine or something. But then I looked down and . . . I couldn't really take it in, you know? It was like my brain couldn't absorb what was happening. And before I could even say anything, it was over!"

They both keeled over laughing, and then Sarah made us go to the bar in Chelsea so we could tell the story all over again, to her roommate.

"But so nobody's heard from him?" I said.

"He must be mortified," Sarah said.

We gave him some time: that week, and the week after. Then one day at work I called his office, and his voice mail didn't pick up. His phone at home was disconnected, too.

I looked over at Sarah. "Martin's gone," I said.

As soon as I said it I felt it was true. Sarah must have heard it in my voice; for the first time since that night, she didn't laugh when she heard his name.

We called Millie, and she invited us over to her apartment that evening to discuss the situation. This was when we saw how nice it was. Her place reminded me of a story I'd heard about an assistant at Condé Nast. "I assume you have other income," the person interviewing her had said, because the salary was so low. At the time, I interpreted that story as having to do with the cluelessness of bosses. But I understood now it was true, true of Millie and other assistants all over the city, that for some of us this life was a game, and for some of us it wasn't. I felt duped, although no one had lied to me. I just hadn't known.

Millie handed us each a beer and we sat around on her Pottery Barn furniture.

"Wow, you have a balcony," Sarah said. "That's great."

"It's tiny," Millie said, dismissing it with a wave of her hand.

There was a new awkwardness between us that wasn't just due to the apartment. It had to do with our understanding how Martin felt about Millie and how she'd enjoyed stringing him along, letting him hope for something that was never going to happen.

It turned out that none of us knew any of his other friends. He'd briefly dated my friend Kim, but when we called her she said she hadn't spoken to him in months. After a few more beers, we decided to go his place. He lived on a shabby block in the East Twenties, and we'd only been there once before, when we were walking home from the movies and somebody had to go to the bathroom. We hung out on his stoop for a while and kept ringing his buzzer. No one answered. Eventually, because of the beer, we had to find a bathroom somewhere else.

There were no stories in the news about anyone fitting Martin's description getting in trouble, or injured, or dying. There was never any news of him at all. He was just gone. I had a hard time accepting that someone we'd hung around with so much could simply vanish. Every once in a while I'd call his numbers or ring his buzzer, but there was never any trace of him. Sometimes I'd ask Sarah where she thought he went and if he was all right, but she never wanted to speculate. She'd give me an odd, weary look, as if my concern was naïve. "If he wanted to be in touch, he'd be in touch," she said.

So I stopped bringing it up. Occasionally I thought about our weird conversation about his funeral. But even in retrospect it didn't strike me as morbid. This was how Martin was—he wasn't afraid to ask a strange question or make a peculiar gesture. It was a way for him to figure out where he stood with you. I guessed he'd wanted that with Millie, too. He must have gotten his answer.

For whatever reason, after Martin went away the rest of us stopped calling one another so much. What had felt like a tight, permanent pack turned out to be loose and temporary. We still met up, just not as often, and the daily phone check-ins slowed to a trickle.

Millie got a new, serious boyfriend. Sarah's roommate left the city for grad school. She and I buckled down at work. We stopped talking about the titmouse and laughing so much at the office.

One day, without warning, Eric died. Janet called and said, "He had a massive heart attack! They found him in bed. It's going to be a mess cleaning that place up, I think he kept the accounts in a shoe box under his bed or something. Anyway, you should probably take the day off. Take the week."

I hung up. Sarah was bent over her desk, her shiny black hair brushing the manuscript pages she was reading. Her hands were clasped over her ears, as they always were when I was on the phone.

"Eric's dead," I said.

"Yeah, right."

"No, seriously."

"Yeah, right."

"Janet just told me."

She looked up and shook her head slightly, as if shaking herself awake. Then, to my surprise, she burst into tears. I reached over and hugged her. We huddled there together, like little kids.

The next day, when we showed up for work, the office was locked. We each got a letter with a severance check from the nonprofit that ran the magazine. I was puzzled but Sarah was irate; she kept talking about breaking into the office and writing to the authors. "There's a proper way of doing things," she kept saying, "and this most certainly is not it." I'd never heard her say things like *proper* and *most certainly*. When I suggested maybe we should just move on, she turned on me like I was a traitor. "Don't you care?" she said.

"Of course I do," I said, but I could tell she didn't believe me.

We attended Eric's funeral together, at a pretty church in the West Village. He seemed to have no family but tons of friends, and they told stories about him as a young man, funny, romantic, and reckless: how he accepted a dare to swim in the East River at midnight, and almost drowned; how he tried to bribe Susan Sontag to publish in the magazine by bringing osso buco to her apartment. He never married, and the magazine seemed to have been his greatest love. Sarah and I nudged each other when we spotted writers we recognized. We didn't talk to anybody. We were the youngest people there, and nobody knew who we were.

After that, we scrambled to find new jobs. With my supposed sales experience, I found a position in market research, and Sarah was hired by a glossy women's magazine. Within a year she was promoted. I remember her calling me from her office, a rare occurrence by that point.

"Guess what I'm doing," she said.

"Why are you whispering?"

"I'm about to have a meeting," she said. "With my *assistant*."

We were on the other side. I got promoted too, and though I didn't have an assistant I had what felt like a real salary, and I left my closet-sized bedroom and rented a studio in Park Slope. Sarah and I were both working long hours, and didn't have much time to hang out. We never saw Millie at all. Sarah moved to L.A. for a few years to help launch a new magazine, then returned to New York. As a market analyst, I drifted away from the media world that consumed Sarah's time, and we rarely crossed paths. She and I would make plans to get together, but it was hard to schedule around our jobs and families. Our arrangements kept falling through. Finally we were able to catch up over lunch, at a garden café near her apartment on the Upper West Side. She was the editorial director of a multimedia company; she asked me about my work and smiled politely through the answer. We showed each other pictures of our children, her five-year-old daughter and my twin boys.

Over coffee she said, "By the way, did you hear that Martin Horst died?"

I set my cup down. Though it was summer and we were eating outside, I felt cold. "No," I said. "When?"

"A couple months ago."

"What happened?"

"Unclear. There were prescription drugs involved. He had a bad back and some other health problems. Maybe it was an accident, maybe it was an OD? Nobody seems to know for sure."

"This was in New York?"

"No, in South Carolina. He'd been back home for quite a while, I think."

"How did you hear about this?"

"The usual. Friends forwarding e-mails. Facebook."

"Martin was on Facebook?"

"No, but Millie is, and she heard about it from his ex-wife. I guess they were friendly. She's an art dealer or something and Millie knows her."

"I didn't know."

"I should've guessed something was up. Martin used to send all these funny group e-mails, especially during the election, he was really worked up about that, but then he went pretty quiet."

For some reason my fingers were trembling. Learning that

Martin was dead—he would've been forty, maybe forty-five?—
was part of it. To think of his dying, to think of the pain that
must have accompanied it, made my stomach hurt. But I was also
shaken to learn that Sarah had been in touch with him, and with
Millie, who'd been in touch with an ex-wife I hadn't even known
existed. A web I was no longer part of.

Across the table, Sarah squinted as the afternoon sun hit her
face. "Oh dear," she said. "You have that look on your face all over
again."

"What look?"

"I'm sorry," she said. "I know he broke your heart."

I wasn't sure what she was talking about. When I thought back
on that time, I didn't register any heartbreak. I did recall Martin, vividly: his hunched shoulders; his attentive, watery eyes; and
his disappearance, a loose thread unraveling a world I was just
beginning to know. But I could barely picture the person I'd been
back then, probably because I was vague even to myself. I hadn't
become anybody yet.

Sarah put on her sunglasses. She'd paid the bill, and now she
stood up.

"Remember when he licked Millie's knee that time?" I said.

"No," she said. "I don't think I was there."

Bruno

The kid came out of the airport security area with his face turned to the windows, scuttling sideways like a crab. He was wearing skinny dark jeans and a red plaid shirt too hot for summer, and his dyed black hair jetted down over his eyes in an aggressive point. Inès had said, "He looks like a dirty little bird you would see in Buenos Aires or somewhere like that. Don't worry, you will recognize him." It was typical of her, this description: fanciful, excessive, weirdly accurate. He knew right away that this was his boy.

"Bruno," he called.

The boy gave a minimal nod, came through the exit, and kissed Art on both cheeks. "*Salut*, Papa," he said.

"Welcome to New York."

Bruno said nothing. As they waited at the baggage carousel, Art asked how the flight was, if he was hungry or thirsty, and received three shrugs in return. So he gave up. Silence accompanied them through the taxi line, and on the ride to Brooklyn. The boy's eyes were trained out the window as the city came closer, his white earbuds firmly implanted. Though it had only been a few years since they'd seen each other, he seemed a stranger. Between twelve and fifteen was a lifetime, Art knew, but the last time he'd visited Bruno was still a child, and they'd strolled through the fields around Inès's country house in Provence holding hands, he was amazed to remember. They'd played catch and wrestled. For a couple of summers he'd been too sick to make his yearly trip, and now his son was a teenager with an eyebrow ring. Inès had said he was having trouble in school, alluding vaguely to the wrong kind of friends. *Maybe you help him on the straight road,* she'd written in her e-mail, another unidiomatic phrase that made perfect sense.

They were almost at his apartment when the boy started nodding and singing along to whatever music was on his iPod. "Hey, baby, you gonna get with me, I show you what to do with that perfect ass. I slap you, I tap you—"

Art poked him and gestured for him to take the earbuds out. "We're almost home."

The boy nodded, taking in the brownstones, the trees, the stores. "It's good, this place," he said sweetly. "I'm glad I come live with you."

"Sure," Art said nervously. He and Inès had only discussed a three-week visit. But he didn't say anything to his son, who he now noticed had flecks of sleep in his eyes. Bruno rubbed them with his fists, the gesture rendering him again the child of Art's memory. He got Bruno inside, gave him a sandwich and a glass of milk, and put him to bed on the futon in his office. Then he took his laptop into the living room and e-mailed Inès: *Wanted to let you know that he got here safely. He said something about coming here "to live." He means for the month, right? Just checking that we're all on the same page.*

It wasn't that he didn't want Bruno here. The whole week he'd been nervous, cleaning up the apartment and rearranging the office; he even found himself, bizarrely, going on a diet, wanting both his place and his person to look their best. But he was never confident about any communication with Inès, who tended to listen to other people's points of view and then do whatever she wanted. This free-spirited determination was part of her charm, and probably also the reason why she'd never married. When they'd met and had their fling, he was on vacation in Paris, recovering from his divorce. Inès had shown him a great time, and he remembered laughing so hard that his stomach muscles hurt. They got really drunk night after night and smoked a ton of pot and had sex in a cemetery. They agreed it was just for fun, a weeklong thing, a release they both needed. Three months later she called to say she was pregnant and going to keep the baby.

The contours of a new life sketched themselves in Art's vision, a French wife, an apartment in Paris, a child. "Should I, uh, move over there or something?"

"Don't be stupid," Inès said. "You don't need to do anything. I am thirty-five, this is my chance for mothering. I want to grab this."

She'd cleared him of all obligations, but he hadn't cleared himself. So he'd taken to spending his summer vacations in France to be with his round-cheeked, blond-haired son, who treated him like the distant relative he supposed he was. Bruno always seemed happy enough to see him arrive and never particularly distressed to see him go. And Inès was also happy—motherhood agreed with her. When her parents died she inherited a stone house outside of Aix, and the summers there were like living in a Cézanne, all haystacks and brilliant sunsets. It wasn't how Art had ever expected to become a father, but it wasn't bad.

He fell asleep in his armchair, the laptop balanced on his knees, and when he woke up Bruno was in the kitchen making eggs. He moved confidently around the kitchen in his tank top and jeans, a cigarette pursed between his lips. He looked like a forty-year-old ex-con fresh from the joint. Bruno nodded for him to sit down, doling some eggs onto a plate and adding buttered toast. There was also coffee.

"Thanks," Art said.

Bruno shrugged Gallically. "I always make for my mother."

"That's nice of you."

"Her cooking is garbage. I cook so I can eat."

Bruno sat down, throwing his cigarette into a glass of water he'd apparently designated for that purpose, since three butts were already floating there. The eggs were creamy, the coffee strong. By the time Art had taken two bites, Bruno had finished his. Then he leaned back in his chair and lit another cigarette.

"So," he said. "Are you still sick?"

Art met his gaze. "No, I'm well now."

"But you had it . . . removed?" The boy's hand fluttered ambiguously around the seat of his chair.

The question started as bravado, but ended in nerves. Art thought, *You little fucker.* He didn't stop staring at the boy, whose gaze finally dropped to the ground.

"I had one ball removed. You know what a ball is, right?"

"Of course I know."

"What's it called in French?"

"*Testicule.*"

"So, I still have one test-ee-cool," Art said, drawing out the pronunciation. "Which is enough."

"Enough for what?"

"For whatever," Art said tightly.

Suddenly they both laughed.

Bruno shook his head, grinning. "It's funny how you say *testicule*."

"I know. I speak French like Inès cooks."

His kid laughed again, and the tension between them eased. Bruno cleared the table and washed the dishes, which impressed Art, and he also emptied the butts out of the glass and set it aside, marking it as his ashtray for the summer. They spent the rest of the day in the neighborhood, Art showing him the grocery store, the park, the Italian social clubs where old guys hung out, monitoring the street traffic. For dinner they ate outside at a café, Bruno ordering and being served, without question, a glass of red wine. Art remembered himself at fifteen, pimpled and sweaty, with three hairs on his upper lip that refused to coalesce into a mustache, agonizing for hours over an excuse to call Alison Kozlowski on the phone. Bruno couldn't have been more different. But they talked easily enough, laughing about Inès, remembering a trip they'd taken to Marseilles when Bruno was very young. When they got home, Bruno went to sleep and Art checked his e-mail, finding an enigmatic one-line response from Inès: *Why don't you see what happens?*

The first week was great. They went to the movies, out to dinner, to Coney Island. In the mornings they drank coffee and read the

Times in the kitchen. Art had taken the week off and was glad he had, not only because a break from work was always welcome. When he'd met Inès, he was an editor at a leftist magazine. He'd made it sound like a bigger magazine, and his own position there more important, than reality could support—foolishly, in retrospect, because Inès couldn't have cared less. In the manner of many intellectual Europeans he'd met, she somehow cobbled together a life out of occasional freelance work and government assistance and for months at a time appeared to do nothing at all. Art's magazine, inevitably, had folded. Now he was editing online content for a website designed for seniors, who ironically were probably the last people alive still buying actual magazines. His twenty-two-year-old assistant did the blog aggregating and headline writing while Art fixed comma splices and assigned pieces on investment strategies to protect your nest egg and the health benefits of broccoli. In staff meetings he was often the oldest person in the room, and sometimes the young faces would turn to him automatically, like tender plants to the sun, when questions about "what seniors wanted" arose. Art was forty-seven and it made him want to scream, but he held his tongue. Too many of his friends were out of work.

Bruno had a little notebook that he took with him everywhere, often spending an hour or two making sketches in a café or jotting down his observations of Brooklyn. Occasionally he left it around the apartment, not seeming particularly protective of it, and Art couldn't resist taking a look. Most of his sketches seemed to be of women (clothed or naked) or of homeless men (clothed, thankfully). He also made a lot of lists: the restaurants they'd been to in Carroll Gardens; movies they'd seen; other mysterious two-word phrases Art decided had to be band names or songs, because in themselves they made no sense.

> *beneficial worm*
> *power sham*
> *lettuce amazement*
> *trifecta bin*
> *shirts trophy*

Since he didn't want to admit he'd looked, Art couldn't ask him about these. But he was often tempted to reference the phrases—to exclaim, "Lettuce amazement!" over dinner, for example, or to say, "Shirts trophy," when he handed Bruno a stack of clean laundry—and found they stuck in his head, sometimes popping into his consciousness at night as he was falling asleep.

He was impressed by Bruno's ability to get around New York, by the attention he paid to the subway map, by his friendliness to people in stores. He'd hang out on the stoop of the building for hours, smoking cigarettes and petting the landlady's beagle. As this kept the dog—ordinarily a howling, roly-poly monstrosity—quiet, he grew popular among the neighbors. One of them told Art, as they chatted on the street corner, how lucky he was that Bruno had come to stay.

"Yeah, Bruno's great," Art said.

"And he's got his future all mapped out already. I mean, NYU," the woman said. "My son wants to be a nightclub promoter. This is a profession? I think he saw it on TV or something. Pathetic."

"Right," Art said, and quickly went upstairs. Bruno was lying on the couch in the living room, listening to his iPod with his eyes closed.

Art shook his foot. "Hey," he said. With the boy's guileless face in front of him, Art didn't know where to start. He wasn't great at confrontation. The cruelest thing his ex-wife had ever said to him, right after the divorce was final, was, "You never even cared enough to fight." He couldn't believe she thought their marriage had failed because they got along too well. Of all the things a man could do wrong, this had been his error? Refusing to be a dick?

Bruno lit a cigarette.

"Are you having a good summer?" Art asked him.

"It's not bad."

"Are you lonely, being away from your friends? Your mom?"

"I don't have many friends. My mother—eh, you know her."

Art wasn't sure what this meant. "Are you looking forward to going back, though? At the end of the month?"

Something like resignation dawned in Bruno's eyes. He swung his feet down to the ground and rubbed his forehead with one hand, the cigarette still blazing in the other. He seemed weary beyond his years. "I've been meaning to talk with you about that," he said.

"Okay," Art said. "Talk."

"I think school in Paris is stupid," Bruno said, then launched into an explanation in French that Art had trouble following: something about there being channels, or tunnels, that students were slotted into and couldn't escape from. He'd had fifteen years to improve his French and never gotten around to it; until now it hadn't seemed like a big deal.

"Anyway," Bruno continued, "so I thought, maybe I come here

and study in America. I stay with you for a time, then I go to university here as resident. For you know, for cheaper."

"For a time?"

"Sure," Bruno said. "For high school."

After that he stopped talking. Art knew this must have been a plan Bruno and Inès had cooked up together. It bore her stamp, which read, *Ask forgiveness, not permission.* Art glanced around the apartment. It had been two years since he'd had a woman here, Vivian from the magazine, who wanted him to pull her hair during sex and whom he'd never called again. Later he heard she'd moved to Colorado and become a Pilates instructor. In other words, he could hardly worry about Bruno cramping his style, when there was so little of it to cramp. But still.

"What is it that you want to study, anyway?"

"International relations," Bruno said.

"Why do you have to do that here?"

"Because here," Bruno said, "is where you need the most help. You need to be educated. To learn that America is not the center of the world."

Art's annoyance quickened his pulse. "I'm pretty sure you go to school to be educated, not tell other people what they don't know."

"Yes, of course," Bruno said. "But Americans really need help. They are messing up the whole world with their terrible foreign policies. Maybe I can work with them, to change minds."

It was in fact Art's own opinion that America was messing up the whole world with its terrible foreign policies. But hearing it articulated so airily by a Parisian teenager made him defensive. Plus, the idea of Inès and Bruno conspiring together pissed him off.

"The world sits back and forces us to take command," he said, "because nobody else is doing anything."

"Nobody is forcing America to do anything. In France we opposed the Iraq war."

"Yeah, you guys are perfect," Art said. "I'm sure the Algerians agree."

Bruno's thin, pointy face reddened. "You know nothing about France."

"And you're not an expert on world affairs either, you little punk."

Bruno spread his hands wide. "That's why I go to school here, to become expert!" he said triumphantly. He grinned as if his case had been won, and with it the battle to stay. Art felt not anger but a sudden torque in his chest that he barely recognized, it had been so long, as excitement.

The dynamic between them shifted, or rather lurched, in a new direction. The relaxing days gave way to activity. Bruno was his *charge,* and there were things to *do.* They had to deal with the paperwork, get him registered at school, buy supplies, procure a medical checkup. Art started to give him a hard time about the smoking, too. Before, they'd been acting almost like roommates but now Art flexed the muscles of authority, and he was surprised how easily the benevolent dictatorship of parenthood came to him; he should have been doing this all along. Bruno, on the other hand, was not pleased. "What happened to you?" he grumbled. "You used to be calm. Now you are like, I don't know. No fun."

"That's right," Art said. "America is *no fun.*"

He cleaned out the office, having determined that if Bruno was going to stay on, he'd need a real bedroom. The boy had been using his laptop occasionally and Art gave it to him permanently, setting him up at the desk. He brought Bruno to work one day, enjoying the looks of surprise on his coworkers' faces when he introduced them to his son.

"I didn't know you had a son," said Samantha, the receptionist.

"I do now," Art said, not stopping to answer when Samantha said, curiously, "*Now?*"

Within two weeks it was all settled: Bruno's curfew, his route to school, his summer reading assignment of *The House on Mango Street*. As Art became more parental, the boy predictably rebelled. He stopped making eggs and doing the dishes. He spent his evenings on the stoop, muttering to himself and blowing smoke in the beagle's face. And the notebook's word pairs grew ominous:

> *Merciless hot*
> *Satan machine*
> *Glad down*

One morning, late for work, Art grabbed his favorite cup out of the cupboard, poured himself some coffee, and choked at the first sip. There was a cigarette butt in it. Bruno was still asleep, or pretending to be, but Art imagined him laughing. When he got to the office, he e-mailed Inès and updated her on the situation. Her reply came almost instantly. *He often behaves this way. Send him back if you want,* she wrote languidly. *You don't have to keep him.*

"Of course I don't have to keep him," Art said out loud. Samantha heard him—the company had an open-plan floor space—and cocked an eyebrow. He shook his head at her and typed back, *Never mind.* He knew Inès didn't count on him to fix her son, or, for that matter, anything at all. Neither did Bruno. If Art said no to the high school plan, Bruno would shrug and get on the plane back to Paris. Art glanced around the office, filled with shiny, twentysomething heads. Nobody expected to stay here long, and everybody openly surfed for other jobs. The horizon of expectations was low. If he left today, he'd be replaced tomorrow. Drilling his fingers against his desk, Art thought, *Enough.*

When he got back to the apartment, Bruno wasn't home. It was a suffocating summer night and the AC units labored mightily in the windows. Art stood in front of one, lifting his shirt to expose his stomach to the cool air. Above the machine's huffing wind he could hear the familiar sounds of his block: traffic, construction, the beagle's harassing wail.

He wandered into Bruno's room, his old office now a scattershot landscape of flung T-shirts and discarded jeans. The boy's suitcase lay open on the floor, its mouth disgorging even more clothes. The air smelled of teenage funk and dirty laundry. Art sat down at his desk. During the months of chemo, he'd spent most of his time on the futon in here, daydreaming of spectacular lives he might one day lead: he'd write a book about his ordeal; get back into political journalism; ask out Samantha, who always flirted with him even though she was so young; and soon he'd be on talk shows and in the *New York Times*. He'd lie on his back, cupping his groin as if he could heal it with the palm of his hand. It had been curiously peaceful, all standard concerns suspended in a liquid solution of *ifs*: *if* I get better, *if* I get through this . . . Strangely, when it all ended and he got his health back, the daydreaming and *ifs* evaporated. He was better but somehow lesser. He stopped imagining anything other than the life he had.

It was eleven o'clock and Bruno wasn't home. Although he

knew the kid was sophisticated, Art was still freaked. He looked around for the notebook, hoping he might find some clue, but Bruno had evidently taken it with him. On the desk was Art's laptop. He'd seen Bruno checking Facebook from time to time, but in general he didn't seem to use the computer much. Now he turned it on and checked the browser history, finding it had been cleared, as if the boy had covered his tracks.

He began to pace around the apartment, fidgeting. He made some coffee, then went through the mail and opened his bills. His mouth dropped when he saw that his credit-card balance was nearly two thousand dollars—charges for music sites, tons of iTunes, and what looked like Internet porn.

His head throbbing, he went back into the office and checked the laptop again. In a folder labeled School he found a long list of obviously noneducational files, and when he clicked on one of the porn videos it brought up images so disturbing that he had to close his eyes, though of course he opened them again right away. "Fifteen," he said. "Jesus." The video concluded and prompted him to visit its home site, where he was invited to "Rate this video! Share your comments here!" Beneath this, a notice instructed him to type the following words as a security measure:

Mice imp

Those word pairs from Bruno's notebook—he was collecting anti-spam phrases. Art couldn't believe a *porn site,* of all places, was trying to discourage spam. On the screen, two women were gyrating around in front of a man holding a gun. Someone was moaning, someone else was shrieking, both out of sync with the video. Staring at it, Art didn't even hear Bruno come in.

He smelled smoke and waved it away, only belatedly realizing it meant the boy was home. He clicked off the porn, blushing violently, and turned around to see him busily stuffing the clothes on the floor into his duffel bag. There was a cut on his forehead and another on his arm, just above the wide leather cuff he wore on his wrist.

"Where the hell have you been?"

"Did you miss me?" Bruno said, smirking.

Art reached up and grabbed his arm, hard. "Where *were* you?"

The boy shrugged.

"Stop *shrugging!*"

Bruno reached for his cigarettes, but Art knocked the pack out of his hand. And then Bruno burst into tears, his mouth contorted, the explanation coming out in rapid, babbling French that Art couldn't understand.

"Hey," Art said. "Hey." He tried to hug the kid but Bruno pushed him away, again grabbing for a cigarette.

Eventually, after he smoked three of them and had a shot of bourbon, the story brokenly emerged. Bruno told it sitting at the kitchen table, his voice soft, his eyes not meeting Art's: he'd gone to the apartment of a woman who'd advertised on Craigslist. But her husband was there, and he wanted to watch. When Bruno started for the door, the man came after him with a knife.

"Are you fucking kidding me?" Art said.

"No," Bruno said, calmer now, though his fingers were still trembling, with some dark substance, whether dirt or blood, rimming the nails.

"What the hell are you doing answering ads on Craigslist? You could've been killed."

Bruno looked around the room vaguely. "There is nothing else to do here."

"You're in New York City and the only thing you can find to do is meet strangers for sex? Jesus Christ, who *are* you? What happened to taking in a goddamn Broadway show?"

The eyes that met his were blank, dark. Unreachable. No wonder Inès wanted him out of her hair, Art thought, no wonder she was willing to send him halfway around the world to a father he hardly knew. This boy—there was something off in him, more than just teenage mischief, some wiring gone amok.

"Like I said, Bruno, you could have been killed."

"Sure," he answered. "Anyway, you don't have to worry about it. I am leaving. My mother will buy me the ticket."

"No," Art said.

The kid looked at him, surprised—as Art himself was. But here he was, sure of what he was doing. He had one ball left: enough for whatever. Enough for this.

"No," he said. "You stay."

Fortune-Telling

The kung pao chicken was what kept me going back night after night. That and the hot and sour soup. Otherwise the Chinese restaurant had nothing going for it. You know those places where there're loads of Chinese people ordering from a separate menu, and you gesture that you want what they're having and suddenly you're eating steamed dumplings and buns with mysterious, delicious fillings and side dishes of spicy, tender broccoli? This was not one of those places. In countless visits I never saw a single Chinese customer. In fact only Mr. Lu, who cooked the food, was Chinese. His wife, Stacy, who took the orders, was blond and hailed from Plano, Texas. Mr. Lu churned out egg rolls and fried rice and kung pao chicken at an amazing pace; you didn't often see him, but you could hear him screaming at Stacy when she went back into the kitchen with the orders. It always sounded like he was outraged by what people had selected, but Stacy told me it was just because all the years of clattering pots and pans had damaged his hearing.

The place didn't even have a name—neither on the door outside nor on the menu. It was just a Chinese restaurant across the street from my apartment. I started going there the week I moved in, having dropped out of college and come to the city to make my name, find fame and fortune, the whole nine yards. The very first time I had the kung pao chicken and the hot and sour soup, the next morning I got a call from a casting agent who wanted to audition me for a detergent commercial. I didn't get the part but still decided the chicken was my lucky dish, so whenever I was feeling down, or tired, or in need of a boost, I'd go back. I felt that way a lot, so I was a regular.

During the day I was temping at a mortgage company, a job so tedious it caused me actual physical pain—backaches, head-aches, stomachaches. The money was good, though, and I'd been temping there for so long they changed my status to *perma-temp*. I made fifty cents more an hour than the ordinary temps, and my boss gave me a plant to put in my cube. All day long I sat in there and proofread people's mortgages, which were passed from bank to bank, back and forth, like chips in a poker game. For legal reasons I had to make sure that the stamps on the front of the mortgage matched these poker-game trails documented at the back. When I was done proofreading a big stack, I filed them in a cool, dark, windowless room we called the Cave. Sometimes I lay down in the Cave and took naps. I didn't mean to slack off, but the idiocy of the work made sleep irresistible. Nobody ever seemed to notice, anyway, just like they didn't when I was gone for two hours in the middle of the day on an audition. They were just as bored themselves, and at times it felt like we were all in a trance, dreaming this shared tedious dream.

After work I sometimes went to a class or an audition, or came home to check my messages to see if I'd been called back for any-thing, which I hardly ever was. Often, too tired to cook, I'd head across the street to the Chinese restaurant. A counter at one end served as a kind of bar, meaning Stacy would bring you a beer if you sat there long enough. When I was done eating I'd occasionally hang out there for a while. It never occurred to me that a young woman sitting alone at a bar could expect a certain amount of attention, that she could be sending out any kind of message to the world at large. I believed that a woman ought to be able to behave exactly like a man did, in any situation. This attitude often got me in trouble. I refused to flirt with male casting agents and directors; I wouldn't wear makeup to auditions for roles where I was supposed to be the attractive ingénue. "In your heart you *want* to fail," one of my actor friends told me once, a statement that, though I didn't realize it at the time, was absolutely true.

It was following one such failed, nonflirtatious audition that I met Simon Robbie. Whether Robbie was his last name or whether he went by two first names was unclear. He was a guy my age who sidled up to me at the counter on a Wednesday night and introduced himself. He was wearing a dirty yellow T-shirt with the name of a Little League team on it, and corduroy pants that were sliding off his skinny hips—your standard hipster look. Also, he had sideburns.

"I'm Zoe," I told him, which was a lie. I was into constructing false personae at this time. The world was my stage, was how I looked at it.

"Nice to meet you," he said, then looked around the place. "What do you recommend to eat at this place? I'm looking for something new and different, some kind of culinary adventure."

"I recommend you go eat somewhere else," I said.

Simon Robbie looked offended. "Hey, I was just making conversation. No need to be a jerk."

"I just meant the food here's pretty standard," I said. I decided that Zoe would be a kind girl from a small town, captain of the History Club in high school. She'd have a fondness for dressing up in period costumes at Halloween—Marie Antoinette, Eleanor of Aquitaine, Madame Mao—and feel seriously disappointed if people didn't recognize who she was. "It's an egg-roll, chow-mein, fortune-cookies-bought-in-bulk kind of place."

"Gotcha," Simon Robbie said. "Hey, did you already eat? I was thinking maybe I'd eat here at the bar with you? Would that be okay?"

"I see no problem with that," I-as-Zoe said, and gave him a friendly smile. I saw Stacy coming out of the kitchen and waved her over. She looked pleased. She thought that a twenty-year-old woman who ate by herself in a Chinese restaurant three or four times a week was in dire need of friends. Simon Robbie ordered three appetizers—scallion pies, wonton soup, egg rolls—and no main course.

"Nothing else?" Stacy said.

"Not for now," Simon Robbie told her. "I like to keep my options open," he said to me, and winked.

"Uh-huh," I said.

While eating he asked me about myself, sometimes gesturing with his left hand as if to say, "More details!" while he shoveled in mouthfuls with his right. The food was greasy and a ring of oil soon appeared around his mouth, wide and shiny, like a clown's lipstick. I told him all about Zoe's childhood on a farm, how her father had to give up the land his family had worked for genera-tions and moved them to a small, grimy town where he worked in a factory, assembling cell phones. I said he hated this so much that the sight of a person talking on a cell phone drove him into a blind rage and one day, when Zoe was sixteen, she came home with a cell phone of her own and he threw her out of the house and ever since then she'd been on her own.

"That's intense," Simon Robbie said.

"Yeah."

"So what do you do now?"

For some reason this was the only thing I didn't want to lie about. "I'm an actress," I said.

"Wow, cool, excellent," he said through a mouthful of egg roll. "What do you act?"

"I do theater mostly," I said. "Sometimes commercials, for the money. You know how it is."

Simon Robbie chewed and swallowed. "No, I meant what kind of *people*," he said. "Show me."

I'm acting right now, I almost said, but didn't. "I don't know if I can do that," I told him.

"Oh, okay, I totally understand," he said. "I'm in insurance myself, and when people ask me questions about it outside of work, I'm like, dude, no more, call me at the office. You know what I mean?"

"You're in insurance?"

"I sell life-insurance policies door-to-door," he said.

I couldn't believe I'd met someone whose job sounded worse than mine. It made me warm to him. "How do you like it?" I asked.

He finished chewing an egg roll, wiped his mouth, and shrugged. "Life is long," he said, "and this is just one phase."

I toasted this philosophy with my beer. Stacy came by and asked if we wanted anything else to drink. Simon Robbie ordered tea, and I said I'd have the same. The place was emptying out,

Mr. Lu's angry cries from the back coming less often now. With the tea Stacy brought some cookies, and I cracked mine open and read the fortune. *You will never win the lottery,* it said. I showed it to him.

"Then why do they print those numbers on the other side?" he said.

I shook my head. The fortune had put me in a bad mood. We sat for a couple of minutes in silence, Simon Robbie opening his fortune—*Be kind to everyone you meet,* his said, which wasn't even a fortune in my opinion, given that it said nothing of the future— and ate our cookies. I drank some weak, bitter tea. "Well, I guess I'm off," I finally said, and waved to Stacy for the check.

"Wait a minute," Simon Robbie said. "I need to ask you a favor."

"I'm not much for favors."

"Please?" he said. "It's important, and I'll buy you dinner. I'll buy you dinner tonight and for the next week."

"That's a lot of egg rolls."

"It doesn't have to be here," he said, nearly pleading.

"Okay, what is it?" I asked.

"It's my mother. She's always after me about a girlfriend, every time I see her. If you could just come over with me, even for ten minutes, pretend that we're on a date, it would shut her up for a least a few weeks. Please?"

"You want me to pretend I'm your girlfriend?" I said. I'd forgotten that I was Zoe, and my tone was incredulous and unkind.

He nodded. Stacy put down the check and he counted out the cash, then looked at me with puppy-dog eyes.

"I only live five minutes away," he said.

I wondered if he cruised the Chinese restaurants in this neighborhood each night, the pizza joints, the Greek diners, looking for a girl who seemed willing to impersonate a girlfriend, if he knew I'd made up Zoe and her cell phone traumas and could tell I was practiced in the immorality of lying. I wondered if he'd give me cash, or if I'd actually have to eat dinner with him every night. Would it be nice to have someone to eat dinner with, or horrible? I had no idea. I was staring at his yellow Little League T-shirt, seeing how it was smudged and smeared with enigmatic stains, and it suddenly occurred to me that he might not be a hipster at all, that it might be a T-shirt from his own long-ago team. It was the saddest thought I'd had all day.

"Okay," I said. "Let's go."

We walked for a few minutes in silence, past a skateboard park and a theater where a movie was just letting out. Simon Robbie sauntered along with his hands in his pockets, pushing his cords even farther down his hips, his mouth pursed as he whistled some kind of tune. I almost reached into my bag for my cigarettes, but then realized Zoe wasn't the kind of girl who smoked. It was important to stay in character no matter what events might unfold. After a few blocks he took my elbow, very gentlemanly, and tugged me down a side street packed tight with little run-down houses. There were no streetlights and the place was dark and deserted. At another time of my life, I might have been scared. But Simon Robbie didn't look very strong; his arms were stringy and thin. I figured I could take him if I had to.

"Here we are," he said, guiding me up the steps of a white house. In the front windows sat three or four cats, their yellow and green eyes blinking out into the night. When he opened the door I was greeted by an overwhelming smell of detergents and ammonia and room fresheners. It was like being hit over the head with a bowl of potpourri.

"Mom?" he called as we walked in, and the cats turned to look at us, crouching down in defensive positions. The living room, as you might expect, was exceptionally clean, with a couch and a television and a round rug made of rags, and everything except the rug was glistening. On the coffee table, magazines were stacked in neat, geometric rows.

A woman came in, smiling. She was younger than I'd expected, with short, neat brown hair and friendly brown eyes. I'd been picturing some kind of dragon lady, and I let out a relieved breath. Simon Robbie was still holding me by my elbow, as if I were a pet he'd led home on a leash. I stepped away and clasped my arms behind my back.

"Mom, I want you to meet Zoe," he said.

"Hey there," his mother said, still smiling. "Great to meet you. Have a seat. Would you like a drink, maybe some lemonade, or a glass of wine? Sit down, please, let's get comfortable."

I glanced at Simon Robbie, who looked like he was about to break into a sweat. I couldn't figure out what about this woman was so terrible. I sat down across from the mother, and he sat down next to me. We were on a kind of love seat, and she was in a recliner. The cats relaxed and resumed their vigilant stares at the outer dark.

"Zoe," his mother said, "that's such a beautiful name."

"Thank you," I said. "I was named for a character in a children's book."

"Really? Which one?"

"I don't know," I said. "My mother chose the name, but she

died when I was young, and my father didn't know which book it was."

"And you never tried to find out? A good library—"

"Of course I've tried," I said, cutting her off. "But no luck." I leaned back in my seat, pleased with how things were going so far.

"You'd think that if you cared enough you wouldn't let the issue drop," the woman said. "About your dead mother, that is."

I looked at Simon Robbie. I was starting to get a sense of what he was grappling with. But I had an advantage: Zoe's mother wasn't real. "Maybe so," I said, smiling wistfully at the carpet, as if long-held grief was welling up inside me.

Simon Robbie put his hand on my elbow again, maybe to comfort me, or possibly himself. Sitting next to me on the couch he exuded a faint, clammy smell of nerves mixed with the residual odor of scallion pie.

"Are you sure you wouldn't like some lemonade?" his mother said, and the pressure on my elbow intensified.

"Sure, why not?" I said. It was the wrong answer. The lemonade was made from a mix, using all the wrong proportions. It was thick and sludgy with particles and so sweet that one sip made my teeth call out in protest. The woman across from me smiled as I set the glass down on a coaster. I was starting to think that this was some kind of demonic ritual practiced by the two of them, that she was a sorceress who demanded her son bring home victims for her to torment. On the other hand, maybe she just didn't know how to make lemonade.

"Delicious," I told her.

"Thank you, dear," she said, and crossed her legs. One of the cats came over and jumped up in her lap. She didn't pet it or anything, just let it settle itself on her thighs.

"Zoe's an actress, Mom," Simon Robbie said.

"How wonderful! What do you act?"

"Funny, that's exactly what he asked," I said, gesturing at him companionably.

"Well, it's a logical question, isn't it?"

I was going to explain my confusion, but decided to let it drop. "Mostly commercials," I said.

"Oh, I love commercials!" she said. "Some of them are so clever these days. They tell a whole story in under thirty seconds. They have this wonderful"—here she snapped her fingers, looking for a word, and the cat jumped down and rubbed itself against my legs—"*economy*."

"That's true, I guess," I said.

"Show me one."

"What's that?"

She gestured at me, commandingly, like a queen. "Act one out. Please?"

I glanced at Simon Robbie but he was staring at the ground. Then I reminded myself that I was still Zoe, not me, though by this stage the lines were getting blurred. I thought about my last callback, for a car dealership. They went with a taller woman in the end, my agent said; I looked too small next to the trucks.

Standing up in that clean, heavily scented room. I motioned at the love seat behind me as if it were a gleaming 4 x 4. "Come on down to the lot at Ed's Car and Truck!" I said loudly, smiling to show as many teeth as I possibly could. "We're practically giving away our inventory of quality preowned vehicles, with no money down and delayed interest payments for up to a year! These deals won't last, so visit us now! At Ed's, we're not just your dealer, we're your friends!"

At this point in the script, the rest of the dealership was supposed to crowd around me, although, as my agent said, they were all men and having them crowd around a young actress as she smiled by the pickup looked like the beginning of some porno movie. But I didn't say anything about this, just stood there, still smiling and a little out of breath. Then I sat down.

"I don't really feel it," his mother said.

"Mom," Simon Robbie said reproachfully.

"What? I just call them like I see them. Would *you* buy a car from that girl?"

"Don't listen to her, Zoe," he said. "That was great. Is that commercial still on?"

"Uh, no. Although I wasn't actually pretending to be a salesperson," I said to his mother. A high-pitched pleading tone surfaced in my voice, the same as it did whenever my agent called with bad news. "I was just advertising their Labor Day sale."

"Those guys at Ed's are sharks," she said. "Don't you feel bad working with sharks like that?"

"I don't know," I said, my voice still squeaky.

"I always go to Millingham Honda. They've done right by me."

I stood up again. "I think I'd better be going."

"You didn't finish your lemonade," the mother said.

"That's okay."

"You didn't like it?"

"It's delicious," I said. "I'm just, uh, full, or whatever the equivalent of that for drinking is."

"Hah!" the mother said, then looked at her son. "I can tell she's lying. She doesn't like lemonade. Probably goes for the hard stuff.

Watch out for this one, babe. She'll lead you down the garden path."

"It was very nice to meet you," I said softly, inching toward the door.

"You aren't even really his girlfriend, are you?" she said. "You don't have love in your eyes when you look his way."

"I do love him!" I whispered desperately from the doorway, all conviction gone. "I love him very much!"

"You don't even know what love is," his mother said.

Red-faced, hands in pockets, Simon Robbie walked me outside. We ambled together down the block, until we were out of sight of those staring cats. As soon as we hit the street I'd started to cry, but Simon Robbie didn't notice at first.

When he did, he nodded his head glumly. "She got to you too," he said.

"She's right, isn't she? You wouldn't buy a car from me either."

"That's the worst part. She only tells the truth. The things that other people think but never say."

"She's like a *witch*."

"She's my mother," he said.

I wiped my nose with my sleeve. If we kept talking about it, I was going to be blubbering like a baby. "You don't have to buy me dinner this week," I said. "Okay?"

He just shrugged. I guessed he was used to getting the brush-off after these home visits. "Sorry about my mom, Zoe," he said. "She does that to everybody."

I left him at the corner, his yellow T-shirt glowing faintly on the dark street, and started back to my apartment. The whole world was colored in hues of truth. I saw the Chinese restaurant clearly as I passed by: a small, grimy place that wasn't worth returning to night after night, that didn't offer any refuge, or even serve decent food. I saw myself reflected in its windows, a girl who was all alone and scared of it, who'd deceived herself into thinking that lying and acting were the same thing. The next day, when I woke up, I talked myself out of this state and got back to the business of living. But ever since then, I've looked back on the night I met the truth-teller as the one moment of perfect clarity I ever achieved— a moment when I realized I had no idea what I was doing or who I thought I was. And often I ask myself: who was she, Simon Robbie's mother? Where did she get her power to speak the merciless truth? And if I ever meet her again, will I still be found wanting?

Acknowledgments

I'm grateful to all the editors of the literary journals in which these stories appeared—especially Sudip Bose, Jennifer Cranfill, Thom Didato, and Don Lee—for their support of my work and of the short story in general. And thanks are due, as ever, to Gary Fisketjon, Jenny Jackson, Amy Williams, and my family, who mean more to me than I can say.